JoAnn Ross

Forever in Honeymoon Harbor

CANARY STREET PRESS

CANARY
STREET
PRESS™

Recycling programs
for this product may
not exist in your area.

ISBN-13: 978-1-335-47495-7

Forever in Honeymoon Harbor

For questions and comments about the quality of this book, please contact us at CustomerService@Harlequin.com.

Canary Street Press
22 Adelaide St. West, 41st Floor
Toronto, Ontario M5H 4E3, Canada
CanaryStPress.com

Printed in U.S.A.

Praise for the novels of JoAnn Ross

"This engrossing and hopeful story will hold readers from start to finish." —*Publishers Weekly* on *The Inheritance*

"Family secrets, complex characters and a glorious setting make *The Inheritance* a rich, compelling read... JoAnn Ross at her best!"
—Sherryl Woods, #1 *New York Times* bestselling author

"Welcome to Honeymoon Harbor, where unforgettable characters come face-to-face with the kind of love that grabs your heart and never lets go." —*Fresh Fiction*

"A wonderfully uplifting story full of JoAnn Ross's signature warmth and charm."
—Jill Shalvis, *New York Times* bestselling author, on *Snowfall on Lighthouse Lane*

"The connection between a deeply conflicted man slowly coming to terms with loss and a woman who understands him adds strength and intensity to a perceptive story that is more than the average friends-into-lovers romance... Verdict: An excellent start to a promising community series with a stunning Olympic Coast setting."
—*Library Journal* on *Herons Landing*

"*Snowfall on Lighthouse Lane* is another deftly crafted gem of a romance novel by an author who is an impressively consistent master of the genre." —*Midwest Book Review*

"A widower gets a second chance at love with his wife's best friend in this...sweet first book in Ross's Honeymoon Harbor series... Fans of cozy small-town romances will be willing to read further in the series."
—*Publishers Weekly* on *Herons Landing*

"It's a cause for celebration when a favorite author gifts us with a new series... Seth and Brianna are a delicious couple."
—*All About Romance* on *Herons Landing*

Once again to Jay, my first and only love and husband of fifty-seven years, whom I recognized at first sight. What's holding me together as I write this is that just as you always believed in me, I'm going to believe what you pinky-swore: that you'll wait for me, and we'll resume the dance we'd already done before that unforgettable summer day when fifteen-year-old me met seventeen-year-old you. Yet right now I miss you more than words can say and will love you forever.

CHAPTER ONE

WESTERN WASHINGTON STATE was well known for its rain, but, as residents of the cities spread along Puget Sound knew, there were many seasons: rain, extra rain—which brought with it the "long dark"—fake spring, disappointment, yet more rain, sunshine, intense sunshine, glorious sunshine, and then the cycle would begin again. The peninsula, located on the far northwest part of the country, did get its share of rain, as much as twelve feet a year in the Hoh rainforest, but Honeymoon Harbor was located in the Olympic Mountains' rain shadow, which tourism brochures and Realtors referred to as the state's "banana belt." Rainfall was actually less than the country's average and the summer days were pleasant and sunny.

Which accounted for another season, known locally as the Double Ws. Weddings and Winnebagos.

While he was always grateful for the income the hoard of vacationers who flooded into town during the summer months provided, as Quinn Mannion watched a trio of motorhomes roll past the wide windows of the pub, he realized this year could prove a problem.

"I'm glad Katie's techie husband got that promotion," he said, as he washed some beer mugs in the bar sink. "But why did it have to be in Austin?" Katie Young had spent the past two years excelling at taking reservations, greeting and seating guests, ensuring that they were kept happy, and, in a pinch, filling in as a server when needed. "And why did it have to happen now? After the usual summer workers have already been scooped up by all the other businesses and the park?"

The Olympic National Park, which advertised work opportunities surrounded by nearly a million acres of glacier-capped mountains, old-growth rain forests, over seventy miles of coastline, and hot springs, was hard to compete with. Hadn't he worked as a lifeguard at Sol Duc Hot Springs resort during summer breaks from the University of Washington?

"I'm assuming you've posted on the employment boards at the college?" Quinn's brother Burke asked from where he was seated at the bar, working his way through an order of wings and a blue cheeseburger.

"Yes. And Lily did her best to find someone." Lily Carpenter, head of marketing and an events planner at Clearwater Community College had married Burke last year. Quinn shrugged as he put the mugs on a rack above the bar. "Like I said, I'm happy for Katie, because they can afford to have a kid now, but the timing could have been better. I even threw the apartment in to sweeten up the job posting."

Quinn had lived in the apartment over the bar after restoring the family pub that had been closed during Prohibition. Like many of the old waterfront buildings, it had sat empty until he'd given up his law practice in Seattle and returned home to brew award-winning craft beer and run Mannion's Pub and Brewery. After a year, once the place was up and running and didn't need constant care, he'd moved to a log house just outside of town on the banks of Mirror Lake.

"The expansion, which seemed a great idea at the time, is going to prove a problem." Last fall he'd obtained a zoning variance to open a small patio of six tables outside on the rocky waterfront. His brother-in-law, Seth, had already laid the stones; the tables, which were late due to supply chain issues at the port in Seattle, were finally due to arrive any day, and landscaper Amanda Barrow had suggested adding pots of herbs. Not only for cooking, but to add ambience and fragrance to the outdoor dining area.

"You'll work it out," Burke said. "You are, as we all know, the perfect big brother."

Quinn had been hearing that all his life. Never from his parents, who'd always allowed their five kids to choose their own paths without being judged. Which was how Brianna had gone from a high-end concierge at the country's elite hotels to running a bed-and-breakfast here in Honeymoon Harbor, and how Aiden had gone from being a vice cop on LA's mean streets to being the town police chief. Gabe, former Wall Street titan, was now building boats and running a nonprofit foundation. And hotshot Super Bowl QB Burke had his own network sports show with the opportunity to do documentaries for CBS

Sports, like their current one on how Teddy Roosevelt, who'd had a secondary role in naming this town, had supposedly saved American football.

"Who knew?" Quinn had asked his brother when told about the story.

"Hardly anyone," Burke had said. "Which is why I'm making it."

"Do you think," Quinn suggested mildly now, "since we're all adults, we can finally drop the damn ranking?" They'd had their share of scuffles over the years due to fraternal competition, which he'd never instigated.

"Fine with me." Burke shrugged his wide QB shoulders. "And for the record, Gabe and Aiden were the ones causing the fights. I stayed out of them."

He was right. Thinking back on it, Burke had been too worried about injuring his hands, which, as he was always reminding their parents when chores were handed out, were his ticket to the NFL. That excuse, which had helped him avoid the most physical tasks on the family Christmas tree farm, had always irked the others, even Quinn, but against all odds, damned if Burke hadn't achieved his goal of winning a Super Bowl.

Quinn had his back turned, rearranging bottles on the glass shelves, when the heavy oak door opened. There were those in his family who believed that his way of seeming to know what everyone was thinking came from him inheriting the gift of Second Sight from the O'Sullivans, a distantly related family of race horse breeders in County Cork. That had always been too fantastical for Quinn's mind to consider. Especially when, at this moment, it didn't take any woo-woo preternatural Celtic powers for him to feel a sudden charge in the air. To know exactly who had just walked into the pub.

Bracing himself, he turned, put a casual, welcoming smile on his face, and watched as Amanda Barrow wove her way through the still mostly empty tables. It was that slow time between lunch and dinner, but Quinn knew he only had a few more days before there'd be no slow time until at least mid-September.

"Well, this is a surprise," he said. Which was true. As long as she'd been in Honeymoon Harbor, except for one memorable afternoon, she'd never come in during the day. Typically, she'd show up a couple evenings a week, all spiffed up after her workday, smelling like a garden of tropical flowers, from either her shampoo or soap.

"I was in Seattle, choosing plants for a new home on the lake," she said, sliding onto the stool next to Burke. She was wearing white capri pants cut off at the ankles—how bad did he have it when he even found her bare ankles sexy?—snow-white sneakers, and a sky blue T-shirt sporting a red wheelbarrow full of colorful flowers backed by a bright yellow sun that read *I'll be in my office*. Below that was the name of her business, *Wheel and Barrow, Honeymoon Harbor, Washington*.

"The thriller writer," Quinn said, as he put a glass in front of her and pulled a green bottle of chardonnay from a cooler beneath the bar. "With the wife whose weavings sell for big bucks in galleries and art auctions."

"That's them." Her smile, which could light up the pub even during the long dark days of a Pacific Northwest winter, brightened her doe-brown eyes. And again, even as his logical mind assured him that it was only a physical reaction to the attraction he'd felt from the day she and her now former husband first came into the pub for dinner, warmth spread through Quinn. "It's true what people say. You do know everything."

He shrugged as he poured wine into her glass. "I handled the guy's incorporation papers when he started hitting it big."

"Which was how he learned about our little hamlet?" Burke guessed. "Hi," he said, turning toward Amanda. "You smell delicious."

"You're married," Quinn said, as a spark of something uncomfortably like jealousy stung.

"Happily," Burke said. He winked at Amanda. "Make that deliriously. But that doesn't mean Lily's going to make me sleep on the couch because I told a beautiful woman she smells like piña coladas."

"Thank you." When Amanda beamed at that, Quinn felt another spike of something that was definitely jealousy. Just as he had a reputation for instinctively knowing things about everyone—which, in truth, merely came from listening—he'd never had the smooth gift for gab his brothers, especially Burke, had with women. "Coincidentally, the homeowner wants to create a tropical vibe in his gardens."

"This isn't exactly the tropics," Quinn said, then immediately wished he could take back his tone, which sounded uncharacteristically gruff and negative to his own ears.

"No, but surprisingly, there are a lot of plants that flourish here, like rhododendron, especially species from Asia that bring more of a tropical look. Gunnera, which is commonly known as Dinosaur Food, also has huge, deeply veined leaves."

"So you're creating Honeymoon Harbor's very own Jurassic Park?" Burke asked.

"Don't start spreading that around," Quinn warned. "It'd only bring in more tourists." Oh, yeah, he was definitely turning on the charm today.

"You don't have to worry," Amanda said. "Like a lot of the tech guys I worked for in California, this one's intensely private. He definitely wouldn't want tourists showing up at his gate." Her brow furrowed at Quinn's atypical attitude. "And here's where I admit that I like tourists. They bring a happy vacation vibe to town. Especially the ones who are here for the weddings in the park and the garden at Brianna's Bed-and-Breakfast.

"Anyway," she continued, turning back to Burke, "there are even species of palms and banana trees that'll grow here. Along with the more typical cannas and hostas. Some need to be wintered over inside, which isn't a problem, since the owner can afford the greenhouse and gardeners to do that."

As Quinn watched her put his anti-tourism negativity behind her, he suspected it was an old habit left over from her abusive marriage, and cursed inwardly at having caused her to revisit that feeling.

"Do you remember the first time you poured this for me?" she asked, looking at him over the rim of the wineglass, deftly changing the topic.

"Sure. The sales guy from Château de Madeline had talked me into a trial offer and I wanted an objective opinion. You were, I remember, quite specific about what you liked about it."

She laughed. And, again, he knew he was atypically romanticizing, but it reminded him of spring birdsong. "I was merely repeating how I heard a pompous waiter describe a bottle Eric had ordered for the table."

Eric, the abusive ex-husband and an actual, true-to-life rocket scientist, was now in a federal prison for trying to sell secrets about US missile systems. A shadow momentarily moved across her eyes before the sunlight returned.

"What I remember most is that I'd just gotten back from visiting him in the hospital, after he'd been found and arrested camping out in the park in the freezing cold. I don't think I'd ever felt more down. I didn't want to go home to an empty house, so, on a whim, I came in here after getting off the ferry."

She turned toward Burke. "Your brother offered his usual hospitality, then asked me to do him a favor by sampling this chardonnay. Then he tried to make me feel better by telling me that it was on the house because everyone got a free dinner on their birthday."

"It's true," Quinn said.

She took a sip of the wine, her gaze turning reminiscent. "I told him it wasn't my birthday." She turned
back to Quinn, lifting her eyes to his. "Do you remember what you said?"

Only every day since. It was one of the few times
in his adult life that he'd spoken without thinking.
"That yes, it was."

"That's it. Exactly. And you know what?"

"What?" Three tables of customers were eating,
two guys who'd gotten off the ferry were drinking draft beers while playing darts, and Quinn
vaguely heard pool balls breaking for a new game.
On one of the two TVs above the bar, the OL Reign
Women's Soccer League team had just scored against
the Houston Dash at Seattle's Lumen Field and the
hometown crowd was going wild. But at this sudden, frozen moment in time, it felt as if they were in
some sort of weird bubble, or like a cone of silence
had settled over them, making Amanda Barrow and
him the only people in the room.

"You were right," she said softly, as if, perhaps, she
felt the odd sensation too. "It was like being reborn.
It had been a very long time since I'd lived just for
myself. Doing what I wanted to do. When I wanted
to do it. The freedom was both heady and scary."

"Scary how?" It crossed Quinn's mind that the
pub was not the place he'd intended to have this long
overdue conversation. He'd imagined many scenarios, perhaps out on the cruiser Gabe had built for
him, over dinner at the family coast house, or better
yet, in bed, after having made love in all the ways

he'd dreamed of. But now that she was opening up, there was no way he was going to shut her down.

"Scary that I might not make the right decision about what to do next with my life. That I might make a mistake."

"We all do that. I made one by being single-minded growing up, and staying that way all through college and law school. I didn't go into the type of law I'd always expected to, but I still stayed on the wrong track. For too long. Especially after I knew, deep down, that it wasn't a right fit."

"I've been lucky," she said. "I always loved growing flowers—although I moved around a lot growing up, so I stuck to houseplants. Mostly succulents, because they don't need as much care. But I dreamed of gardens."

"And now you create them," Burke said, unknowingly bursting that private bubble they'd been in as he rejoined the conversation.

"I do." She shook her head, perhaps experiencing the same jolt of time and place Quinn felt, then bestowed a quick, easy smile on his brother, reminding Quinn of a time, not that long ago, when there'd been an aura of reserve around her despite her friendliness, which he'd originally put off to shyness. Or being new in a town that was so closely knit together, it probably felt like her first day in a new school.

Although she'd always been happy to talk about her work, he'd sensed an invisible barricade around her, like the wall of thorns and vines in Disney's *Sleeping Beauty*, which he'd recently watched with

Gabe and Chelsea's daughters while he'd been over to their house for dinner. Getting past that emotional barricade had been neither quick nor easy. But over the past eighteen months, Quinn had begun to feel as if he'd made progress. That there were times, like just a minute ago, when she considered him more than just some friendly fixture behind his bar.

"And I love every minute of my work," she was saying to Burke as Quinn dragged his mind back to the conversation. "Speaking of which," she said, turning back to him, "I picked up the herbs Jarle wanted for the patio. It's going to smell fabulous."

"That's great to hear. I just hope we'll be able to open it so people can enjoy them."

"Oh, dear." She frowned again at his uncharacteristically negative tone. Little vertical lines of concern appeared between her brows and his hands itched with the need to rub them away. "I take it you still haven't found anyone to replace Katie?"

"I've asked everyone in town, including the guys at Cops and Coffee, if they had any applicants they didn't need. Being ex-cops, they'd run background checks on everyone who applied to work there for the summer. One applicant had apparently spent twenty-four hours in a Port Angeles jail and paid a fine for driving while high. So, I opted against even checking with him."

"I can see how he might prove a risky hire," Burke said.

Another motorhome passed, painted with a huge American eagle along the side. Fortunately, because

Honeymoon Harbor had started out as a farming and lumber town, the streets had been built wide enough to turn a wagon around. Which kept the humongous RV from wiping out the cars in the oncoming lane.

"What makes people decide to sell their homes and all their stuff and move into a scaled-down house on wheels?" Quinn asked. Even Seth's parents were somewhere in New Mexico, last Quinn had heard. From what Brianna had told him, Ben Harper's initial reluctance to retire from the family construction company and take to the road had nearly done in her in-law's decades-long marriage.

"Perhaps they're seeking adventure," Amanda suggested.

"Does that sound appealing to you?"

"No." Her sleek, glossy hair, a few shades lighter than her brown eyes, skimmed her shoulders as she shook her head. "But, having experienced more than enough unwanted travel adventure, I'm more interested in a quiet, predictable life."

"Predictable can be boring." Quinn wondered if she found him quiet and predictable. Which could work in his favor after her rocky marriage. Unless, conversely, she thought he was boring.

"Some might think so," she agreed easily, thankfully oblivious to his thoughts. "But, as I said, I moved around a lot growing up, then again during my marriage, so having found this place, where I fit, I'm more than happy to allow my roots to settle in…

"And, bringing the topic back to my reason for coming in today, I was thinking that, since you're closed on Mondays, I could get your herbs planted tomorrow without disturbing any customers. I have some cedar pots with a self-contained watering system that should get them through the dry summer months."

At that moment, Jarle, who formerly worked as a cook on Alaskan crab boats, came through the swinging door from the kitchen with a half rack of baby back ribs in one hand and a mile-high cheese and bacon double beef patty burger with a side of fries in the other. It wasn't often the six-foot-seven tall chef with a butcher's chart of a cow tattooed on his arm acted as server, but whenever he did, he never failed to stop the buzz of conversation.

"The tourism bureau should list Jarle as a scenic sight," Amanda murmured. "When we were plotting out the plants, which aren't nearly enough for all his cooking, but will add to the ambiance regardless, I realized it was too bad the town council had turned down Viking Fest. Because putting him on a poster would bring in people from all over the state."

The event had been suggested during a tourist-free summer caused by the Covid pandemic, which had given the members of the tourism board time to discuss more ideas to draw in outside dollars to their remote corner of the country. When you lived in a state where summer was glorious but brief, there was basically a three-month tourism window. The season currently kicked off with the spring Heritage Day festival, followed by the Sawdust Festival, a logging competition meant to not only honor the early settlers, but also those still providing the nation with lumber, mostly from sustainable working forests, making Washington the country's second highest producer of lumber, second only to neighboring Oregon.

Another of the earlier tourism draws still in operation was the Theater in the Firs, an open-air theater, literally set in the forest. Seth's parents had met at a production where Ben had been doing the lights, and Caroline had been a Southern belle who'd driven into town in a pink Cadillac. A few years ago, Quinn's parents had turned the barn at the family Christmas tree farm into a summer theater to draw in summer income.

Like most towns, there were Memorial and Veteran's Day parades, which were mostly attended by locals, along with whatever tourists happened to be in town, but weren't that much of a draw on their own.

The Fourth of July offered yet another parade, food trucks, and fireworks over the harbor, and then there was the Wooden Boat Festival, which, last year, had included a Bachelor Auction where Brianna, Chelsea, and some of their friends had conspired to set up local vet Cam Montgomery with local business owner Megan Larson. The date—dinner aboard a tall ship—must've gone well, because Cam had proposed a few weeks afterward, atop the Ferris wheel at Lucky Harbor.

"Lily told me about some drama regarding the Viking idea," Burke said. "Apparently, Margaret Meany, a history teacher at Honeymoon Harbor High, pointed out that the Vikings had never sailed west of New-foundland.

"While Margaret might have been right, according to Brianna, who was on the Zoom call, Mildred Mayhew jumped in to point out that there was no proof that Sasquatch, aka Bigfoot, was real, but he was certainly a local legend. So, what was stopping them from going with Vikings?

"That was when Kylee, who'd photographed all the guys in the bachelor auction shirtless, had suggested dressing Jarle up in a horned helmet and animal skins for a Vikings Day poster."

"Oh, I'd pay to see that," Amanda said.

"You're not alone. Lily said the meeting got side-tracked when the women on the call voted for Viking Fest, just for a chance to see Jarle in animal skins."

"Brianna told me about that part," Quinn said. "And that Dad, who was on the call as mayor, had wisely kept out of the discussion, hoping that more reasonable heads would prevail."

"And they sort of did," Burke continued, "when Chelsea, in full librarian mode, threw a bit of cold water on the idea, pointing out that Viking clothing was actually made from wool, with wealthier people going for a more comfortable linen. Animal skins were worn. But only on top of the other clothing, for warmth.

"Then Mildred, being determined, pressed again for Viking Fest, and everyone started arguing that it wasn't fair to single out one group. That if they were going to have a Viking Fest to celebrate the Scandinavians who'd settled here, they should also have an Irish fest, an Italian fest, a Mexican fest, an Asian fest, and then things really began getting out of hand.

"According to Lily, Chelsea then pointed out that if they were going to celebrate early settlers, they should also have an Indigenous People Fest, since the Olympic Peninsula's Jamestown S'Klallam tribe has been here for ten thousand years. A lot of people liked that idea, but because Edna Kallapa from the tribal traditional food and culture committee wasn't on the call that day, having taken her daughter to the health center for what turned out to be tonsillitis, they decided to table the idea for this year."

"We always get a big crowd for the Fourth," Quinn said.

"It'll be even better this year," Burke said. "Because instead of fireworks, the committee voted to have the college's IT team create a light show in the sky with drones that'll be set to music. Gabe funded a really strong program. The light show will be fun and all, but they've also been working on the effects of climate change using drones' ability to predict and tract storms, study various earth situations in depth to detect areas of possible flooding, then work out ways to prevent it, along with helping with agriculture."

"I'm all for that," Quinn said. "Given that this place is only a few feet above the water."

"I'm definitely not a tech guy, but apparently drones are able to do that better than even satellites because they can zero in on wide range areas with much more clarity."

"That's wonderful. And good for the students and Gabe for working to save our planet," Amanda said. "But that aside, I really love the idea of the light show."

After agreeing, Quinn delivered a mug of Surfin' USA, this summer's homage to the Beach Boys to a wiry man who, despite his age, had spryly climbed on a stool down the bar. Magnus Ragnarsson had been coming into Mannion's since it opened for a daily glass of beer, claiming it contributed to a long life. Since his family had held his ninety-sixth birthday celebration here last year, Quinn figured he might have a point. A few months after that party, his wife of seventy years had died of a sudden heart attack, which was when he'd moved into a water-front studio apartment on the other side of the ferry dock. Seth had turned the eyesore of an abandoned shuttered sawmill into housing for low income in-dividuals and families, while Amanda had created a beautiful greenspace and children's park in front.

As Quinn shot the breeze with Magnus, he heard that now familiar sound and glanced over to see Amanda laughing at something Burke had said.

He'd watched her bloom after leaving her hus-band, not unlike one of her flowers. That protective reserve she'd worn around herself had faded away and she'd made close friends. First with Kylee and Mai, playing a role in their wedding after designing the yard for the cottage they'd bought to bring their adopted baby girl home to. Through them, she'd met

Brianna, which was how Quinn had gotten to know her when she'd come in for an order of wings with Brianna and Chelsea.

He was supposed to be the guy who knew everything. Which just went to show how wrong the people who believed that were. Because he'd never picked up on the signs of emotional and physical abuse her husband had been putting her through. Fortunately, Aiden, who'd been on enough domestic violence calls early in his big-city cop career, had spotted them, convinced her to let him help, and had, quite possibly, saved her life.

"You know, this is damn good beer," Magnus told him, his thick mustache whitened with foam. As he held the mug up, the sun shining through the wall of windows had it gleaming a rich burnished gold. "So, I have a question."

"Okay." Like those with Quinn's own grandfather, Magnus's conversations could go veering off track easily.

"How come a guy who's smart enough to have been a big shot–city lawyer and now brew award-winning beers like this doesn't have enough brains to take that gal off the market?"

"What gal would that be?" Quinn asked.

It was Magnus's turn to look down the bar. "That pretty brown-eyed landscaper gal. She got shed of her bad husband nearly eighteen months ago. If you don't make a move soon, some other hotshot's gonna move in and you'll have missed your chance."

Deciding it would be disingenuous to insist he

didn't know what Magnus was talking about, he asked, "Is it that obvious?"

"Son, when you're my age, and don't have that much going on in your own life, you tend to get your entertainment from watching others." After nearly a lifetime in the States, the elderly man's voice still carried a bit of a native Icelandic tilt up at the end of a sentence. "Which is how I learned, a long time ago, to pick up on the fact that girl is, as my great-granddaughter Alice would say, really into you."

As he looked back at Quinn, his eyes were a little hazy from cataracts. But, through the clouds, a knowing light gleamed. "Take her fishing."

"Fishing?" Although Quinn had considered several scenarios for an easygoing, no-stress first date, fishing had not been on any of his carefully thought-out lists.

"That's how I got my Anna." Magnus looked upward, as if the connection with his wife was as strong as it had been when she'd been alive. "I took her out salmon fishing on my boat. Then I grilled a nice fillet for her, along with some fresh corn. Women like men who can cook.

"Fortunately, like your Jarle, I taught myself while working on a fishing boat. It was either that or the crew eating out of cans the entire season... Yep." He nodded his head, which had gone bald, save for a bit of white fluff at the crown. "That's the ticket. Your brother built you a great cruiser. Take the girl out on it."

"I'll keep that in mind." Thanking Magnus for the

advice, Quinn wished him a good day, and headed back down the bar to where Burke and Amanda were still engaged in what appeared to be a lively conversation.

CHAPTER TWO

PIPER LOWELL COULDN'T believe her luck. After arriving at SeaTac, wanting to save the money she'd have spent on a rental car, she'd opted for a nearly four-hour bus ride to Honeymoon Harbor, which, at first glance, reminded her of the village her mum had grown up in. Located in North Wales, Betws-y-Coed was the gateway to Snowdonia National Park, which boasted verdant forests, dazzling lakes, snowcapped mountains, and tumbling waterfalls. Also, both had the same Victorian feel, with quaint shops and restaurants.

Now, just when she'd begun to worry that perhaps her parents had been right to be apprehensive about her impulsive decision to make this trip, she'd been given a sign. An actual sign. One posted in the front window of the red brick building, advertising a job for a hostess/server. And even better, the job came with a rent-free apartment.

Wiping her suddenly damp hands on the front of her jeans, she took a deep breath to calm her nerves, dragged a hand through her mass of copper hair and pushed open the door that looked as if it had been a prop from one of those old-time Hollywood black-

and-white American gangster movies her British
father had gotten into streaming during New York
City's quarantine days.

The inside of the pub was rustic, but inviting. The
ceiling was stamped tin, which also was a throw-
back to olden times and the tables had been crafted
from heavy wood. The bus had arrived at a fortunate
hour, given that only three of the tables were occupied, suggesting that either the business wasn't all
that successful, or perhaps this was merely a slow
time of service. After all, back in New York, many
restaurants weren't even open midday. Across the
room, five tables faced large windows that offered
a view of a bright white ferry with green trim that
was pulling up to the dock. A second tier of tables
sat on risers above the first.

Apart from the tables, in an alcove set off by a
brick arch, were a dart board and two pool tables.

Her gaze moved to the long, wooden bar across
the room, where a tall man with thick, raven black
hair was talking with a man and woman seated on
stools.

"Hi," he called out. "You can take a seat anywhere.
We're currently without a hostess." His voice was
deep and warm, echoing the welcome in his blue eyes.

"I know." Her voice broke, maddening her when it
revealed her nerves. "I saw the sign. I'm here about
the job."

"Well, that's a piece of good news." His smile was
equally welcoming. Americans, she'd discovered,
were far more open with their emotions than the Brit-

ish. "Why don't you come sit down and we can talk about it?"

Nerves rattling, she wove her way through the empty tables to the bar and sat down a few seats away from the man and woman engaged in conversation. Now that she was closer, she took another, closer look at the man. "You're Burke Mannion!"

"That would be me." His smile, warm like the bartender's, creased his cheeks, but was framed by dual dimples that she'd seen plastered all over magazines in her current home city. "Are you a football fan?"

She decided it would be rude to point out that only in the U.S. was the game he'd become rich and famous for referred to as football. Which was ironic because unlike the international sport his country called soccer, there were only two players on an American football team who ever actually kicked a ball.

"I've spent the past two years in New York," she said. "And attended all the Knights home games with my parents. My dad's a crazy avid fan. Everyone was very surprised when you retired so early."

"I was surprised myself." Another grin flashed, more appealing than the first. She'd only ever seen Burke Mannion on magazine covers, the jumbotron screen during games, and TV interviews, but as handsome and hot as he'd appeared, he was triple that in person. He tilted his head. "You're not American."

"I'm British." She acknowledged what her accent had already revealed. "But I've dual citizenship because my mum gave birth to me while she was in America, working at the consulate in San Francisco. I've spent the past two years in New York, while my parents are stationed at the UN." Desperate for the job offered on the flyer, she wanted the pub owner to know that she'd be having no visa problems.

"Handy about the dual citizenship," the man holding her future in his hands said. "I'm Quinn Mannion, pub owner, brewer, and older brother of the football hero." The smile he shot his brother suggested it was easy sibling teasing, something she'd never experienced, being an only child. "Can I get you something to drink? A Coke, maybe?"

"Just water, thank you." Piper's mouth was dry. Her lips parched as if she'd crawled across the Sahara to get to town, rather than taking a scenic bus ride.

"Water it is." He arched a brow. "Ice?"

She nodded. "Thank you."

He filled a glass and placed it on the table. "So," he said easily, "As I said, I'm Quinn Mannion, the QB's older brother and owner of this pub. And you'd be?"

"I'm Piper Lowell."

"Have you ever worked in a restaurant before?"

"Yes, I have. My grandparents have a restaurant in Cromer, Norfolk. That's a seaside resort from British Victorian days."

"Honeymoon Harbor is a Victorian town."

"I noticed the resemblance right away." And had thought it to be another sign that she belonged here. "Cromer prides itself on its restaurant scene, which is locally famous for its Cromer crab."

"Another coincidence. We have Dungeness crab here."

"I saw that." There were several items featuring it on the menu posted in the window next to the poster. "Cromer crab is cooked in several ways, but the traditional way is seasoned, then stuffed into the shell with a salad garnish. I worked there during summers, so I've had experience not only in a restaurant, but handling a busy tourism season. We didn't have an official front of house. Everyone just pitched in, but I've watched *Top Chef*, and took note of how that works during restaurant wars."

She saw the humor in his eyes and belatedly realized that might not have been the most ideal thing to admit. Especially since whoever took on the role of front of house in that TV show typically ended up going home.

"That's more experience than most applicants would have," he said. "My former hostess Katie's husband was just transferred to Austin. That's in Texas."

"I know. I've seen the *Austin City Limits* music show on TV."

"Well, as happy as I am for Katie and her husband, because it was a promotion for him, it left me trying to find someone late in the summer hiring season." He folded his arms, displaying biceps that revealed he did more than just serve up drinks behind his bar. "What brings you all the way across the country to us?"

"I'm taking a gap year before going to college," Piper said. "I've seen a great deal of the eastern part of the country while living in New York, and taking weekend trips with my parents to Boston, Philadelphia, and Washington, DC. We also went up the coast to Maine last fall.

"After seeing so many Instagram reels of Washington State, especially this peninsula, I decided it'd be an interesting place to start exploring the western side of the country." It wasn't the truth, the whole truth, and nothing but the truth, the way she'd heard stated during trials on American television *Law & Order* programs, but it was, she decided, close enough. "I'm especially interested in your rain forest. I've been to rain forests in Thailand, but yours looks very different in the videos."

"I don't mean to interrupt, though I'm doing exactly that, but you might be interested to know that Washington's rain forest is a temperate one," the woman seated next to Burke Mannion said. "But you're so lucky to have been to Thailand. I've been studying rain forests for a job I'm working on—I'm a landscape architect—and read that over thirty percent of the country is covered in tropical rainforests, and Indonesia's forests have a diversity of plants equaled only in Amazonia."

"I went on a tour with my parents and our guide said that over twenty-five thousand species of flowering plants have been catalogued within the country, with two thousand species of orchids growing on Borneo alone," Piper said.

"I've heard that. Along with the fact that forty percent of those plants exist nowhere else on Earth. You were fortunate to have seen them. This job I'm working on has me determined to take a trip there. Maybe at the end of December, after Christmas, which is a slow time for my business."

"That would be the best time to go," Piper said. "It'd still be warm, but not stifling hot, and the rains will have mostly stopped. Except for the beaches, which can still get storms. I spent a year there with my parents. They're very into saving the planet."

"A worthy goal," Burke joined the conversation. "So, they're environmentalists?"

"Mum says everyone must be an environmentalist these days if we're to survive. But that's not their day job. They're both British civil servants. My dad's a trade minister assigned to UNCTAD, the United Nations Conference on Trade and Development, and Mum currently works as an interpreter there. Which is why we were in New York City."

"I've been there," Quinn said. "Not Thailand, but New York. And the UN was one of the places we visited. My mom's a retired school teacher and principal, who lived in full-time teaching mode when my brothers, sister, and I were growing up. One summer, we took a trip from DC to New York, with stops in Philadelphia and Boston. I doubt there was a historical marker or statue that we missed."

She laughed at that, feeling her nerves untangle a bit. "Sounds as if our mothers would get along great." She decided against mentioning her parents having had dinner at the White House.

"So," he said, getting down to business. "Why

don't we go down the bar, and you can fill out an application?"

The bar was long with a curve at the end. "This looks really old," she said, as she ran a finger along the gleaming but somewhat battered wood before sitting down on one of the stools.

"It's from the 1800s," Quinn said. "My brother-in-law, Seth, restores old buildings and found it in a salvage yard in Virginia City. That's an old Victorian mining town that's in California, not the state of Virginia. Seth says it's supposedly from an old brothel."

"Really?" Piper's dad loved American Western movies, which had her imagining beautiful women in scarlet-as-sin satin corset dresses showing off a scandalous amount of leg adorned in striped black stockings.

He shrugged. "That's what the seller claimed. But he might have been thinking it'd up the price if it had a more interesting past. I'll be right back." He went behind the swinging doors to the kitchen and returned with a clipboard with a single piece of paper on it.

"Have you received many applications?" she asked as she took the pen attached to the top of the clipboard. Although she'd been careful with her spending, the trip had drained most of her savings and she didn't know what she'd do if she didn't get this job. With her parents having been reluctant about her taking this trip, the last thing Piper wanted to do was to have to call them and ask for money.

"You're the first," he said. "Which, from what

you've already told me about your experience, makes filling out this application a formality. If you want the job, you will need to be eighteen to get your MAST certification to service alcohol in Washington State, which isn't a big deal, since I can always work the tables in a pinch."

"I'm eighteen. And what's a MAST certificate?"

"It allows someone between the ages of eighteen and twenty-one to serve alcohol as long as they're supervised by someone over twenty-one. Which would be me. Or Jarle, who's the cook, who'll you'll meet in a bit. It requires taking a course, which is available online, which shouldn't be any problem for you."

He went on to list her duties, which weren't that different from when she'd worked for her grandparents. "You'll also have meal and rest breaks. If you choose to eat here, your meals are free. During the summer, because we're still having trouble finding workers, there may be times when you have to work a six-day week. With Mondays off."

"That works for me." It wasn't as if she planned to have a busy social life. And once Quinn Mannion learned the true reason why she'd come to Honeymoon Harbor, he might send her packing long before the tourism season was over.

She was considering that possibility when he surprised her by naming a base salary higher than she could have made in New York. "That's very generous," she said, thinking that her parents, proponents of everyone deserving a living wage, would approve. And that was on top of not having to pay rent. If she could have even been able to find a place, which hadn't appeared likely.

"Have you ever worked in the States before?"

"No. But I was volunteering at an after-school rec center put on by New York City's Parks and Recreation Center before everything shut down."

"That must've been tough on the kids," he said. She liked that his first thought was one of compassion. "So, here's how taxes work here. The US is one of only two countries in the world that imposes citizenship-based taxation rather than residence-based taxation. This means that all US citizens are required to file an annual tax return no matter where they live in the world.

"But, given your status as a dual citizen, you won't have to worry about double taxation, because we have a tax treaty with the UK. I can help you with the paperwork. Typically, and in your situation, you'll pay taxes to whichever country you reside in for the majority of the tax year. Which, by the way, is a different time period here in the States than the UK. But if you're going to spend most of your gap year in this country—"

"I plan to." Dearly hoped to.

"Then we'll set you up for US withholding tax."

"Do you get a lot of British workers?" Piper was surprised by the clarity with which he explained that.

"Again, you'd be the first. But before I got into brewing beer and opened this place, I was an attorney in Seattle with clients who did business all over the world. Advising them on tax law was part of my job."

"That's quite a change in occupation," she said as she started filling out the simple form.

From the plaques and trophies on the glass shelves on the wall, it appeared his beer had won a lot of awards. Still, even though this seemed to be a very nice pub, it had to be a downgrade from his previous occupation.

"It was."

"I'm going to be an attorney."

He folded his arms and looked down at her from his considerable height. "Do you have a specialty in mind?"

"I'm focusing on humanitarian issues. I intend to work at the ICC. The International Criminal Court," she clarified.

"I've heard of it," he said dryly, which had embarrassed color—the bane of all redheads—flooding into her cheeks. Of course an attorney with high-profile international clients would know of the court whose mandate was to investigate and try individuals charged with the gravest crimes of genocide, war crimes, crimes against humanity, and crimes of aggression.

"That's quite a lofty goal," he noted.

"And an important one. As former UN secretary General Kofi Annan said, 'This cause is the cause of all humanity.'" When she'd reached an age when most teenagers would be getting their driving permits, she'd lived in a country where adult women weren't legally allowed to drive. Which was, unfortunately, the least of the repressive behavior against women she'd witnessed. "My parents have been posted all over the world, so I've seen people suffer a great many inequalities. And while I realize it may sound idealistic, I want—no, *intend*—to be an agent of change."

She saw something flicker in those deep blue eyes, which she took as doubt regarding her determination. Even her own parents had gently suggested that university was a time of exploration, to discover possible life choices. She'd often wondered if that was because her mum had once planned to do the same thing she intended. As important an occupation as being an international interpreter was, having served at various embassies and consulates like the UN, Piper occasionally wondered if her mother had ever regretted sidetracking her own plans to change the world when she'd become a mother.

"The sign says the position comes with an apartment?" she asked, changing the topic back to her potential job.

"It's on the second floor," he confirmed. "When I had the building refurbished, my brother-in-law contractor created an office space and the apartment. I lived there my first year in business. It's small, but it worked for me. I also had a small kitchenette added, so I wouldn't have to come down here every time I wanted a sandwich."

"I'm sure it'll be fine," she said. "Better than fine. I'm currently staying at the motel by the lighthouse and they told me when I arrived today that the room was only available for two nights."

"What were you planning to do?"

He didn't sound judgmental the way her parents had responded when they'd first heard her plan, as if she wouldn't be able to take care of herself. They were, she'd decided, a contradiction to the old saying about opposites attracting. Although they were certainly adventurous, going places many people couldn't find on a map, neither was impulsive. Which made sense, because growing up, she'd had a front seat to all the world's problems as they'd discuss their work over the dinner table each night. The work they did, the decisions they made, not only reflected on their home country, but also had the power to impact people's lives. Often in a life or death way.

When Piper realized Quinn Mannion was waiting for an answer, she forced a smile. "I wasn't certain. I'd gone online looking for work and it seemed that everything's filled. Including jobs at the national park."

"Those usually fill months in advance," he said. "The only way you'd get one now would be if someone quit."

"So I was told. But I had two days to come up with a plan and decided to trust in the universe giving me an answer." This time, her smile was real. "And it did. When I saw the sign in your window, I knew I was meant to work here."

Those creases in his cheeks deepened as he smiled at her assertion. But he didn't seem to be laughing at her. Then he glanced over to the door as a group of young women came in.

"Since, as you already know, we're short-staffed, I've got to get back to work. Fill that out," he said, pointing at the form, "then we'll go over the particulars of the job, and I'll show you the apartment."

"Yes, sir. And thank you, Mr. Mannion. I promise you won't regret hiring me." She hoped.

"It's Quinn. We're not big on formality around here. As for hiring you, one thing both the law and tending bar has taught me is how to be a quick judge of character. Summers are always crazy busy, but I have no doubt that the universe also came through and gave me the ideal person for the job."

"So, you believe in fate?"

The smile reached eyes as blue as the waters outside the windows. "I'm half Irish. How could I not?"

PIPER WATCHED AS Quinn deftly prepared cocktails— two strawberry margaritas, a watermelon martini, and a mojito—to go with the order of fried calamari the waitress had turned into the kitchen. After delivering the drinks, he returned, took her application, skimmed it, and declared it perfect. Then he opened a wooden door and led her up a set of stairs to an apartment.

Expecting a cramped place beneath some bare eaves, she was surprised by the cozy space. There were dormer windows in the back offering a stunning view of the harbor and still snowcapped mountain, which the tour guide she'd viewed online from New

York told her was Mount Baker, part of the Cascade Range that, in this state, also included Mount Rainier and Mount Saint Helens—which had blown its top, sending ash all around the world for two weeks.

Her mother, who remembered seeing that eruption on a BBC report when she was a child, was concerned about her daughter living in what her Science Channel–loving father knew was called the Ring of Fire, for all the still active volcanoes. Since the mountain towering over the harbor wasn't smoking, Piper decided she was safe enough. Though she definitely wasn't going to tell her parents about the blue-and-white tsunami and earthquake evacuation signs she'd seen from the bus window.

There was, as he'd told her, a living room, kitchenette, bedroom, and a bathroom with a large walk-in shower. Everything was spotlessly clean. "How long has it been since you've lived here?" she asked, instinctively running a fingertip over a tabletop polished to a glossy sheen. The fragrance of lemons floated in the air.

"Three years," he said. "From time to time, a new employee has stayed here, but it's sat unused most of the time. I could use it as extra office space, I suppose, but it's easier for me to use the one I had built off the kitchen."

"My mother's a clean freak," Piper said. "But I think you may have her beat."

He laughed. "I have a friend, Megan Montgomery, whom you'll be meeting. She owns a cleaning company that does our after-hours janitorial work, and while her business has grown enough that she doesn't actually do the work herself these days, she has a crew come in every two weeks to polish this place up so it doesn't start looking like Miss Havisham's House."

"*Great Expectations*," she murmured. "I had to read that in school."

"Me too. I suspect most students do," he said. "It's an important tale of social standing and wealth not being as important as loyalty and compassion. My dad, who'll you'll undoubtedly meet if you stay the entire summer—which I'm hoping you'll do—is a living example of that being true. He was supposed to go into his family's banking business. But instead, after living for two years in Nepal, he returned home, married his high school sweetheart and now he runs a Christmas tree farm.

"He's also served as Honeymoon Harbor's unpaid mayor since I was a kid. He keeps threatening to quit, but no one will run against him. Personally, I think—no, I know—he enjoys it. Even though he says at times, like during a recent annual festival planning committee meeting, it's a bit like herding cats."

"My father has often said the same thing about his work. As has my mother, working at the UN." She focused on what, to her, was the intriguing fact he'd just shared. "You grew up on a Christmas tree farm?"

"I sure did." His eyes lit with reminiscence. "The running family joke is that my parents had five kids in order to have free labor. My sister, brothers, and I spent much of our time planting or trimming trees, because they don't grow into that conical shape on their own. We'd gripe, like kids do. But looking back, it was a pretty great life."

"I think it sounds wonderful." When she'd been seven or eight, her parents had planned a trip for them to visit a Christmas tree farm in Scotland during the holidays. But then some crisis had sprung up in some long-forgotten country that had caused them to cancel the trip.

"The Mannion Christmas tree farm puts on a big event from the day after Thanksgiving up until Christmas Eve," he said. "My folks started out just selling trees, then, over the years, it's become an event people come from all over to participate in. There are sleigh rides, which are really more like a wagon hitched up to a tractor, music, lots of lights, hot apple cider, and cocoa. Lots of families have been cutting their own trees for multiple generations. If you're still in town for the holidays, I think you'd enjoy it."

"It sounds grand." And perhaps impossible, given that she might not still be here by Christmas. But not wanting to blow her chances for this job, she kept that to herself.

CHAPTER THREE

"I'M AFRAID," Gloria Wells said.

Jolene Mannion looked up from shelving bars of soap wrapped in the Thairapy Salon and Spa lighthouse logo a graphic design student at Clearwater Community College had created for them. It was one of the many beauty products she and her mother made and sold at their Thairapy Salon and Spa. "About what?"

"Getting married." At the same time, her mother was boxing up the special orders customers from across the country had ordered through their website.

"Why would you say that? Michael Mannion is a perfect catch. He's rich, he's traveled the world, he's an amazing artist, but also an entrepreneur, and a good man with how he's created those working studios for all the local artists in that building he bought. He's kind, generous, smart, and, he's really, really hot."

Brother of John Mannion, Honeymoon Harbor's mayor, and uncle to all five Mannion siblings, he'd aged well. Like George Clooney, if Clooney's eyes were the blue all the Mannion men had been gifted with, instead of brown. "The only problem I can see is a lot of women are going to be very unhappy about you taking him off the market."

"He's famous."

"I suppose so. In art circles. But he's so down-to-earth, you'd never know it."

"He's been to a royal wedding." Gloria ran the tape runner over one of the boxes, and stuck the address label on it. "And danced with a princess of Montacroix." Coincidentally, an earlier royal wedding of that same family in the early 1900s had resulted in the town's name change.

"They're friends." Though the video clips and photos, showing the princess's dress flaring out as Michael had twirled her, had admittedly dominated entertainment news, TikTok, and Instagram reels for a surprisingly long time. "From when he painted her portrait."

"That's what I mean." Gloria threw up her hands. "Who does that?"

"Dance? Or paint?"

"Either. Both! All you have to do is Google his name and there are pages and pages of him with rich, stunningly beautiful women. He was on the red carpet at Cannes with Lady Gaga!"

"You were on the red carpet at the Emmys."

"The daytime ones. With my daughter." As if realizing she'd sounded as if she'd been scoffing at the event that had, up until now, been the highlight of her life, color flooded into Gloria's cheeks. "Please don't think I was insulting you. I was never so proud in my life."

"I know." Her mother had informed everyone she'd met that day that her daughter had been nominated for an Emmy. Including the young woman bussing the luncheon table.

Which took Jolene's mind back to when, for a woman born literally on the wrong side of the tracks, she'd been living her dream life. She'd escaped Honeymoon Harbor, and had been living in Beverly Hills, in the same 90201 zip code where Jason Priestly and Luke Perry had hung out. She'd come close to winning an Emmy in the Outstanding Makeup for a Limited Series or Movie (Non-Prosthetic category). While the Creative Arts Awards hadn't been included in the big prime-time Emmy extravaganza show, they'd been held in the very same theater, and until her marriage to former Honeymoon Harbor bad boy turned police chief, Aiden Mannion, the highlight of her life had been being able to fly her mother to Los Angeles to be her date, even though she'd lost to yet another Henry VIII costume drama.

Gloria Wells had not led an easy life. Losing her parents when she'd been a teenager had led her into the arms of Jake Wells, which in turn had resulted in her getting pregnant at sixteen, and becoming the married mother of a newborn at seventeen. Unfortunately, Jolene's father turned out to be a low-rent criminal who'd grown and sold marijuana before it had been legalized, cut and sold timber from federal lands, illegally harvested oysters and clams he sold to Seattle restaurants and markets, and finally, while drunk, had decided it would be a good idea to take his S&W .38 to Port Angeles and rob the state liquor store.

That crime had ended with him being incarcerated
in the Clallam Bay Corrections Center. Six months
later he'd been killed when a huge tree limb from
an old-growth Douglas fir had crashed down on him
while he'd been clearing winter debris from hiking
trails on a trustee prison work crew.

But Gloria had persevered, graduating from high
school, then studying cosmetology at Clearwater Community College, and after getting her degree, she'd
begun cutting hair in their trailer outside town.

Because her mother was every bit as talented as
many of the hairdressers Jolene had worked with in
Hollywood, the salon had thrived, and after a series
of unfortunate events, Jolene had returned home to
work with her in the old lighthouse keeper's house
that Seth Harper, Brianna Mannion's husband, had
remodeled into a hair salon and day spa.

Making it a family affair, Sarah Mannion, who'd
received her interior design certificate after years of
helping friends decorate their homes for free, had
gifted them with a design palette to encourage relax-
ation, using cohesive beach glass blues and greens
she'd described as "secret garden meets seaside."
Even before Jolene's mother and Michael had started
dating, he'd chipped in by painting a mural of a tropical beach on the reception room wall of the spa,
which, if the wall was taken out of the building and
auctioned off at Sotheby's, could probably go for as
much as seven figures. More of his prints decorated
the private massage and skin care rooms.

The decor was casual enough for local clientele, while sophisticated enough for the occasional wealthier brides who'd come from all over the country to get married in a town whose name got it included on many destination wedding lists in bridal magazines and online.

"Then there was that possible affair he had with Caroline Harper," Gloria said, returning the conversation to its earlier track as she put another box together.

Jolene understood her mother's concerns about marriage, having been so badly burned once. But Michael Mannion was the polar opposite of her father. She wondered if, perhaps, her mother subconsciously believed that she didn't deserve the celebrity artist.

"Caroline Harper would never have an affair." She might not know what was giving her mother an attack of pre-wedding anxiety, but about this, Jolene was certain.

"You weren't living here then. Back when Caroline had left Ben."

"I heard all about it from Brianna. And they weren't really separated."

"They were living apart."

"True. But Caroline only moved out to get Seth's dad's attention. To shake up his life enough that he'd live up to his promise to retire and travel." Which was how they ended up spending much of the rainy months following the sunshine around the country in that flashy motorhome with the rocky Washington coast painted on the sides.

"She and Michael were dating," her mother insisted. "They were seen out painting together. And Mabel Marshall told me, while I was giving her a cut and color back then, that they were seen having dinner together at Leaf."

"Mabel is the worst gossip in town. Even worse than Mildred Mayhew, which is saying something, since Mildred gets paid for writing *Honeymoon Harbor Herald*'s 'Seen Around Town' column. Which is basically just gossip she takes from the Facebook page. Men and women can be friends without adultery taking place."

"I know that. And it's what Michael said when I very casually mentioned Caroline during some time we had alone during that Thanksgiving dinner at the Mannions during my cancer scare. He told me that he'd first met her years ago when she and some girlfriends were visiting the peninsula on a road trip. It was just before a performance at the Theater in the Firs, and he'd had his eye on her, because, well, as he'd pointed out, it's not every day that a pretty girl drives into town in a pink convertible. But before he could hit on her, there was a thunderstorm, and while they were all sheltering out of the rain, Ben moved in."

That had Jolene laughing. "Ben Harper is probably the least likely guy in the world to move in on anyone."

"You didn't know him when he was young."

"I seriously doubt he was that different. It's hard to get five words in a row out of him. One of the reasons their marriage has worked so well for so many years is probably because Caroline talks enough for both of them. Even now, after decades here in the Pacific Northwest, she's still a quintessential Southern belle. Besides, I've heard the story of the breakup, and Seth claims she made the first move when *she* hit on Ben that night."

"Oh. Well." Gloria blew out a breath. "Even so, that doesn't mean that Michael might not have been carrying a torch all those years."

"You can't have it both ways, Mom." Jolene moved on to straightening the bottles of shampoo and conditioner that invariably got moved around by clients always looking for that perfect item that would make their hair look like some celebrity's. Having done hair and makeup for many of the country's top actors and pop stars, Jolene knew all that went into the perfection viewers saw on the screen.

She'd enjoyed her previous life. It had allowed her to travel the world and develop close relationships with stars she'd never have met if she'd stayed here in Honeymoon Harbor. Styling for a movie was never a one and done, not like she and her mother did when they sent a client out of the salon. In movies and television, you had to be constantly available to take care of any bad hair days. Often, she'd spent an entire day of shooting on the set, jumping in between shots to ensure that the actor's hair exactly matched the previous shot.

"Either he's the playboy of the Western world. Or he's been carrying a torch for a woman he only talked to for a few minutes decades ago. They're friends. Nothing more."

"That's what he says."

"And you don't believe him?"

There was a long silence while her mother began checking items off a printed-out order list as she packed a new box. "I want to." She blew out another breath, then dragged a hand through her hair, which was a sapphire blue today. Gloria's hair changed color nearly as often as the peninsula's weather. "Really, I do."

Realization dawned. Having learned from a *Hollywood Reporter* breaking news article that her actor boyfriend had dumped her and gotten engaged to his co-star while filming a reboot of *The Thorn Birds* in Australia, Jolene had harbored a few trust issues of her own. And although she'd moved on, she had to admit that the memory of that already twice-divorced actress flashing a diamond the size of the iceberg that had sunk the *Titanic* occasionally stung. Not because her heart had been broken, but that she'd been foolish enough to give it to such an unworthy person.

"He's not Dad, Mom."

"I know that. If I couldn't trust him, I wouldn't be marrying him. Or have Caroline officiate at our wedding."

Caroline and Ben Harper came home every year for part of the summer and one of the highlights of one homecoming was when Seth's mother, who'd gotten ordained online, had officiated at Kylee and Mai's Hawaiian theme wedding.

There was a long pause as Gloria looked out the window as the ferry passed by, chugging toward the landing, followed by the usual parade of seagulls, diving for fish the boat would churn up.

"Your father was my first love. I know we were married too young, but so many teenage boys in his situation would've just told me to get an abortion. Or dumped me to raise you alone. But he insisted that I have you, not that I personally would've considered ending my pregnancy. Women have a right to choose and I knew I wanted you. But also, instead of ghosting me like a lot of guys might, he was excited about starting a family. A concept he admittedly had romanticized ideas about, having grown up with a violent father.

"Of course, marriage and parenthood were more difficult, especially when you're teenagers and don't have a clue or enough money to even get through the week. But I did love him. And although I'd already loved you before you were born, when you were first put into my arms, I was swamped by a tsunami of love. The delivery room nurses later told me I cried. I don't remember that. Just that you were, and still are, the most amazing thing I've ever accomplished."

"Damn it. Now you're making me cry," Jolene complained. Their family might not have ever been Disney rated, but she'd always known that while her parents' marriage had its ups and downs, they'd both always cared for her. As well as they could.

"Your father had many flaws," Gloria said on a

sigh, ruffling those blue waves as she ran her hands through her hair. "But, for the record, he never cheated on me."

"I never considered that he had." In a town the size of Honeymoon Harbor, she definitely would've heard any rumors about her dad playing around on her mom. Especially from those bullying mean girls who'd been the bane of her high school existence.

It was Jolene's turn to sigh. "I loved him too, Mom. Especially how he made me laugh." He might have been far from what society considered a normal dad. But he'd had a seemingly endless supply of lame dad jokes, which, even in her teens, when she was trying to be cool, always managed to make her laugh.

"He was flawed by an illness he couldn't overcome." Jolene had known addicts in California. She'd done their hair and makeup and had worked on sets with them. Except for the sexual harassers, which had gotten her drummed out of the business when she'd joined the #MeToo group of women telling their stories, they were mostly good people driven by addictions they couldn't control.

"And again, Michael is not dad. After all you've been through during your life, including the terribly tragic way you were widowed, you deserve some happiness. So, how about you stop creating problems where there aren't any?"

Having been born to a teen mom, Jolene had often thought that their relationship was, at times, more big and little sister than mom and daughter. This was one of those times. "I suppose many brides have pre-wedding jitters," she allowed. "Heaven knows, I've done hair and makeup at enough weddings to have witnessed quite a few. Some real meltdowns."

"Did you have one? You're so strong. I can't imagine you ever having a meltdown. But did you at least have jitters?"

Jolene thought back on her relationship with Aiden. "It depends on whether you consider having a panic attack while watching Christmas movies and getting drunk on a bottle of Baileys and two pints of Rocky Road and Cherry Garcia ice cream after he'd casually asked if I could ever consider marrying a cop as having had jitters."

"Why would you panic? He's certainly not the town bad boy he was growing up. And you used to hate Christmas movies. You claimed they were unrealistic."

"Well, yeah, that was back when I was cynical about love. But my best friend, Shelby—who I'd called to talk me off the ledge—insisted I give them another try. Because although those movies might be supersweet, they were also all about finding true love in the most unexpected places between the most different people, who face obstacles, then live happily ever after."

"Well, that certainly fits the two of you," Gloria agreed.

"I know. That's what terrified me. It was all so easy—I couldn't trust it."

"Because of your father and me." Her mother's

face fell and a sadness Jolene hadn't seen for a very long time shadowed her eyes.

"No... Okay, maybe only a bit because of that, but don't forget, I'd also watched a lot of celebrity marriages break up. Not to mention having my own boyfriend dump me for his co-star after I'd gone all the way to Australia to visit him on location when he'd been making that movie."

"Which failed miserably at the box office," Gloria remembered. "As it should have, because while he was admittedly good-looking in a pretty boy sort of way, he was terrible in the role. The entire idea of a remake was ridiculous anyway, since everyone knows that Richard Chamberlain will always be the only Father Ralph."

Having thought exactly the same thing at the time, Jolene laughed. "I love you, Mom."

"I love you more." It was something they'd said going back as far as Jolene could remember.

"I *am* happy." Gloria looked around the room Seth Harper had remodeled, and Aiden's mother had designed. "Why wouldn't I be?" she asked in a way that had Jolene wondering which of them she was trying to convince. "I spend my days working with the best daughter in the world, whom I adore, in a beautiful studio, in the most beautiful place on earth."

Having worked in quite a few beautiful places, both in California and around the world, Jolene couldn't disagree. "Still, sharing your life with that one special man will make it even better. Michael

Mannion is like the proverbial cherry on the top of a hot fudge sundae."

"That would be true," Gloria agreed, color rising in her cheeks as her mind appeared to wander somewhere sexual Jolene had no desire to go. "I'm lucky to have him."

"And he's lucky to have you. Because you're better than any model, movie star, or princesses he may or may not have dated. You're special. And there's no one else I'd have rather had for a mom."

"Look at what you've done." Gloria reached for a tissue and began dabbing at her eyes. "You've made me cry and now my mascara is going to run. I'm going to have to redo my makeup before my dinner with Michael."

"No, you won't." She gave her mother a hug, took the tissue and dried her wet cheeks, which were still unlined despite being in her fifties. "Because that mascara is one I developed for crying actors. You could run out of here and jump into the harbor and it still wouldn't run."

"I think I'll pass on that idea," her mother said, reclaiming the natural calm that had helped her survive so many of life's storms as she began putting away the remaining packaging. "What are you and Aiden doing tomorrow night?"

"He's got some sort of joint policing meeting with the neighboring counties. So I'll probably just play with some ideas I have for using more florals from Blue House Farm in our face creams."

"All work and no play... How about pizza from

Luca's and a TV night with Lorelei and Rory? The reunion."

Their *Gilmore Girls* marathons had been a feel-good tradition for mother and daughter for as long as Jolene could remember. There were so many plot lines they could recognize from their own lives.

"The wedding episode," Jolene said. After ten rollercoaster seasons, Luke and Lorelei had finally gotten married in the reboot. "Though your wedding is going to be better."

"It's going to be exactly like I'd dreamed back when I was playing with Wedding Day Barbie and Ken," Gloria said. "Back when I didn't realize how disappointed poor Barbie's wedding night would've been because of his lack of manly equipment."

Jolene laughed at that idea. "You can't blame her for running off with G.I. Joe in those old car commercials."

"He literally left poor Ken in the dust," Gloria said on a laugh. "And I'm very happy that you managed to overcome your holiday movie cynicism because watching them together helped lift my spirits during my cancer scare."

And hadn't that been the scariest time of Jolene's life? And the reason she'd come home. And reunited with Aiden, who'd refused to give up on them, despite her doubts and fears? "But back to then, to make matters worse, when Aiden came over to the house and found me hungover, I still wasn't thinking straight and told him that I was afraid to even think about marriage because it was too easy to love him because he was sweet and perfect and we got along so well."

"I'm admittedly no expert on relationships, but it would seem to me that would be a good reason to get married."

"Of course! To any rational person, it would be. But—and I've never told this to anyone else, but I'm going to tell you, if only to show that you're not the only crazy woman in our family—I told him that I couldn't even think about marriage because we hadn't had our dark moment."

Gloria, who was putting the filled boxes into the cart they used to take them out to the car to deliver to the post office, looked back over her shoulder. "What's a dark moment?"

"It's that moment, when all is lost, and the hero—or in a romance, perhaps when the couple—knows they can never be together. In a movie, it's usually at the end of the second act leading into the third. Novels can have a looser structure, but it has to happen before the climax."

"That's fiction," Gloria argued. "It's obviously only there to add drama to a storyline. I've had enough drama in my life. I'm perfectly happy to marry Michael without us ever having our dark moment. And, with any luck, we never will."

"Aiden said much the same thing," Jolene admitted. "When he suggested we just skip it." Which they had. And look how well their marriage had turned out. There were times she'd wake up after a night of delirious lovemaking, watch the man she considered the most handsome of the Mannion men making breakfast for her while wearing nothing but a pair of boxer briefs, and she'd be amazed that she'd gotten so lucky.

CHAPTER FOUR

"This is going to be so pretty!"

Amanda turned. She'd been so occupied planting the lemon thyme that brightened fish dishes so nicely, that she hadn't noticed the girl—Piper, she remembered—come outside. "Thanks."

She stood back, folded her arms, and looked at the work in progress. The planters were of varying heights and widths, not solely for design interest, but to allow for both the eventual sizes and heights the herbs would grow.

"It's going to work out well," she decided. "You probably haven't had a chance to see Sensation Cajun, but I did a garden patio there too. Bastien Broussard—he's the owner—wanted it to resemble one of the hidden courtyards in the French Quarter where he and Desiree, his wife, grew up. So, Seth Harper laid weathered stone for a floor, and found some aged brick that he used to build a high wall and planters around the perimeter to create an aura of intimacy. Fortunately, I'd been to New Orleans and had a good idea of what he wanted, so I went with lush plants and a fountain in the middle. The fountain works well, not just as a visual element, but the falling water also works as ambient noise to soften the sound of conversation at other tables." Amanda didn't mention that the patio had appeared in *Southern Living* magazine in an article about how Southern style could fit into any part of the country. Even the very different Pacific Northwest.

"It sounds wonderful," Piper agreed. "But I think this is going to be just as special. The pub has a very different vibe from New Orleans, and with the pots, there won't be anything to detract from the view."

"You're right about the vibe, and the view is the main reason Quinn decided to add a patio. Did you know that an ancestor of his once owned it?"

"No. Admittedly, this is only my second day, but he doesn't seem to talk all that much."

Amanda laughed. "He's a quiet one all right. He's an extremely generous man, as you'll discover, but thrifty when it comes to using his words. Though when he does speak, he always seems to have exactly the right thing to say."

"Are you two a thing?"

"A thing?"

She lifted her thin shoulders. Although eighteen, she was still growing, Amanda could tell. She was all long slender arms and legs. "You know. Like boyfriend and girlfriend. Though I suppose that sounds a little silly at your ages."

Despite suddenly feeling nearly as old as the faded pink bricks Seth had discovered for Sensation Cajun's wall, Amanda laughed. "You'd think with all the words in the English language, someone would come up with one to describe that sort of relationship once you get past your teens," she said. "Or at least college age. But no, Quinn and I aren't in any sort of partnered relationship. We're just friends. I went through a difficult time a while back and he and his brother Aiden were both there for me when I needed someone."

"Quinn seems really nice."

"He's the best. All the Mannions are pretty special. I'm an only child." Amanda was surprised to hear herself volunteering that. She'd learned early not to talk about her life. First it might be social workers. Then truant officers from schools. Other kids. "I always wondered what it would be like to have a brother or sister. Watching the Mannions and hearing stories from when they were growing up, sometimes I envy him."

"I'm an only child too. Were you ever lonely?"

It was more than an idle question, Amanda sensed. There was an expression on the teen's face that resembled the wistfulness Amanda had often felt. Having grown up on the road with her father with no woman to talk with, then losing him in a car accident the week before her high school graduation, had led to her marrying in a mistaken attempt to create the type of family she'd always dreamed of. She decided to answer honestly.

"Most of the time. My mother left when I was young. And my dad and I traveled a lot. He was a professional poker player."

Piper perked up at that idea. "Like in the tournaments on television?"

"Sometimes." Amanda felt her heart clench at the memory of the police arriving at the motel door, telling her that her father had been killed in a head-on collision after some joyriding teens crossed the center line. The car had been totaled, but the next day, when she picked up his personal belongings at the police station, she discovered a check in his wallet from the casino he'd been returning from.

He'd called her on the way, telling her he was bringing home a big surprise. He hadn't told her that he'd won a jackpot that would pay for her entire four years of college. He'd won the big one, just as he'd always dreamed. Unfortunately, he hadn't stayed alive long enough to enjoy it.

"That's kind of cool," Piper said, drawing Amanda out of a memory that still ached deep in her heart.

"It had its moments." Like going out for hot fudge sundaes at two in the morning. Or springing for a dinner at some chain steakhouse. Or, when she turned sixteen, she'd woken to a bouquet of pink roses, a pink birthday cake with her name written in white frosting on the top, and a gift-wrapped box. She'd unwrapped it to discover a slender gold chain necklace strung with sixteen gold beads on it. The chain and the beads had turned green by her eighteenth birthday, but at least he'd remembered to celebrate the occasion. At the time, she'd wondered if her mother had even remembered the day she'd given birth to the daughter she'd left behind. "Actually, sometimes it was like living an adventure. Other times, I was very lonely."

"That's how I felt," Piper said. "Because my parents work for the government, I've traveled to a lot of places people twice my age may never experience. On the other hand, during the times they'd be stationed in some location considered too dangerous for families, we couldn't be together. I'd be able to stay with my grandparents during the summers, which was great. But during the school year, I'd be enrolled in a boarding school. They were always nice ones, nothing like anything from Dickens or how all the posh public boarding schools in Britain are rumored to be, but ones with diplomatic kids from around the world. So we all had that in common, but it wasn't the same as being with family."

"Life always has its ups and downs, doesn't it?" Amanda had certainly had more than her share. "I suppose the trick is to learn to appreciate the hills, then you can deal with the valleys."

"That's very wise."

Piper seemed very adult for her age. Amanda supposed it was the British upbringing. And, though she hadn't had to bring up herself as Amanda had done, she guessed a child of diplomats would have very strict house rules. Because, if you screwed up, you'd not only embarrass your family, but possibly your entire nation. Which, in turn, could be a very heavy responsibility for a child to carry.

Putting that thought aside, she smiled. "Thanks. But it's not original. I learned it from Quinn during a difficult time in my life. It's supposedly a quote about the music business, but, as Quinn told me, the idea can also apply to life. I can't carry a tune or play an instrument, but I've always loved music. All kinds. Something Quinn and I share. Although he can't entirely appreciate my BTS fandom."

"Maybe he's just jealous," Piper suggested. "I know I wasn't the only fan who went into mourning after they went on hiatus while each took turns serving their mandatory Korean military service. Because they're all really, really cute."

They shared a laugh at that, and in that brief moment, Amanda felt a sense of bonding. While the girl was technically a young woman, she gave off a youthful aura of loneliness that Amanda recognized all too well. Given their shared backgrounds, while their circumstances growing up sounded very different, she'd experienced that feeling of being on the outside. More of an observer than a participant.

"Want to help?" she asked.

"May I?"

"Absolutely." Amanda handed Piper a trowel. "Most herbs have small root systems, which make them ideal for container gardening. Although the weather isn't as changeable this time of year, it can get warm in the sun, so some of the pots have built-in reservoirs that make them self-watering for the chives, parsley, marjoram, and mint that prefer constant moisture. Rosemary, thyme, and basil prefer to dry out during watering, so they'll be in those pots."

She pointed at a second group. "I've already assured Quinn I'll drop by daily to check on them."

"That's really nice of you."

Amanda shrugged. "I often stop by in the evenings anyway. And it wouldn't say much for my business if people came to dinner and were surrounded by dying plants. I worked as a plant stylist for restaurants in various cities in California, and now here. I design the live decor, continue maintenance on the plants, sometimes taking ones that are beginning to look a little stressed back to my nursery and caring for them, while filling in the gaps with new ones."

"I never realized that was a job," Piper said. "But it makes sense, because you're right. I'd be really bummed out by having a plant dying next to me while I was eating." She gasped. "Wow. What is that?"

Amanda followed her gaze to where a playful breeze was creating little whitecaps on the deep blue water. A blue heron was stalking on tall, spindly legs in the shallows along the rocky beach, its head bobbing from side to side on its long S-shaped head. Then it suddenly ducked its long, dagger-like beak into the water, coming up with a fish before flying off with its catch.

"That's our famous Great Blue. She's heading to Herons Landing Bed-and-Breakfast," Amanda said, pointing toward the large yellow house with a bowed front on a cliff above the water. "It's an original Queen Anne Victorian. There are old Douglas firs in the back where herons have been returning to for years."

"Like coming home," Piper murmured.

Amanda glanced at the girl's face. Although she'd seemed carefully guarded earlier, her expression now looked as if it had *wistful* written across it in bold neon marker. And didn't she recognize that feeling? It was how she'd spent her life until she'd landed here in Honeymoon Harbor. Until then, she'd lived her life like a feathery bit of fluff that flew like little tiny parachutes off the head of a dandelion at the end of its short life cycle. No longer drifting, her roots were now planted deep in the town's loamy soil.

"Nature is remarkable," she said mildly, not knowing Piper Lowell well enough yet to get any deeper into the personal part of their conversation. Instead, she pulled two small bottles of water out of a cooler, handing one to Piper and decided to take a short break.

"We're on the monarch migration flyway, and I've encouraged everyone in town to plant milkweed to help feed them on their journey. They've become endangered due to climate change and pesticides."

"That's tragic," Piper said.

"It is. Which is why many of us are working so hard to protect them. Brianna, Quinn's sister, who runs Herons Landing, has a beautiful butterfly garden. Because monarchs have such a wide path, and their number is so much less than it once was, it took a season for them to find it, but once they did, they return every year."

"I'd love to see it."

"I'm sure she'd love to show it to you. You'll undoubtedly meet her soon. She gets a lot of take-out lunch meals from the pub for her guests."

"I tried to get a reservation there before I arrived in town, but they're booked solid for the summer."

"She was once a high-end concierge and it didn't take long for her reputation to spread."

"That sounds like a cool job."

Amanda laughed. "It does, doesn't it? But wait until you hear some of her stories. She'd reached the level where she was more like a butler to high-end guests, some of whom, apparently, were unreasonably demanding. She even has a questionnaire on the reservation page of her website. I've gotten the feeling that it's more a case of her choosing who she wants in her B and B than being in competition with other places in the area."

"I didn't even get to that stage."

"That's too bad. I know she would've loved to have you, but look how well it turned out. You have a lovely apartment right above your workplace."

"For free," Piper added. "So, it did turn out well. I told Quinn that although I didn't have a job or place to stay lined up, I'd decided to leave it up to the universe. Guess what he said to that?"

"I don't know. What?"

"That the universe had sent him the perfect person for the job."

"Quinn said that?"

Piper nodded. "He did. I was surprised, too, because, you know, he doesn't look like a guy who'd be

into that sort of stuff. But I asked him if that meant
he believed in fate."

"And what did he say?"

"He smiled and said he's half Irish. So, how could
he not?"

"Good answer," Amanda said, even as thoughts
began tumbling through her head. Somehow, in a
brief time, this teenage girl had discovered something about Quinn Mannion that she never would've
thought to ask. And if she had even thought of it,
would she have had the nerve to come right out and
ask him? Because then that question might lead to
another. One about whether he possibly, just maybe,
believed that fate had led her to Honeymoon Harbor. And to him?

She shook her head. What was she? Sixteen? What
was it about Quinn that had her feeling like a girl waiting for that one special boy to ask her to the prom
not that she'd ever been to one—while, at the same
time feeling oh, so much like a woman? A woman
whose hormones spiked whenever she walked into
the pub.

"We'd better get back to work," she said, deciding to ponder on all this later. The break over, they
resumed planting the herbs.

"It really is going to be wonderful," Piper said. "I
once ate at a restaurant in Florence that had herbs
growing outside where some tables were set under
the trees. There were little fairy lights strung through
the trees. It reminded me of *Lady and the Tramp*."

"I'll bet." Amanda patted down the last bit of potting mix, then asked, "What are you doing for dinner?"

"I figured I'd get some takeout. I saw a Mexican place that looked good. Then thought I'd watch some TV." A bit of wistfulness returned, reminding Amanda how it felt to be that age, and alone on your own.

"Want some company? There's a park down by the lighthouse. We could sit by the water, have some tacos, then either go to my house or come back here to watch TV. There's a historical Kdrama I've been wanting to stream."

"I love Kdramas!"

"Then let's get the rest of this flat planted, and we'll have more time to spend in Korea's Joseon Dynasty."

AFTER FINISHING THE PLANTING, they stood back to admire their work. After sending Piper inside to get ready to get takeout from Don Diego's Mexican restaurant, after gathering up the pots, Amanda had just entered the pub's restroom to wash up herself when she heard a familiar voice coming from one of the stalls. Apparently the girl hadn't bothered going upstairs to the apartment.

"It's not a bar, Mum. It's a pub. A very respectable one. I'm not working in some dive full of alcoholics. It's very popular with everyone in town."

There was a pause. "No, I haven't. Not yet."

Another, longer pause. "I'm waiting for the right time, and no, I'm not returning home. We'd agreed that I could take this gap year. Anywhere in the world, you said. Well, *this* is where I want to spend it."

Another pause.

"I realize that. But I've spent my entire life living wherever you and Dad get appointed to, or getting dumped on my grandparents or boarding school whenever I'm an inconvenience for you—" Her voice had been rising in volume and tone when she seemed to have been interrupted because there was yet another pause.

"All right," she said on a long sigh. "I realize you have little choice in the matter. And if I were a mother, I wouldn't want to put my daughter in danger either. And of course I loved being with Nana and Granddad. But you raised me to be independent. I'm grateful for that now that I'm able to make my own decisions. And right now, I'm deciding to stay in the States, hopefully here in Honeymoon Harbor, and—"

Another pause as Amanda heard her draw in a deep, shuddering breath. "I know. And I truly do understand. But you don't have to worry. I'll be fine. Really. I just need to do this, Mum. So very much." Her voice was trembling, as if she were on the verge of tears.

This time, the pause went on longer still. Amanda knew she shouldn't be eavesdropping. Yet something told her that Piper was facing what could be an impending problem, and with her parents in New York, and her not knowing anyone in town, someone had to be available to protect her from whatever it was her mother was so obviously concerned about. "I will. I promise. Meanwhile, I love you. And give my love to Dad."

As soon as she heard the call winding up, Amanda stepped outside, counted to ten, then walked in with a smile she hoped didn't look as forced as it felt.

CHAPTER FIVE

"BRIANNA TELLS ME that you've finally found some-one to take over Katie's job," Sarah Mannion said to Quinn as they shopped together at the waterfront farmer's market. Jarle and Quinn usually took turns sourcing much of the food for the pub and today was Quinn's turn. Since his mom was shopping for the family's big Fourth of July barbecue, they'd de-cided to use the task to spend some one-on-one time. Which wasn't always easy to get in a family as large as theirs. "She met her when she stopped to pick up a lunch basket for a couple staying at Herons Land-ing and reported back that she's a young English girl named Piper Lowell, and is very charming. How's she working out?"

"Surprisingly well, considering she walked in off the street three weeks ago without a recommenda-tion. She claimed to have worked at her grandpar-ents' restaurant back in England, and apparently she wasn't lying." He didn't add that he really hadn't had any options but to take a chance on the teenager who claimed the universe had sent her to his pub.

Sarah laughed. "As well as you're doing with your second career, there are times when I think you would've made a dynamite prosecutor. It's intriguing how, although you're right up there with Brianna when it comes to generosity of spirit, you're also the most cynical of my children."

"I'm not cynical." The description both surprised and stung, just a bit. "Merely careful."

She patted his arm. "Which is a good thing. Sometimes I worry that your father and I instilled firstborn syndrome in you. You always felt the need to be perfect."

That was the second time in recent weeks he'd been accused of what was definitely not his favorite topic. But, because it was his mom, he laughed it off. "Maybe perfection is a fault I inherited from both of you."

She laughed and linked arms with him before waving to Bastien and Desiree Broussard, who were shopping for Bastien's Sensation Cajun restaurant and Desiree's Ovenly boulangerie. As they made their way through the aisles, Desiree had one arm beneath her baby bump, which had Quinn wondering if he'd ever be a father. And if so, would he be a good one?

He knew dating hadn't been easy for his sister and brothers. Though they'd all managed to make it work and were living in what seemed to be idyllic marriages, here he was, the eldest, the supposedly "perfect" one, still struggling. He knew *who* he wanted. He just didn't know how to accomplish it without risking his friendship with Amanda.

"That's nice you gave the girl the use of the apartment," his mother said, breaking into thoughts that had been tumbling around in his head for too long.

He shrugged. "I needed an incentive to get someone to apply. And it's not like it was being used. Megan said when her team went there to clean it the other day, they found it—and I quote—'neat as a pin.' She told me the girl was so tidy that I probably didn't need to have it professionally cleaned. But tourism season is crazy busy, so I didn't want to have Piper worrying about dusting and stuff after a hard day's work."

"See, there's your generous side," Sarah said. "And your father and I certainly can't take credit for that because you were born with it. You always took care of your brothers and sister without having to be asked. Do you remember when you were in middle school and we were called in for a meeting with the principal and your teacher after you fought with Thane Covington?"

Of course he remembered. Even at twelve, he'd belatedly realized that his behavior had put his mayor dad and high school teacher mom in a small-town public spotlight. And not in a good way. "He made Brianna cry."

Thane Covington IV, the guy who'd gotten their debate team disqualified for cheating, which could have hurt Quinn's scholarship chances, had also stolen Brianna's candy when she'd been trick-or-treating with friends. It had been the first year she'd been old enough to go door to door without their parents.

"While I'll never condone fighting, I will admit

that your father and I felt quite a bit of pride that you'd stood up for your little sister."

Quinn shrugged again. "It's what big brothers do." He decided not to bring up punching his now brother-in-law for deeply wounding Brianna's heart when he'd told her that although he loved her, having lost his army nurse wife in a suicide bombing in Afghanistan, he wasn't willing to risk losing anyone else he loved.

"Like helping Burke with his paper route that winter," his mother said, oblivious to his thoughts. Not that it had been any big secret. One look at Seth's face when he'd shown up at the farm to grovel had undoubtedly told the story. Fortunately, nobody had asked. And neither he nor Seth had told. Though, from the uncharacteristic blasting he'd gotten from his sister later, she'd undoubtedly dragged it out of her now husband.

The winter his mother remembered had been an unseasonably cold one with sleet icing up the roads. Pairing up with Burke, and having to wear the traction cleats he usually saved for hiking in snow and ice in the mountains, he'd taken the hilly streets, because his brother had been afraid of slipping and breaking his passing arm. Which wasn't just an ego-driven concern, because getting a football scholarship was how Burke planned to pay for college.

"So," Sarah said, "getting back to Piper Lowell, what's she doing on the Fourth?"

"I didn't ask." With the Fourth of July falling on a Tuesday this year, the annual family celebration was happening the day before the holiday, which made it convenient given that Mannion's was closed on Mondays.

"Obviously you can't leave the girl to spend the day alone up in that apartment. Has she had time to make any friends yet?"

"Mom, she works for me. I'm her boss. Not her social secretary. I have no idea what she does during the hours she's not working."

"Well, she's young and new in town. Since she's working full-time at the pub, and not in school, she probably hasn't had the opportunity to meet anyone her age. You should invite her to spend the day with us."

"The entire day?"

His mother considered that as she picked out yellow ears of corn for the cheesy bacon corn side dish she'd learned from Gloria, who'd gotten it from a chef friend of Jolene's. They'd brought it to a Mannion Thanksgiving dinner and it continued to be a hit at family gatherings.

"Unless she's already made other plans, she's coming to the barbeque. The Fourth is a family affair, and even better this year with you not having to work. Unless she has plans to go back home to New York."

"She doesn't." He didn't mention that it was Magnus who'd bothered to ask. Which, he admittedly should have done. But he'd had other things—another person—on his mind.

"Then she'll be part of *our* family for this holiday." She'd turned on her mom voice, the one that brooked no argument. It had served her well wrangling four sons—Brianna had never caused her any problems—and during her years as first a teacher, then principal at Honeymoon Harbor High School. She'd also been inviting people to holiday dinners all his life. He wasn't sure how she found all those who'd be spending the day alone, but they usually ended up at the Mannion family table. "I'll stop by the pub and invite her," Sarah decided.

"I can do that."

"Of course you can. But, as you pointed out, you're her boss. If you invite her, it'll sound more like an order. Also, there's the fact that, being British, she might not be all that enthusiastic about celebrating our Independence Day."

"She has dual citizenship from her mother, so you never know."

"Well, isn't that convenient?" Sarah said with a quick smile. "I've been wanting to meet her anyway. Brianna says that she's very sweet and pretty. But seems a bit shy, which is another reason I suspect she hasn't reached out and met anyone."

"She's reserved," Quinn allowed. Which he personally didn't mind since she wasn't always trying to engage him in conversation. And she portrayed just the right amount of friendliness to customers, being welcoming without making people feel as if she wanted to be besties just because they'd chosen to eat at his pub. It was, he'd discovered with the few hires who hadn't worked out, a delicate balance. "It's probably because, despite the dual citizenship thing, both her parents are British and work for the British government, so I'd guess the American side, which she has because she was born in this country, isn't all that emphasized in her family."

"Isn't that interesting... Well, whatever the reason, she's spending the day with us."

And that, Quinn knew, was that. Even if Piper wanted to spend the Fourth exploring the town, or just staying inside, reading a book, or streaming something, everyone familiar with Sarah Mannion knew that resistance was futile. It was also why he wasn't at all surprised to see her show up at the pub later that afternoon when the lunch crowd had mostly left and they were allowed a short breather.

He called Piper over, went through the necessary introductions, then, claiming the need to check with Jarle to see if there was anything they needed to take off the menu before the dinner rush, escaped into the kitchen.

"So," Sarah Mannion said after Quinn had introduced Piper to his mother. "What are your plans for tomorrow, dear?"

"Since the pub won't be open, I suppose I'll just stay in and read. Or walk around and take in the sights. Maybe drop by the park. There were some girls in last night celebrating a bachelorette party. After I took a group photo of them, they invited me to the wedding at the gazebo."

"That sounds lovely."

"It did at the time, but maybe they only invited me because they'd been a little buzzed on mojitos. I wouldn't want to feel as if I were crashing the wedding. I was looking through my tourism guide and it says that I can take a ferry to Victoria out of Port Angeles. I've been to one of the eastern provinces of Canada, when my parents were part of a group representing the UK at the Commonwealth Day."

"Quinn told me they're both in government service. That's very admirable."

"It is," she said. "Nana and Granddad told me they'd initially hoped Dad would take over the family seafood restaurant, which they'd taken over from their parents, back through the generations into the late 1800s. My many-times-great-grandfather was a fisherman, and his wife started up a small shop selling the cod and herring he'd catch. Then later, their daughter had a small take-out shop, selling fish and chips to the tourists who came to town on the train to the beaches. That gradually expanded into the restaurant I worked in. They're in their seventies and could afford to retire comfortably, but are still working. Two of my uncles are also fishermen, though these days they mostly fish for crabs and lobsters."

Piper was surprised to hear herself sharing her family's ancestry. She'd been taught at an early age that even the seemingly most innocent comment could reflect back on her parents. And even the entire Commonwealth. Which was why she'd probably lived the most boring personal life of any teenager ever.

"Isn't that a coincidence?" Quinn's mother said. "My father's family began fishing here in the 1800s. Although Dad no longer goes out on the water, except recreationally, he still has boats that he leases out to others for a percentage of the catch income. So," she said, "apparently fishing wasn't in your father's blood."

"Not even a little bit. The only way he wants to see fish is on a plate. The way he tells it is that he always had a yearning to see the world, so he figured that by going into the DIT—Department of International Trade—the government would pay for his travel."

"That was a clever plan."

"It was. Because he's certainly spent his life traveling. My mum's multilingual, and is an interpreter, so they've been fortunate to arrange to be posted in the same places."

Piper knew she'd experienced more in eighteen years than many people would in a lifetime and had seen parts of the world that she never would have visited had it not been for her parents' careers. Yet, during those times when she'd stay with her grandparents, she'd find herself worrying about them and wishing that she could live a normal life, like those kids whose families, like her dad's, went back generations in Cromer. The difference was, they had stayed.

She'd met Quinn's sister, Brianna, briefly, when she'd come to fetch takeout for a couple staying at her bed-and-breakfast. That had her wondering why Brianna and all the Mannions had returned home. She'd hoped for years that her parents would have chosen to do that same thing, either to her mother's home town of Betws-y-Coed in Wales, or her father's in Cromer, but they still seemed to possess no inkling to settle down.

"Well, then, you definitely must visit Victoria, while you're here," Sarah said, breaking into her thoughts.

"I plan to. After Commonwealth Day, we took some family holiday time to Toronto, Montreal, and Quebec City." She smiled, remembering that trip. "Quebec was my favorite. It reminds me of an old historic European town. My mum and I spent a wonderful day at Quebec's Rue du Petit Champlain, which is a historic shopping district dating back to the 1600s. It's very quaint, with cobblestones, like Cromer— and here. We bought so many locally made gifts for friends we had to buy an extra piece of luggage to carry it all back to New York."

"It sounds like a wonderful place. John and I should visit. Living so near the border, we've been to Victoria many times. And the rest of British Columbia, along with Banff, in Alberta, but that's as far east as we've been. Quebec has always been on my bucket list. I'd love to see the cobblestone streets. Ours are made from ballast from visiting ships.

"My son-in-law Seth's family were the early builders of this town. He's explained that cobblestones were superior before modern paving because they didn't create ruts and allowed rain water to drain so the roads wouldn't flood and turn the ground muddy. It really was an ingenious system." Her voice drifted off for a moment as she appeared to be studying Piper.

"I suppose, being British, you may not be all that excited about celebrating our upcoming Independence Day," she said, segueing into a different topic after that brief pause, during which Quinn had reappeared at the bar to pull a pint for a fiftysomething man Piper knew to be a retired police officer from the coffee shop next door. Then he disappeared back into the kitchen.

"To many of us, the fourth is merely a day between July 3rd and July 5th," Piper allowed. "Though last year, the British embassy in D.C. created a cheeky play list for the day. Every song was 'Baby Come Back.'"

Sarah's warm laughter reached her eyes. "I did my post-grad study at Oxford," she divulged. "Studying Jane Austen. I'd already left to teach the books in Japan when the embassy in London had their annual barbecue and fireworks, but I don't remember any negative conversations about it, although a few of the snarkier students did comment on how much Americans love their fireworks."

"Well, we certainly have our share of fireworks on Guy Fawkes Day and New Year's Day. I remember Dad once described the American Revolution as an eventually amiable divorce. He also pointed out—no offense—that the United States isn't the only former colony to have declared independence from Britain over the years, so it's not really a major deal. Especially since our two countries have always been each other's allies."

"Your father sounds like a very wise man," Sarah said. "I believe I'd like him."

"Everyone does," Piper said.

"I suppose likeability would be an important factor when it comes to negotiating trade deals around the world when compromise is required," Sarah mused. "Although I'm admittedly biased—my husband is unrelentingly likeable. Which is why, I suppose, Honeymoon Harbor residents seem determined to keep him as mayor."

"Quinn told me he's been mayor for many years." Piper had found it an interesting coincidence that both her family and Quinn's father served their citizens.

"John keeps swearing he's going to retire and just putter around the farm, or maybe have our son, Gabe, teach him how to make a boat, but then year after year, no one volunteers to run, so he stays on. He complains every election, but I know that he truly loves the job."

"He sounds very nice."

"He's a very special man. We were teenage sweethearts," she said. "Although we had to keep our romance secret, because my parents didn't approve."

"Really?" If John Mannion was anything like his sons—and so far she'd met two—she couldn't imagine anything his mother's parents could have had against him.

"It's a bit of a long story I'll share some day when we have more time. At any rate, since the Fourth of July is on Tuesday, we're having our annual barbecue on the third, but any day we can get the entire three—now four, with Chelsea and Gabe's girls—

generations of Mannions together at one time is a cause for celebration. Especially after all those years my children were scattered to the four winds. So, would you like to join us?"

It took Piper a moment to catch up. "Are you inviting me to your family barbecue?"

"I thought you might enjoy it," Sarah said. "Of course, if you decide to go to Victoria, as you were considering, I'll certainly understand."

"I can do that anytime." Piper's heart was beating so fast and hard, she wouldn't have been surprised if it jumped out onto that roughly hewn wood plank floor. "I'd very much like to attend, Mrs. Mannion. Thank you."

"Then it's settled. And please call me Sarah. We're not that much for formality around here."

It was the same thing Quinn had told her. "Yes, ma'am. I mean Sarah."

Even knowing that she might be making a mistake and later regret accepting this invitation, Piper couldn't resist the opportunity to meet all the Mannions. Because of her parents' occupations, she'd never attended any of the big family celebrations always cited in the annual Christmas card letters from relatives she'd never met, though she did at least know the basics of her ancestry. Her mother's family could trace their roots back to before the English Reformation of the 1600s. Her many-times-great-grandmother had been a lady in waiting to Henry VIII's first wife, Catherine, and had, the records showed, even accompanied her to Kimbolton Castle, where the former queen had lived a quiet, prayerful life after having been banished from court in favor of Anne Boleyn.

"It's a ways out to the farm, too far to comfortably walk," Sarah said. "But Brianna already offered that she and Seth would be happy to drive you. All the rooms are filled at Herons Landing, but fortunately, this isn't a weekend guests will want to stay indoors all day, and for those who do want to come and go, or perhaps have a lunch ordered, she's got that covered. This year, she's hired a full-time employee to help out."

She glanced toward the door where a family with three young children entered the restaurant along with a couple whose pink faces showed that they'd spent the day either in the mountains or along the coast.

"I only meant to drop in for a moment to invite you, so, I'd better let you get back to work. Quinn's got your number, so Brianna will call you this evening and you two can work out the details."

With a wave of her hand to Quinn, who was back behind the bar, Sarah Mannion sailed out of the pub, mission accomplished.

After seating the family first (Piper had learned while working at her grandparents' restaurant that it was always best to get toddlers settled in a high chair with oyster crackers and crayons), she led the couple to a window table they'd reserved. After handing out menus, listing the daily specials, and taking drink orders while giving them time to decide on what to eat, Piper watched Quinn pull a draft beer, pour a glass of wine, and mix the drinks.

"I like your mother," she said as he rimmed a glass with salt, then stirred in tequila, grapefruit and lime juice, simple syrup, then added ice and topped off what she'd learned was a Paloma with a fizz of soda water.

"So do I," he said as he garnished the glass with a slim wedge of red grapefruit. Then moved on to making a Shirley Temple and pouring a ginger ale.

"I do have one question. Does anyone ever say no to her?"

He shrugged. "Rarely. Her charm offensive is her highest level superpower, of which she has many."

"She invited me to a barbecue at your family's farm."

"I know. She told me she was going to."

"You don't mind?"

He paused in placing the glasses and coasters on a tray. "Why would I mind?"

"Well, it sounds like a family event and I'm not family."

"She's never made any distinction. We all grew up with people who wouldn't have anyone to spend the holidays with at our table. Which is probably another reason why my sister is so comfortable running a bed-and-breakfast."

"That's very special. That she'd invite so many people."

His eyes warmed with affection. "*She's* very special. I'll admit we were probably all so used to her energy and generosity, we'd started taking it for granted until last summer, when she was in an accident that could have turned fatal. Which definitely got all our attention. It's also what brought Burke home from New York."

"He quit playing football to come home for your mother?"

Piper had heard many reasons bandied about on New York radio and television shows, but never anything about his mother.

"She was the reason he came back. The reasons he stayed are complicated. You'll probably hear more about that eventually. One thing we Mannions like to do is spin tales."

"You don't."

A smile quirked at the corners of his mouth. "I don't have to. Everyone in town already knows them all, and for those who don't, there's always someone to tell the story."

Since she'd passed the test with flying colors, earning her MAST certificate, he handed her the tray of drinks to deliver, essentially declaring their brief conversation closed.

CHAPTER SIX

RATHER THAN CALL, as Sarah Mannion had told Piper she was going to do, Brianna dropped by the restaurant shortly before closing.

"Hi," she greeted Piper. "I was out doing some last-minute shopping for ingredients for my contribution to tomorrow's barbecue, so I thought I'd drop by in person to work out details for tomorrow with you. I was hoping to catch you before your shift ended."

"Thank you. And I'm now officially off the clock... Unless you need me?" she asked Quinn.

"Jarle and I can handle things. Why don't you two go upstairs and don't be worried if you hear some noises down here," he told Piper. "I'll be staying after hours prepping for the barbecue."

"This is very kind of you," Piper said, as she and Brianna entered the apartment a minute later. "Please, sit down. I haven't done much grocery shopping yet. But I do have tea. And biscuits." Her mother had insisted she pack both, as if she were traveling into the uncivilized American West on a wagon train in the 1800s.

"Tea sounds lovely, thank you."

Piper opened a cupboard. "I have Fortnum's Earl Grey, Queen Anne, and Breakfast Tea."

"I bought my mother a tea-a-month gift from Fortnum & Mason a few years ago," Brianna said. "She's quite the tea drinker and told me it had become her favorite brand. I'd love a cup of Earl Grey."

"Coming right up." Piper got out the kettle that had come with the fully stocked kitchenette, took out a package of milk chocolate digestives biscuits, and placed them on a plate. "For dunking," she suggested.

As the water heated, they chatted a bit about Brianna's visits to London and her former life plan that had her becoming the chief concierge at the city's Claridge's Hotel.

"Not the Savoy?" Piper asked as she placed the cups of hot water and the plate of cookies on the table.

"I certainly wouldn't have turned down an offer." Brianna ripped open the bright blue-green package. "But Claridge's has been loved for more than a century, and, as a five-star hotel in the heart of Mayfair, has hosted royalty, movie stars, and global dignitaries."

After dipping her tea bag a precise three times, Brianna let it stay in the cup to steep. "After that, my pinnacle was going to be the Hôtel Plaza Athénée. Which might not be Paris's flashiest hotel, but it's definitely the most luxurious and romantic. But what makes it truly iconic are the glorious views of the Eiffel Tower."

"My parents and I stayed there once when they

were there for an international trade conference. It's quite different from a bed-and-breakfast."

"Isn't it?"

Piper dunked a cookie into her tea as she considered whether the question in her mind would be too rude. Then, thinking she couldn't have been the only one to wonder, asked, "May I ask what changed your mind?"

"It started with a terrible guest. Doctor Dick." Taking the tea bag from the cup, she placed it on the saucer. "Which is admittedly a very rude name and I refrained from calling him that out loud, but it fit. Many of the megarich are very nice, but there are some that land at the other end of the scale. And this one definitely did.

"Usually I brushed it off, but he really got under my skin, accusing me of not doing my job. At the end of the day, I went home to my apartment, and to unwind, started looking at Honeymoon Harbor's Facebook page, catching up on things. That's when I saw that the Victorian that we kids used to break into—it was rumored to be haunted—was for sale. It was as if a lightbulb had turned on over my head. I went in the next day, resigned, and came back home and hired Seth to be the contractor. I'd been secretly in love with him from the first grade when he shared his Ding Dong—"

"His Ding Dong?"

"It's this exquisitely wonderful chocolate-covered junk food cake my mother, being a farm-to-table cook before that was even a term, would never let

me have. Believe me, the first taste was Nirvana."
Brianna sighed, as if reliving that moment.

"Perhaps you fell in love with the Ding Dong and
not the boy," Piper suggested, thinking how Brianna
must have crushed her job as a concierge because she
already had her chatting with her as if they'd known
each other for years.

"That was undoubtedly part of it, but it was everything about him. His sweetness, his cocker spaniel
brown eyes, his generosity... Whenever my friends
and I played Barbie wedding growing up, my Ken
was always Seth. Then Zoe came to town our freshman year of high school, and we became best friends
and he and Zoe fell in love. I loved her so much, I
couldn't even be jealous.

"After they married, she became an Army nurse
in Afghanistan and was at the end of her deployment,
getting ready to return home so they could start a
family when a suicide bomber breached the gates at
her base. She died."

Piper gasped. To her, Remembrance Day, during
which her family had represented their country all
over the world, had always been more of a chore, or
duty. She'd never personally known anyone who'd
died in a war. Or had any family members forced to
live with the loss. "That must have been terrible."

"It was tragic," Brianna agreed. "I wasn't living
here then, but—and I'm not telling you anything
the town didn't witness, so it's not a secret—Seth
was still grieving and suffering from survivor's guilt
when I came back to town. As we worked together,

turning Herons Landing into my bed-and-breakfast, we found that we made a perfect team. And fell in love." She took another sip of tea.

"That's a lovely story." It could have been from one of the romances Piper had started reading in secondary school.

"Of course, neither of us would have wished Zoe's death, but I suspect that Seth was probably ready to move on when I came back from Vegas. My coming home just hurried things along.

"Anyway, I wanted to tell you about the rest of my sprawling family to hopefully make introductions easier tomorrow. Trying not to make the tale sound like an episode of *Finding Your Roots*, the town's name was changed from Port Vancouver to Honeymoon Harbor when European royalty visited here on the advice of their friend, President Theodore Roosevelt, during their honeymoon sightseeing trip across America. Roosevelt had designated part of our peninsula forest to be the Mount Olympus National Monument in order to preserve the native habitat of elk. Which are now named after him."

"I saw some on the bus ride into town," Piper said. "They're magnificent."

"They are, aren't they?" Brianna agreed. "I've lived with them all my life and they still take my breath away… Anyway, to honor the newlyweds, the town council, headed by a Mannion mayor, voted to change the town's name from Port Vancouver to Honeymoon Harbor. The vote was nearly unanimous. Except for Nathanial Harper, who voted against the change. The resulting acrimony resulted in a feud that lasted more than a century. It had diminished over the years, but was officially over when my Harper mom and Mannion dad got married. Then Seth and I finished it off.

"My brother Aiden went from town bad boy—not that he was really ever that bad, just acting out—to police chief, which our dad pretty much tricked him into doing. Our mom can talk anyone into anything—"

"I've gotten that impression."

Brianna laughed. "Of course you have. But watch out for Dad. He has mad ninja skills that have you agreeing to things you never saw coming. Not that he'd have any reason to use them on you, but Aiden had almost been killed in LA working a police case with a federal task force and was having a rough time getting over his partner dying. He'd come home to withdraw from the world, and after an appropriate length of time being a hermit out at our coast house, Dad talked him into filling in as sheriff just until he could find a replacement. That was five years ago."

This time Piper laughed with her.

"Anyway, he's married to Jolene Wells, who also grew up here and had a career for several years working in Hollywood as a makeup artist. And, making things even more complicated, Jolene's mother, Gloria, is marrying my uncle, Michael Mannion. He's an artist who's traveled the world." She paused, tilted her head, and studied Piper. "Hearing from Amanda and Mom how you grew up traveling the world with your parents, you and Uncle Mike probably have a lot you could talk about."

"I'd like that."

"Burke, who tells me you've met, was, of course, a famous football player. He's married to Lily, the events director at Clearwater Community College. She's another family member you'll have a lot in common with, because she's traveled, and worked, all around the world.

"And then there's former Wall Street wizard Gabe, who now has a business building beautiful boats, runs a charitable foundation, and invests in start-up businesses that don't have enough clout to get financing from financial institutions. He's married to Chelsea, the town's head librarian. They adopted two girls, Hannah and Hailey, who you'll meet.

"Oh, and speaking of girls, Kylee and Mai will also be there. They married a couple years ago and have adopted a darling little girl. They're both photographers and met while Kylee was photographing WWII American graves in Italy and Mai was there to visit her grandfather's grave. He'd been one of the Japanese Americans who fought for our country during the war.

"And," she added, "since you already know Quinn, I think that pretty much sums up us Mannions. I added Kylee and Mai because they're an additional part of the family we've made."

Piper was grateful for Brianna giving her an overview of the Mannions. She'd already Googled them, and had found some basic information, but it was helpful to have a more personal insight than the dry facts she'd found in online articles.

After saying good-night to Quinn's sister, and agreeing on a time to leave for the barbecue, she went into the bedroom and stood looking at her closet, trying to find something appropriate for the most important party of her life.

QUINN CAME OUT of the kitchen as Brianna came downstairs. "So, did you give her a diagram with all the photos with lines connecting them like a police movie murder board?" he asked.

She slapped him lightly on the arm. "I'm not that anal retentive. I merely wanted her to have a heads-up on who everyone is before she's tossed into the crowd."

"She's gotten along well with Amanda. I assume, given her parents' work, that she's used to dealing with crowds."

"True. But there's no point in not making things easier on her. And speaking of Amanda, you do know that she's coming to the barbecue?"

"She mentioned it." He picked up a rack of short ribs and carried them into the walk-in refrigerator.

She followed him in. "And?"

He shrugged as he placed the ribs on a shelf, where half a dozen other racks were marinating. "And what?"

"What are you going to do about her?"

"Why? Has she said anything about me?" Oh, hell, Quinn thought, he'd regressed to high school.

"We talk about you from time to time. It's obvious that she likes you."

"And I like her. Which is probably why we're friends."

"Quinn!" She put her hands on her hips. "I mean *like* like. So, again, what are you going to do about it? You can't tell me you don't feel the same way. I've watched you watching her. And how you change when she comes into the pub."

He left the fridge, closing the heavily insulated door behind him, Brianna right on his heels. She could be, he considered, as persistent as their mother when she got an idea into her head. Who else would've tackled a project like that old ramshackle house that, had it not been on the historic record, probably would've been torn down long ago? Like this building, he considered.

"I don't want to risk our friendship."

"You do know that people can be friends and be in love too," she pointed out. "Look at Mom and Dad. They're best friends. So are Seth and me. I can't imagine marrying someone I didn't consider my best friend."

"Now you've jumped to marriage?"

She cocked her head and gave him a long look. "Well, at a certain age, giving a woman your class ring and asking her to go steady seems a little silly. Make that a lot silly. So, quit acting like high school and go for it. Like Cam did with Megan. They had lunch together for months until he finally decided playing it cool wasn't working for him."

Cameron Montgomery had been the new vet in town whose house Megan cleaned once a week. Quinn had been a sounding board when he'd decided to make a move. A big move. Not only did he ask all Megan's friends to bid on him in a charity bachelor auction, guaranteeing to cover whatever it cost, he'd booked a replica of a 1700s tall ship for a dream date.

"I'm not really into big gestures like Cam pulled off." It wasn't his nature.

"So? What makes you think Amanda would even want some elaborate, grand gesture? She lived with a guy who swung to dangerous extremes when he wasn't on his meds. She's been there, done that, and if it hadn't been for Aiden, she could have ended up dead. You're the opposite of her ex. You're steady, dependable—"

"You do realize you're making me sound as dull as a stick."

"You're perfect for her," she persisted, ignoring his complaint. "From what I read in the various papers that covered the story, and the little she's talked about it, it sounds as if her marriage was a roller coaster through hell. If she found you boring, she wouldn't come in here so often. And do you honestly believe that she checks the plants in *every* restaurant and shop in town each and every day?"

She dragged a hand through her hair. Quinn had seldom seen his calm, cool, collected sister frustrated. This was one of those times. The other was when he'd punched Seth. But they'd all put that behind them. "That would be unlikely," he agreed.

"You think? So, here's the deal. The barbecue will provide the perfect playing field for you. All you have to do is call your play, then make your move. And he scores!" She threw her arms up into the air like a referee when a player crossed the goal line.

"Those football metaphors would work a lot better on Burke."

"Sorry, but I don't know any beer metaphors. Just do it," she advised, her voice softening as she lifted her hand to his cheek. "You've always been my strong, brave, big brother. Even when you'd come to drag Seth, Aiden, Burke, and me out of Herons Landing back when it was a dangerous, falling-down wreck. Although you could be really bossy, I always knew that you were doing it because we could've gotten hurt in there.

"You've created your dream here, Quinn. You were brave enough to give up a hugely successful career and walk away without looking back. And look how well that's turned out. Okay, love is admittedly scary. Seth and I were both scared. For different reasons, but I hate to think what would've happened if he hadn't overcome his fear of loss after Zoe's death. I do know we would've missed out on the wonderful life we've created together."

She blew out a breath. "So...be happy, Quinn. Be loved. After all the years you spent being not just a brother, but a trusted sounding board and advisor to us, it's your turn."

"Okay," he said.

"Super." She went up on her toes, and pressed a

light, sisterly kiss on his cheek. Then left, but not before turning in the doorway. "Don't mess it up," she instructed, wagging her finger, then breezed out the door, leaving Quinn to realize, for the first time, how much like their mother she was. Although he'd never before noticed it, Brianna was Sarah Mannion's Mini-Me.

CHAPTER SEVEN

NOT KNOWING HOW long she'd be staying in Honeymoon Harbor, or what she'd be doing while there, Piper hadn't packed many clothes, deciding that, on the outside chance she did end up staying for the entire summer, she could always buy more. She'd brought along a few pairs of jeans, T-shirts, shorts, and her go-to casual dress, a short-sleeved print midi dress inspired by the one Kate Middleton had worn to host a picnic and treasure hunt for children at the RHS Hampton Court Palace Garden Festival. Just as her late mother-in-law had done before her, the Princess of Wales had set the style for a new generation of British women.

Piper opted for the dress, not only because it was pretty, but the print could hide any stains or spills. Then, not knowing exactly how rustic the Mannions' Christmas tree farm might be, instead of the pretty canvas espadrilles Kate had worn, Piper decided on a pair of classic white trainers.

Belatedly realizing she didn't have a hostess gift to bring to the barbecue, she called Amanda and asked if she could run down to her nursery on her break and pick up some flowers.

"No problem," Amanda had assured her. "While I don't have as many cut flowers as Jim Olson does at Blue House Farm, I do keep a cooler of them on hand for arrangements. What would you like?"

Piper thought of all the care and consideration that had gone into the diplomatic dinners her parents had hosted and realized she should have been paying attention. "I don't know," she said. "It's a barbecue." Not like they were hosting the Queen of Norway or a trade diplomat from China. "Something simple?"

"How about daisies?"

"I like daisies. They're happy flowers."

"They are. And perfect for a summer picnic. I'll put a bunch together and bring them by in a bit. And there's no charge."

"Oh, I couldn't let you—"

"Consider it payment for all your help planting the pub's herbs," Amanda cut her off. "See you in a few."

THE ROAD TO the Mannion Christmas tree farm twisted in tight switchbacks lined with tall trees, which gave Piper the feeling of driving through a green tunnel. "We don't have anything like this in England," she said, looking out the window at the towering green trees piercing the blue sky.

"They're Douglas fir," Seth Harper, Brianna's husband, told her. "They're one of only four species that can reach three-hundred-feet tall. The tallest recorded is in the Hoh Valley in the Olympic National Park."

"We'll have to take you there one of these days," Brianna said.

"Amanda told me about the rain forest."

"It's amazing. Many of the trees are ancient. There's a cedar that's almost a thousand years old."

"Which is how long Douglas firs can live, under the right circumstances," Seth said. "Although, since Honeymoon Harbor was founded by fisherman and loggers, the really old ones can only be found in the park, where they're protected. These—" he waved a hand toward the towering firs they were driving past "—are third, maybe fourth growth."

"England is losing our trees," Piper said. The topic was a frequent one at her family's dinner table whenever they returned to their home country. Her father was a naturally optimistic person, but not when it came to deforestation. "My dad says that we've cut down nearly all the oak trees our Victorian ancestors planted to try to restore the trees that had been lost to the ax in earlier centuries for shipbuilding."

"It's a problem worldwide," Brianna said, "which is why Seth uses reclaimed lumber whenever possible."

"It's a drop in a bucket," Seth admitted.

"True," Brianna agreed. "But we can hope that with more and more people being affected by climate change in their everyday lives, more countries will find ways to turn things around."

Every so often, there'd be a gap in the trees, offering a glimpse of meadows abloom with a dazzling display of wildflowers that could have washed off the canvas of an impressionist painting.

They passed acres consisting of neatly planted

rows of flowers surrounding a blue clapboard house, which she took to be the Blue House Farm Amanda had mentioned. Just beyond it, Seth took a fork in the road and, suddenly, they were in a forest of conical-shaped trees in shades ranging from a soft blue-green to a bright, lighter shade. Rising from the center of the forest was a large, apple-red barn with *Mannion's Family Christmas Tree Farm, established 1983*, written on the side in bright white paint. Below that read *Delivery or Cut and Carry.* And below that was a banner announcing that the Theater at the Farm would be debuting July 10, with *Grimm Tales.* A large poster featured witches, wolves, frogs, and fairies and promised a fresh adaptation of the Brothers Grimm's beloved classic fairy tales certain to entertain young and old alike.

The road dead-ended at a pair of red gates that had been opened, and after driving a bit farther down a tree-lined driveway, they reached a two-story white house with a gray slate roof. Shutters the same gray color framed the windows, while the front door's red hue, the same as the barn and gate, offered a cheery welcome. A riot of hydrangeas, in shades of pink, blue, white, and pale green formed a hedge in front of the house on either side of the door.

As soon as she got out of the SUV, Piper breathed in the tangy scent of the trees, the tinge of salt riding on the air, along with the mouth-watering aroma of meat on the grill, coming from behind the house. They went around back, her carrying her flowers, Brianna carrying pans of fudge brownies. When she turned the corner, she was grateful Quinn's sister had taken the time to fill her in.

The backyard was a beehive of activity. Long plank tables filled part of a large flagstone patio. At the other end of the patio, she saw Quinn and Jarle manning four large grills, two with chicken and ribs, the others with oysters and Dungeness crabs. Two Australian shepherds, their muzzles white with age, were seated on their haunches eyeing the ribs with the intensity they might have directed toward a herd of sheep or cattle they'd been bred to guard.

More tables were lined up, already covered with enough side dishes to feed an army. As Brianna and Seth walked toward them with Brianna's pans of brownies, Sarah, who'd been placing silverware into little buckets, turned and came hurrying toward them.

"I'm so glad you came," she said, her face wreathed in a welcoming smile. "And, oh, you brought daisies! They're one of my favorites."

"The Bellis perennis, better known as the English daisy, has been popular for centuries," a young man standing nearby offered. "The name *daisy* comes from the old Anglo-Saxon *daes eage*, which means *day's eye* because of the sunny center and the fact that the flowers close in the evening.

"It's an old folk cure for a variety of ailments. Henry VIII is reported to have eaten English daisies to help with his stomach problems. And perhaps his gout. It was known to ease aches and pains, and a form of it, arnica, from a type of daisy that grows in the Alps, remains popular today. It's also edible, and has more vitamin C than a lemon."

"I make a tea with it," the brunette standing next to him offered. "It has a subtle lemony flavor and is perfect for drinking with spring colds." She smiled. "Hi, you must be Piper from the pub, right? I'm Sage Fletcher. Soon to be Sage Fletcher-Olson." Her smile brightened as she waved her left hand, which was wearing a topaz brown and gold ring that perfectly matched the color of her eyes. "And this is Jim, my fiancé. I'm in marketing, and Jim owns Blue House Farm."

"We passed that on the way here," Piper said. "Your gardens are beautiful."

"Thank you," he said. "The farm has been in my family for three generations."

"That's very special." Piper wondered how it must feel to have roots that ran as deeply as they seemed to in Honeymoon Harbor.

"It is," he agreed. "My parents left it to me to run when they moved to Arizona."

"And he's done wonderful things with it," Sage said enthusiastically. "In fact, business actually grew during the days when the country was shut down due to Covid because people stuck at home started growing their own herbs and veggies. Jim had already been considering selling seeds, because they're so much easier to ship than the actual plants themselves. Once we added a variety of seeds to his online business, sales just boomed."

"Sage is not only beautiful, she's savvy when it

comes to business and social media," Jim offered. As he gazed down at his fiancée, love and admiration shone in his gaze. It reminded Piper of the way her father often looked at her mother. Although their globe-trotting life wasn't for her, she did hope to someday have the type of relationship they—and, it appeared, Jim Olson and Sage Fletcher—had.

"Let me put these in water while Brianna and Seth introduce you around," Sarah said.

Once again, as Quinn's sister led her through the crowd, Piper was grateful for Brianna's primer and those times when she'd appeared at official functions with her parents, which had taught her to memorize names of people she'd be introduced to. Over the next few minutes, she met a dizzying number of people of all ages. She and Amanda were chatting when a tall redhead who looked as if she could play for the WNBA, arrived, dressed in a flowing flowered midi skirt, lipstick-red camisole top, and red Converse high-tops to match. Since the woman with her was a petite Asian-American, dressed casually in a white shirt, light wash jeans, and white sneakers, Piper concluded they must be Kylee and Mai. Between them was a young girl with a shiny doe-brown ponytail that flew out like a flag as she broke free of their hands and ran toward Quinn, grabbing him around his legs.

Her high-pitched "Quinn! Give me a pony ride!" rang out over the crowd.

He lifted her up, put her on his back and, apparently not the least bit self-conscious, trotted around the lawn. "He started doing that when she was a toddler," Kylee, who was now standing beside Piper, said. "We're hoping she'll outgrow it before adolescence."

"When we first decided to adopt," Mai said, after introductions had been completed, "people told us that it wouldn't be fair to a child not to have a father figure."

"Which was a crock," Kylee broke in. "Because I was practically adopted into the Mannion clan when my parents couldn't accept me being a lesbian, so she has a bunch of surrogate dads."

She glanced over at the eldest of the surrogates, who'd left the grills to Jarle while he romped around the lawn, making neighing noises. "At her first birthday party, Quinn made the mistake of putting her on his back and giving her a ride."

"She's lucky. My grandfather gave me pony rides on the seaside beach where they had their restaurant." Until now, that memory had been deep in her past. Her own father, while loving and caring, was far too British proper to be seen prancing around a yard filled with people who might judge him less seriously.

"I read on the town's Facebook page that you'd worked at your family restaurant in England," Kylee said.

Piper had discovered the page while doing her research on the town. But had never imagined appearing on it. "I'm on there?" The idea was both intriguing and appalling at the same time. She also doubted Quinn would have said anything, so it must have been customers where she'd come from.

"Oh, you don't have to worry," Mai assured her quickly. "That page is mostly about local events. And, admittedly, from time to time who's seeing who. We garnered quite a bit of conjecture when I moved from Hawaii after meeting Kylee in Italy. But none of it was negative."

"On the contrary, there were so many people hoping we'd get married, we finally caved and tied the knot to shut them up," Kylee said. Then laughed. "Just kidding! They were openly rooting for us, and if there was anyone in town who wasn't supportive of us becoming parents, they didn't share their feelings openly. It was the same with Brianna and Seth. Everyone knew they thought they were keeping their relationship secret, but we all kept quiet about it because we didn't want to put pressure on them. Honeymoon Harbor is a wonderful, caring place. As you'll notice, kids still feel safe riding their bikes down the streets, and residents sit on their front porches—and socialize with their neighbors."

"That's so true," one of the women who'd joined them said. "Of course we've got our gossips. Be careful what you say in the market, because if Mabel had lived back in Boston during the American Revolution, she would've beat Paul Revere sounding the alarm about the British coming. I'm Gloria Wells. And this is my daughter, Jolene Mannion."

"You two own the salon and spa," Piper remembered, then addressed Jolene. "And you were nominated for an Emmy for that TV miniseries set in Ireland, which was, by the way, much better than that dreadful and historically incorrect Henry VIII drama that stole your award. You're also married to Aiden Mannion, right?" A Mannion male she'd yet to meet.

"I am. Unfortunately, he's only going to be dropping in for a short time, because the Fourth of July weekend is a busy one for police, what with all the drunk driving and boating. And thanks for the compliment about my work. Brianna told me she'd filled you in on our clan," Jolene said.

"She gave me the condensed version, but I would have recognized your name anyway. I watched both series, loved yours, and never finished the other. I was really annoyed when you were robbed at the Emmys."

"I think I already love you," Jolene joked.

"I hope being thrown into this crowd doesn't make you too uncomfortable," Gloria, who Piper recalled was going to be marrying yet another Mannion, said. "Even without the invited guests, the Mannion clan are a large and occasionally rowdy group," she said, glancing over toward a flag football game going on.

"I'm used to being thrust into a crowd where I don't know anyone thanks to traveling all over the world with my diplomat parents. Though Brianna filling me in on details did help."

"I've always thought of Honeymoon Harbor to be like Stars Hollow, if *Gilmore Girls* had been set in the far northwest corner of the country," Jolene said. "Which is partly why so many of us ended up leaving, because when you're young, you want to be able to figure out your own life and find your own way, which is hard to do when people know all about you and have their own ideas and expectations about what paths you might choose along the way."

"That's exactly why I'm taking this gap year," Piper said. "With my parents working for the government, I've never really felt I had any independence to just be myself. I already know that I want to be an international human rights attorney, thanks to living in countries where so many people are wrongly treated. But that's a career. There are so many other personal aspects of my life I want to figure out first."

Jolene nodded. "I so get that. It's why I left here for Los Angeles. It was scary because I didn't know anyone. But the upside was that no one knew me. So, I could choose to be whoever I wanted. Which was great while it lasted. All the Mannions have their own version of that same story. But, eventually, we all realized that there was no place like home, so we clicked the heels of our metaphorical ruby slippers, and well—" she swept her hand around all the activity buzzing around them "—here we are."

"From what I've seen so far," Piper said, "it's a lovely town and I can understand you wanting to come back home."

The concept of coming home might be foreign to her, given that the closest thing she'd ever had to a home was those occasional summers with her grandparents, and although she planned to eventually settle in The Hague in the Netherlands, a country she'd enjoyed during a too-brief year there as a child, right now, she couldn't think of any other place she'd rather be.

After being introduced to even more people, all very welcoming, she was at one of the tables, trying to choose from the bounty of food when someone who seemed not much older than her, appeared beside her.

"You can't go wrong with the sweet chili lime wings," he said, a smile brightening a tawny face dotted with freckles across his nose and cheekbones. His short, ebony afro accentuated rich, dark brown eyes. "The maple whiskey bacon ones are great, but the sweet chili lime are the bomb."

"I know," she said. "They're a bestseller at Mannion's. Quinn's brother Burke told me that he started making them back in high school to bring to football team meetings."

"That you know about their popularity tells me that you'd be Piper. You're working Katie's old job at the pub, right?"

"Right," she said. What Jolene had told her about everyone knowing your name seemed to be true. "And you are?" She'd had guys hit on her before, but she usually brushed them off because she didn't take a year off school for romance, but to discover herself. This one, though…well, there was something about him that made her want to know more.

"I'm Jamal Washington. I work for Gabe Mannion. Since I wasn't going back home to Virginia for the holiday, I'm one of his mom's Fourth of July orphans."

"You build boats?" The idea had intrigued her when she'd first heard of it, but she hadn't yet had time to go visit the shop.

"I don't work all that much with the wooden parts, unless someone needs a hand, then we all pitch in. I mainly do all the wiring." She assumed her surprise must have shown on her face because he smiled. "Gabe will do the occasional skiff, canoe, or kayak, more as a favor for someone, but most of the boats coming out of Mannion Boat Works need motors." His smile widened in a way that had her heart doing a little flip. "And that's where I come in. My granddad and dad both work at Newport News Shipbuilding. It's a major employer, and a lot of my family has worked there. They've built everything from tugboats to battleships, tankers, submarines, ocean liners, even aircraft carriers. My dad worked on the *John F. Kennedy* nuclear aircraft carrier. He was really proud, which I get, but I guess I had a bit of rebel in me, because I didn't want to follow in their footsteps. I wanted to find my own path."

"I can relate." Piper put a few of the sweet chili lime wings on her plate, along with a scoop of pesto pasta salad, some Rainier cherries, and one of Brianna's fudge brownies.

"But you also ended up in the boat business," she pointed out.

"I did. And I fully recognize the irony. But Gabe's shop is much smaller and more personal. Still, it took a long and winding road for me to get here."

"I'd like to hear about that," she surprised herself by saying.

"Tell you what…" He filled his own plate with ribs, macaroni and cheese, two local grilled oysters Piper knew were from Kira's Fish House, because she'd gone with Quinn on an early morning shopping trip there last week when he'd wanted to show her the amazing variety of available fresh Pacific Northwest seafood, and two of Brianna's brownies, which had been cut into precise squares. "How about we go claim that bench beneath the tree where it isn't so chaotic and swap life stories?"

She looked at the tree he was pointing to, and saw a wooden bench just large enough for two beneath the leafy canopy. "Mine is too long and complicated to summarize," she said.

"Works for me. I'm a sucker for long, rich stories." He had such a killer smile. She warned herself that she was undoubtedly not the first girl he'd won over with it. And likely wouldn't be the last. But although she'd never admitted it to her family, she'd always felt a little claustrophobic in crowds, so it wasn't actually like she was falling for it. She just needed a bit of breathing space. *Liar.*

"So," he said as they settled down on the bench, plates on their laps. "Tell me all about yourself and feel free to go on as long as you like, because I really like your accent. I could listen to you all day."

She felt the color rise in her cheeks. "Does that line really work?"

He shrugged. "I don't know. You're the first girl I

ever tried it out on. Partly because you're the first girl with an English accent I've met. But it isn't really a line. I really do like your voice a lot. You remind me of Emma Watson, and—this isn't a line either—I had a huge crush on Hermione."

Piper laughed. "There's a coincidence. I wanted to be Hermione."

"One more thing we have in common," he pointed out.

Unable to resist his charm, along with the fact that he was really, really, cute, Piper shared an abbreviated version of her nomadic life up until having landed in Honeymoon Harbor.

"You are," he said, his eyes no longer laughing, but full of sincerity, "the most interesting girl I've ever met."

Not accustomed to such a straightforward compliment, Piper felt the blush returning to her cheeks. "It's my parents who are interesting. I was just taken along for the ride."

"You want to save the world," he pointed out.

"Not the entire world. Just the oppressed and badly treated people in it." Millions of them. Even knowing she couldn't save them all, Piper at least wanted those people causing their suffering to pay for their despotic, evil behavior.

"See?" He pointed a long finger at her. "I've never met anyone with so lofty a goal. That's a really big deal. And I don't have a single doubt that you'll succeed."

Again, flattered, she nevertheless laughed. "You just met me. How could you possibly know that?"

"Because you're a visionary. That's both interesting and special. And, throughout history, it's the visionaries who've done amazing things none of the rest of us would think of. Or dare to do even if we did."

She lowered her gaze to her plate. On the rare occasion she'd told anyone about her life plan, they'd either scoff or patronize her. All except for her parents and Quinn. And this boy, on a day that was turning out to be one of the best she'd ever experienced, believed in her.

He went on to tell her how he'd always been interested in how things worked. And solving problems, which had gotten him in trouble a lot growing up. Like when he was five years old and took apart his mother's toaster.

"But I did get it put back together," he said. "Though she wasn't happy that the family went two weeks without toast until I managed to figure it out."

"That's very impressive at five," she said. "A lot of people would just buy a new toaster. And punish you in some way."

"My dad, who's an amazing welder, backed me up. He told Mom that I was a natural for the boat business."

"Which you've proven correct."

"True. But not in the way he was expecting. Like I said, those boats were too big to feel personal to me. I liked going to the launching ceremonies, but I never felt any internal pull. Then, one summer, because I have mad computer skills—no bragging intended—"

"That's a skill worth being proud of," she said. "I often have problems with apps on my phone."

"Different strokes," he said with a shrug. "Anyway, that got me a summer job after my freshman year at the University of Virginia, working for an architect who was designing what was going to be an art gallery on the water. Architects need to know how to make things work, which was still my thing, but when I took that job, I'd graduated from toasters to building computers and drones."

"I heard tomorrow night's fireworks are going to be done by drones," she said.

"Yeah. I taught a weekend open-to-the-public workshop there," he said. "Lily Mannion, who's in charge of special events, said that it was one of the most popular ones and raised a lot of money for the school's food bank—sorry, sounds like bragging again."

"I didn't take it that way. It's a simple fact you should be proud of. Especially since the money went to a good cause. I've seen too much famine around the world, usually caused by weather conditions or wars, but knowing there's hunger in the US, or my country, seems so wrong. So, well done, you."

"Thanks. But getting back to my winding road tale, as much as I enjoyed my work that summer, learning all about the principles of architecture, and as beautiful as that building was going to be, it just didn't speak to me, you know?"

"I do. It's like, I love watching Jarle cook. He's taught me a lot of techniques that someday I'd like to try out cooking for myself and friends. I've discovered that I enjoy cooking. But it's not something I'd want to do day in and day out for a living."

That grin that she was so drawn to flashed again. "Exactly. It's obvious you're brilliant. We think alike. But, getting back to the gallery, I realized that even if I stuck around school long enough to get a degree in architecture, I wouldn't be the guy actually doing the work. Making the architect's vision come to life. Or finding new ways to change the plans when something was unworkable, while keeping to the original intent."

"Because, while you had the vision, I'd imagine the relationship between the architects and contractors would be complex."

"Try confrontational," he said. "And I'm not a fan of conflict. Also, in the mix, you've got the owner who's paying for the building—in this case, a zillionaire who'd made a fortune on Wall Street, but knew zilch about design or construction. And who didn't like anyone saying no to the dramatic changes he kept wanting to make."

"Because function would ultimately have to trump design or a building could end up collapsing," Piper said.

"Exactly. Again, I've never met anyone I was so in tune with. I don't suppose you'd marry me?"

Knowing it was a joke, she shrugged, and said, "I'm sorry, but I'm only eighteen and I have plans—"

"To put the world's bad guys behind bars," he said with an exaggerated sigh. "Which I suppose is more important than getting married to a mere boat builder."

"Building boats is a special occupation," she said, not wanting to let him think she was some sort of do-gooder snob. "I'll probably get married someday," she said, "if I can have a marriage like my parents. One that's a true and equal partnership."

"As it should be," he said. "My mom's a librarian. Which you wouldn't think would be a perfect match for a boat welder. But dad builds other stuff, like a wrought iron fence around our yard, and instead of watching TV all night, they listen to audio books together. Plus, they collaborate on cooking dinner. So, I get what you mean. I'm twenty-one, and not ready for marriage either. But maybe we'll stay in touch." It was his turn to shrug. "And who knows what the future will bring? Which I realize is too heavy a conversation for a first date."

"You consider this a date?"

"Well, sort of. We're definitely not mingling. Though we are starting to get looks, which is par for the course in this town, so don't freak out if we end up as a mention in the paper's 'Seen Around Town' column or the Facebook page as a possible budding young summer romance."

"Please tell me you're kidding."

"Small-town living," he said easily. "Anyway, to finish up, I sort of did what you did, but instead of taking an official gap year, I dropped out of a school I'd worked my tail off to get into, which didn't exactly thrill my folks. Then I took off and wandered across the country, taking gig jobs to pay the bills while figuring out what else might appeal to me.

"I was nearly at the end of the literal road, a few miles from the opposite coast from where I'd started, when I took a tour at the Northwest Boat Building School, just south of Port Townsend. It's to this region's busy marine trades what UC Berkeley is to Silicon Valley, which intrigued me."

"Well, you do have those mad computer skills..."

He shook his head. "That really does sound like bragging, hearing it repeated back to me. However, having built a kayak in my high school shop class, I originally went there to check out the wooden boat building course, thinking that might be something I could get into. But then the guy leading the tour took us to the systems' side of the school, and I fell in love. Suddenly I had the opportunity to learn all about plumbing, mechanics, wiring, hydraulics, diesel, even new solar techniques—all the stuff that makes up the heart of a boat. It was like taking Mom's toaster apart. But on a much larger scale."

"Which makes sense, since you like to figure out how things work."

"You were listening."

"Of course." She decided not to say that she was finding him the most intriguing boy she'd ever met.

"Anyway, to paraphrase Joseph Campbell, following my bliss put me on a track that was out there, waiting all along, because it turns out there's a huge shortage of boat tech guys, so before I even finished the nine-month course and could put my résumé online, Gabe called and offered me a job after one of the instructors at the school recommended me.

"One thing in my favor was that I'd gotten to work on *Clean Bay*, a zero emissions pump boat built at the school, which was epic, and Gabe's been wanting to become more green. I'm now living the life that was meant to be."

"That's a wonderful story." And although Piper didn't want to point out yet another thing they had in common, Jamal Washington was interested in saving the planet with technology, while she intended to use the law to save the oppressed.

"I like to think so. Although my mom would've rather had me stay back East. Since she's the one who gave me Campbell's book to read when I was in middle school, I kid her that she's to blame for my having found my bliss here on the Olympic Peninsula. I am going home for Christmas, though."

"Gabe invited me to visit his shop," she said. "I just haven't made it out there yet. The pub's been super busy."

"Yeah. Tourism time. When you decide to drop by, give me a call beforehand and I'll show you around." He dug into the pocket of his jeans and pulled out his phone. "Let's exchange numbers."

She hesitated, reminding herself that as nice as he was, she hadn't come all the way across the country for a summer fling.

"Too soon?" he asked.

"Maybe. If you're looking for a summer girlfriend, I've no idea how long I'm going to be here."

"I wasn't looking," he assured her. "But, you know, sometimes the best things happen when you're not looking. But hey, it's summer. You're a girl. And I'm pretty new here too and could always use a friend. Just to hang out with. No expectations, no strings."

That sounded reasonable enough. It wasn't as if she had all that much free time anyway. She handed over her phone. "I only have Mondays off. And the pub closes at nine." Fortunately, Quinn had left the breakfast business to Desiree's Ovenly boulangerie and Cops and Coffee.

After they'd exchanged numbers, he said, "There's a meteor shower coming up. Want to watch it with me out at Mirror Lake this Sunday night? The skies are supposed to be clear and those who've seen it before say the reflections on the water are really spectacular."

Sitting by a lake, in the dark, with a cute guy, watching stars. No, Piper decided. That was playing with fire.

"There's going to be a group of us," he assured her. "Other students from the boat school and some friends from the local college."

It was tempting. But her personal life was currently complicated enough. If she got up the nerve to go through with what she'd come to Honeymoon Harbor to do, she might not even be here next Sunday.

"Can I let you know?"

"Sure. Like I said, we'll just keep it loose and hang. No expectations."

No expectations was the same thing she'd been telling herself for weeks as she'd planned this trip. But as she was discovering since working at Mannion's, that mindset was a great deal easier said than done.

CHAPTER EIGHT

"YOU HAVE A wonderful family," Amanda told Quinn as they strolled through the rows of fir, pine, and spruce trees as the barbecue wound down. Although the sun wouldn't set this far north until nine o'clock, with another hour of light after that, it was currently the golden hour, that exquisite time when the light was soft and diffused, creating a warm, glowing effect over the snowcapped Olympic Mountains in the distance.

"I definitely lucked out," he agreed. "My brothers and I had our moments growing up. It couldn't have been easy on our mom, raising four boys, all so close in age, but although we had our share of fights, we always had each other's backs.

"There was this one time when Aiden got suspended from school for three days for beating up a guy on my debate team. The guy got caught cheating, costing our team the state trophy, which seemed important at the time, because that win was going to be one more thing to add to my scholarship application forms. Although my parents earn a comfortable-enough living, their income couldn't cover sending five children to college."

"While I normally don't believe in settling problems by fighting, good for Aiden," she said. "There were times growing up when I fantasized having a big brother or sister to stand up for me. Still, it must have been special, growing up on a Christmas tree farm."

"It was harder work than most people imagine, but yeah, it was great," Quinn agreed. "Dad was supposed to take over the family bank."

She tilted her head in a thoughtful way he'd noticed before, when she'd been planning how to add the herbs to his new patio. "No offense intended, but having gotten to know him a bit these past years, I can't see him as a banker."

"Neither could he. But he's a natural born peacemaker, so rather than cause a big family fight, he compromised. He got a degree in business, to appease his authoritative father, but since he'd always liked growing things, he also minored in agriculture and horticulture."

"He told me about that. We had a wonderful conversation about the underground volcanoes, Ice Age and other paleoenvironments of this area. Did you know ten to eleven thousand years ago, there were actually cacti growing here in the peninsula's rain shadow?"

"I did. There's nothing Dad loves to talk about more than soil. Did he tell you about living in Nepal?"

"No, we just were able to have a brief conversation while he was turning burgers, but that's wonderful. He must have so many stories."

"He does. Unlike a lot of people, he didn't go there

for the mountain climbing or to seek enlightenment. He originally went to assist communities with fruit tree propagation, planting a variety that would provide fruits year-round, and to build a water system. But, as he tells it—ironically—living and working with people who were able to find love and joy with so little validated his belief that he'd never be happy following in his family's banking footsteps. So, he ended up finding enlightenment after all, while not having been seeking it."

"That may explain why he's always seemed so Zen. Except after your mom's accident. I took a plant and some pastries from Ovenly to the house, and although Brianna told me she was recuperating well, it was obvious that your dad was still very stressed-out."

"They were high school sweethearts," Quinn said. "Coming so close to losing her had to have been unthinkable for him. It sure as hell was to all of us."

"I've heard bits and pieces of their story and love it. I realize not everyone is able to live their dream, but I'm certainly grateful every day that I'm able to spend my days doing work that makes me happy."

"You won't get any argument from the guy who gave up law to brew beer."

"We're both fortunate to be able to have chosen occupations that we enjoy." She paused to run her fingers along the tips of green needles on one of the perfectly shaped trees. "Although, I suspect many people think of landscapers as the guys who mow lawns and blow away leaves—who are definitely essential workers—I've always considered my work to be a bit like creating a painting. I can envision the completed image of gardens in my head as I design."

Having watched her plan on her sketch pad, where he saw circles of varying sizes, he'd imagined she'd been envisioning the completed patio, which had, as he'd hoped, increased business. "Then you bring those images to life. Like Monet."

"Oh, I do like that comparison." As a blush rose in her cheeks, Quinn wondered if she realized how stunning she was, even without wearing makeup, usually clad in T-shirts or jeans, sometimes with a flannel shirt or hoodie, depending on the weather. "I remember a quote I saw in a gallery next to a print of his *Garden at Giverny*. It read, 'I must have flowers, always, and always.' I identified with that feeling. But, of course, he was worlds more talented than me and his work will last forever."

"Maybe so. But your gardens are living and allow people to experience them in person," Quinn said. "Breathe in the scent. Enjoy the colors, and feel happy, like the mood you created at Kylee and Mai's house, or the tranquility for Brianna."

"Kylee's very high energy, and her main wish was to be surrounded by joy. Brianna wanted something more welcoming, and restful, since people come to her to unwind."

"My point exactly. The ability to evoke emotion that matches your clients takes every bit as much talent as painting some flowers. Probably more, because someone with your talent had to design and plant those gardens Monet captured in his paintings."

"That's very flattering, but—"

"It's true. And you're far too modest."

Again that color rose in her cheeks, making Quinn question again how someone with all her abilities couldn't realize how very special she was. While, unfortunately, everyone in Honeymoon Harbor knew too much about her disastrous married life, he also wondered about her childhood, which she never talked about—at least not with him.

He supposed he could ask Brianna if she'd ever said anything, but there were three problems with that. The first was if there was something in Amanda's past that she wasn't eager to have others know about, Brianna would never share a secret.

The second problem was that he wouldn't honestly want her to. Because he wanted—no *needed*—to get to know this woman on her own terms. To have her feel close enough, safe enough, to share her past, and her feelings, with him herself. She'd already been with one controlling man. So, he didn't want her to sense any similarity to her ex in him. And the third was that the last thing he wanted was his sister telling him, again, what he already knew. That he was acting like he was in high school. Which wasn't really accurate because he'd never acted that way in high school.

As they turned back toward the house, Quinn could hear Brianna in his head, telling him that patience was all very good, but the clock was running out and it was time for him to call the play.

"There's a beer festival on the coast at Orcas Beach

next weekend," he said, offhandedly. "It's not as big as the annual Washington Brewer's Festival, but in a way, that's a plus, because while it draws a good crowd, it's more laid-back."

"And you're planning to enter?"

"I'm already registered. Although it's a busy time for the pub, Jarle assures me he can handle things. And we just hired his cousin as a part-time bartender. Axel moved down here to retire, then decided that he was getting bored and missed the comradery of pub work. So, we've worked out a loose schedule and he's filling in for me while I introduce our new brew to those on the coast. And now that Jarle's a partner—"

"I didn't know that."

"That's because he doesn't want it to get out. He says that if his relatives learn that he's part owner of a successful American pub, they'll all want to borrow money. So, he's a silent partner. But, now that he's put cooking for fishing crews behind him, he wanted to buy in. I'd already planned on asking him if he'd consider being a partner because he's valuable in more ways than just his cooking."

"That's wonderful. And I promise my lips are sealed." When she made the universal sign of a key locking her lips, Quinn considered calling an audible on his planned play and kissing her. Then reluctantly stuck to his game plan. "But now that he and Ashley are getting married, it's nice that he'll have the stability a partnership will bring."

"That was my thought. Along with selfishly not wanting some other place to steal him."

"Not happening," Amanda said. "I've watched him. After all those years at sea, he's definitely found his home place."

"He has." Quinn wondered how they'd gotten off track. "So, about the beerfest," he said, returning to the original topic. "Although it's only one day, I was thinking of taking a long weekend."

"That sounds like a great idea. And it's supposed to be lovely weather at the coast."

"True. And, well, my idea was that it would be better if I had someone there to enjoy it with me. What would you say to coming along? I know it's a busy time for you—"

She didn't hesitate. "I have a great crew. Some are even interns from the college horticultural program. So, I doubt Wheel and Barrow will collapse if I go away for three days. I love the coast and it sounds like fun. I've never been to a beerfest. Now I can cross it off my bucket list."

"You had attending a beerfest on a bucket list?"

As she smiled, the sun caught little bits of gold in her brown eyes. "No. But, confession time, I've been known to write things on daily lists for the satisfaction of crossing them off."

Having done the same thing himself, Quinn decided that was yet more proof they were meant to be. "Sounds reasonable to me," he said. "My family has a house on the coast."

"I know," she said. "Aiden was originally considering stashing me there for safety when everything was happening with Eric. But then it turned out some friends—a former Portland homicide detective and her Navy SEAL husband—had room in a safe house that they usually used to hide women and kids from abusive partners. In spite of all that was going on with the manhunt, for the first time in years, I had an almost normal Thanksgiving with a woman who was also staying there with her six-month-old baby and four-year-old daughter." A soft smile touched her lips. "Despite the circumstances, I had my first almost happy holiday in years."

If Quinn had anything to say about it, she'd be having a lifetime of happy days.

CHAPTER NINE

"I FEEL A little foolish buying a wedding dress," Gloria said as she and Jolene walked toward the Dancing Deer Dress Shoppe. "I'm nearly sixty years old and this isn't my first marriage."

"Your first marriage was when you were sixteen and pregnant," Jolene reminded her. "It took—what?— ten minutes at the courthouse?"

"A little longer. We had all those forms to fill out and I had to go to the restroom to throw up from morning sickness."

"You've just made my point." They stopped beneath the blue-and-white-striped awning. "This may be your second marriage, Mom, but it's going to be your last chance to be a bride. God knows you deserve it. And, as the person you asked to walk you down the aisle, there's no way I'm allowing you to back out. Besides, it'll be fun."

"I'll bet the only thing that'll work for me will be some boring old lady lace mother-of-the-groom dress. Or worse yet, a lace pantsuit."

"There's no way you could look old. Or boring. So, stop fussing and I'll buy you an ice cream cone when we finish shopping."

"That's what I used to say to you."

"Exactly. If the whining fits…"

They were greeted by Velvet, web designer, sales clerk, and more recently a partner in the business, who'd proven that marriage and motherhood hadn't turned Honeymoon Harbor's former Goth girl into a soccer mom. She was wearing a black T-shirt pronouncing *The Future Is Female* and a red-and-black-pleated tartan miniskirt with black boots with rainbow-hued soles. She'd also been responsible for drawing younger customers from all over the peninsula for her curated collection of goth, punk, and emo attire.

"Hi! This is so exciting. Doris and Dottie have been gathering up possibilities since you called. We're all so excited for you!"

Doris and Dottie, the owners of the Dancing Deer were two still spry twins in their eighties who'd married twin brothers. After a tidal wave had taken out their building down the coast in Oregon, they'd relocated to Honeymoon Harbor, undaunted and savvy enough to add a bridal section; they'd been doing a booming business with their *You Bring the Groom— We'll Supply the Dress* slogan. It had been Velvet who'd suggested they offer rentals, especially for those brides who came from out of town and didn't have the desire or room to keep their wedding gown preserved in a box forever. Or until some future daughter might or might not want to wear it.

Although she'd been in the store countless times since her return, especially since the sisters had started selling the bracelets her mother made in their accessories section, Jolene's gaze was drawn to a darling little girl with a tumble of black curls, clad in pink overalls and a sparkly T-shirt. She'd built a Lego castle and a sword-wielding Lego knight was fighting a green dragon, while a Lego princess was watching from a tower window.

"Cordelia's day care is having a week long chicken pox shutdown," Velvet said, her hazel eyes, emphasized with heavy cat liner and kohl shadow, following their look. "I swear, Thorn and I wonder every day how we created a fairy princess child. Although, it's possible that in a former life she was a queen of the sea. It would be fitting, since the first time she kicked was when we were at the coast. It's as if she felt the tides pull, which is why Thorn and I decided we'd wait and let her choose her name. Which she obviously did. Cordelia has Celtic roots meaning daughter or heart of the sea."

"She's adorable." Jolene and Aiden had been talking about starting a family, and the sight of Velvet's daughter created an inner tug she'd been feeling more and more often.

"I like that parents are going back to traditional names," Gloria said. "And you've done such a wonderful job with her. I love it when she comes in for a haircut. She tells such fanciful stories."

"She's a chatterbox, that's for sure," Velvet said, today's nose ring sparkling in the morning light shining through the window. "In that respect, she's definitely my daughter."

"You and Thorn are both so creative. Maybe those genes passed down and she'll become a novelist, or write screenplays," Jolene suggested.

"Now there's a thought." Velvet laughed. "My daughter in Hollywood."

"Mine was." Gloria's glance toward Jolene was brimming with pride. "Jolene was nominated for an Emmy, you know."

"Mom," Jolene complained. "I doubt there's a person on the peninsula, or maybe even the entire state, who doesn't know that thanks to you broadcasting it every chance you get."

"It's a special thing," Velvet said. "You both have a right to be proud. Let me run in the back and get Doris and Dottie. They're finishing up their quarterly tax return."

A moment later, two elderly ladies came out of the back office. Dottie was dressed in a flowing floral top over her generous curves and red clamdiggers, while Doris was in a crisp white shirt and taupe linen slacks. Dottie had accessorized with a trio of bangle bracelets in the colors of the flowers on her top; Doris was wearing her usual pearls.

"Oh, we've been waiting for this day!" Dottie said. "And we're delighted you're getting married here in Honeymoon Harbor instead of jetting off to a destination wedding."

"Michael was the jet-setter," Gloria said. "But he's happily settled back home and we want to be married with all our family and friends in attendance. Which made the farm the obvious place."

"It is! And I heard Sarah will be back in town to officiate."

"She will. As it turns out, I was lucky that she wasn't booked. She's become quite in demand. Apparently the motorhome crowd has a strong community who chat in various Facebook groups and more and more people have turned to her to officiate their weddings. It's mostly people renewing their vows or widowers or divorced people who are remarrying and want more of a celebration than signing papers at the courthouse."

"I think that sounds like a wonderful idea," Velvet said. She grinned at Dottie and Doris. "There's no age limit for starting a second career."

"It's a wonderful idea," Doris said. "I always felt that inside that Southern belle exterior there was a spiritual core. Her performing weddings sounds like another step along her life's path."

"And do we know about that," Dottie agreed. "Especially given the Dancing Deer's journey. And although neither of us were blessed with children, we have Velvet as the daughter of our heart, and now little Cordelia as our granddaughter."

"Proving that you never know what life will bring," Doris agreed. Her expression softened and her eyes warmed as she watched the Lego princess tie a long silk cord to the windowsill, then climb down, landing between the jousting night and the dragon.

"Here, Mr. Dragon," Cordelia said in a high, sweet voice. "Would you like a piece of gumdrop? I brought you a red one because they're my favorite."

She put the small red piece of plastic in the dragon's clawed hand, them lifted it to his mouth.

"Dragon likes gumdrops," he said in what sounded like a happy growl.

"Oh, goodie. That means we can be friends because I have a lot of gumdrops. Would you like to have tea with me in my castle room?"

"Tea and gumdrops?" the dragon asked.

"Yes," the princess assured him, then she turned to the prince, reached out, and took his sword away. "You're invited too. But you can't bring your sword."

"What if the dragon wants to eat you?" the prince asked in a voice between the princess's high-pitched one and the dragon's growl.

"I only eat gumdrops," the dragon protested.

"I have cupcakes with pink frosting and sprinkles on top too," the princess said. "It will be a lovely tea. But also, fire breathing is not allowed. Okay?"

"Okay," the dragon agreed readily.

She turned back toward the prince. "See?" she said. "Love is love. Even for dragons."

"Your daughter's an old soul," Gloria told Velvet.

"Thorn and I think so too." Her hazel eyes moistened as she watched Cordelia show the dragon and prince how to climb up to the window on the silk cord. "Sometimes I just can't believe how lucky I am." She blinked, clearing her gaze. "I wouldn't claim to be clairvoyant, but I can sense things," she said. "And I know that you and Michael are going to have a very special wedding and wonderful life together."

"And with that," Dottie said, returning the conversation back to Gloria and Jolene's reason for having come to the shop, "let me show you what we've put aside for you. Of course, this is just the first group. If we don't have exactly what you want, we have a local seamstress who does beautiful gowns. Also, we can send away for a dress and alter it when it arrives."

"I don't know if I'm excited or nervous," Gloria said beneath her breath to Jolene as they followed the sisters toward a rack hanging next to the far wall beside the alcove where the wedding dresses were displayed. "Probably both."

Surprisingly, nothing on the rack of dresses were the muted lace gowns Gloria had expected. Instead, there was a rainbow of choices. "They're all so pretty!"

"Dottie insisted that these were appropriate for a casual outdoor wedding," Doris said. "And in your case, I totally agree."

"The fact that you change your hair color so often proves that you love color as much as I do," Dottie enthused.

"I change my hair every new moon," Gloria said, revealing something Jolene had never known. "When I was younger, and my life was more—" she paused, as if seeking the word she wanted "—*challenging*, I always saw each new moon as a chance for a new beginning."

"We all use whatever gets us through the day," Dottie said. "Doris and I certainly know about new beginnings. And I especially do, after losing my Harold."

Jolene knew he'd suffered a cerebral hemorrhage

while playing a game of doubles pickleball with his
twin brother during a peninsula-wide seniors pickleball tournament. The brothers had been hands-
down favorites to win state. It had Jolene thinking
of her father's sudden and unexpected death. You
never knew what might be waiting for you around
some unseen corner, so you might as well appreciate the good times. Such as wedding gown shopping
with her mom. And going home for a quiet dinner
with her husband, then lovemaking that could range
from slow and sweet to fireworks hot and explosive,
but never failed to leave her feeling like the luckiest
woman on the planet.

"That was such a tragedy," Gloria said.

"It was. I still miss him. Every day. And especially
during the nights." A reminiscent smile touched her
lips even as her eyes moistened. "And those occasional nooners during my lunch break on slow days
here at the shop."

Dottie had never been one to filter her thoughts,
and often drew criticism from her two-minutes-older
sister. But not today. Although it may have been a
trick of the light, caused by the morning sunlight re-
flecting on the lenses of her glasses, Jolene thought
she caught a glimpse of a tear in Doris's eye.

"I don't know what I would've done without my
Doris and Hayden," Dottie continued, Hayden being
Harold's twin brother and Doris's husband. "It was
all so sudden, like a bolt of lightning from a clear
blue sky. My mind was so muddled. If I'd been capable of coherent thought, I'd have worried that I'd

come down with sudden dementia. There were so many thoughts and memories tumbling around, I couldn't catch and hold on to any of them."

"I know that all too well," Gloria commiserated. "I was fortunate to have Caroline and Sarah for emotional support. John Mannion took care of all the details, and as worried as I was about Jolene, it was almost as if we'd switched roles, and she was the one who was comforting me."

There was a long moment of silence. Then Doris returned to her usually bubbly self. "Well, today isn't about the sad times," she said. "This wedding is going to be like your new moon, Gloria. The start of a wonderful new life with a wonderful, caring man."

"He wouldn't even let us pay him for the mural on the spa wall," Gloria said. "How generous is that?"

After all agreed that Michael Mannion was the catch of a lifetime, they got down to business. Dottie rolled the rack into the larger dressing room, and after telling them to call if they needed anything, left mother and daughter alone.

"I don't know where to start," Gloria said.

"Neither do I." The women definitely knew their customers. Every dress on the rack looked so perfect that Jolene's first plan of putting aside the definite *No* dresses wasn't an option.

"Your father wasn't really a bad man," Gloria said, as she stripped down to her underwear. "We were both young, and I'll admit to having been reckless in those days, but when I told him I was pregnant, he didn't hesitate to do what everyone thought at the time was the right thing."

"The right thing meaning getting married before either of you had graduated high school," Jolene said, wondering what all the adults around the couple had been thinking.

"There was a stigma about being an unwed mother. At least both sets of parents certainly thought so. It's a small town." Her words were muffled by the tiered, ombre turquoise dress she was pulling over her head. "People talk." She laughed, a soft sound that sounded more wistful than happy. "Fortunately, I quit worrying about that years ago.

"So, following our parents' advice, he dropped out of school and got a job at the old paper mill, which paid enough to put a roof over our heads. At first we were like kids playing house. It didn't seem so bad because we were crazy in love."

Crazy being the definitive word, Jolene thought, but did not say. Her mother had been talking about her dad more recently than she had for most of Jolene's life. She supposed it was her way of putting it in the past and, like her new moon hair theory, allowing herself to move on to new possibilities with a new love. "But we were pretty much on our own. His parents blamed me for 'trapping their son' and mine blamed him for 'ruining their daughter.'"

Having watched how difficult life had been for her mom, there'd been no way Jolene was going to risk making the same mistake during her teens. Though, to be perfectly honest, keeping her virginity hadn't been all that difficult because there'd only been one guy at Honeymoon Harbor High that she'd wanted to have sex with. She'd admittedly been frustrated when Aiden, who'd his own reasons for keeping their relationship secret, had possessed far more self-discipline than she had.

"That's when he started drinking," Gloria said. "To shut out all the negativity coming in from both sides. At first it was just a couple of beers. Then a six-pack. Then he moved on to the hard stuff. Like I said, he wasn't a bad man. He had a sickness, and a predilection for addiction."

"Grandpa Wells drank. A lot." Jolene remembered being afraid of the huge, gruff timberman who'd refused to ever call her mother by her given name. Whenever forced to acknowledge her existence, he'd only called her *that girl*. "It was probably an inherited illness."

Her mother shrugged. "Inherited or a learned behavior for coping, I never knew. He tried, going to so many AA meetings. But they never took. And looking back, the one thing that kept me with him was that, unlike the way his father treated his wife, he was never violent with me. After every bender, he'd bring me flowers. Sometimes from the market, other times he'd either pick wild flowers or steal from someone's gardens. For a while, he took a second job at Blue House Farm, and the Olsons let him bring home flowers and vegetables, which helped with the groceries.

"And I wish you could've seen his face when you were born. It was as if he'd won the Powerball lottery. He loved you from your very first minute. Even before that. He loved feeling you kick. It awed him that we could have created such a miracle. That's always how he thought of the pregnancy. Never as a burden, but an opportunity to have a better life, a better family than the one he'd grown up in."

An opportunity that, unfortunately, he'd never achieved. "He made you cry," Jolene said. Her mother had always put on a brave face, but the walls in the trailer were thin, and she'd spent many nights lying in bed, listening to her mother's weeping. She belatedly realized that although she'd hear their arguments, she'd never heard him shout the way her grandfather was prone to do.

"He did," Gloria allowed, "but he certainly did his share of crying too." Another sigh. "He wanted to be so much more. And the saddest thing of all was that, as terrible as it probably sounds, I'd honestly believed that getting sent to prison was the best thing that ever happened to him. It had been a serious wake-up call. And since the local chapter of AA even had meetings there, and one of the other prisoners was his sponsor, he'd managed to stay sober for the longest time in years.

"John Mannion had even offered him a job working on their Christmas tree farm when he got out. I always suspected that Sarah talked her husband into it. She and Caroline continued coming to the salon even when people were gossiping about me. Looking back, standing up to the gossips was probably the reason they'd started coming to me in the first place when I was still working out of the trailer. So, he had a good job working for good people waiting for him, and us to come home to."

Personally, Jolene wasn't as optimistic that her dad would have ever been able to change, but she understood why her mother needed to believe that.

"You did your best under difficult circumstances," she said. "And you've definitely earned a happier, easier life."

"I'm gloriously happy." Her brow furrowed beneath the bangs she'd cut last week as she studied herself in the mirror. "Except these tiers make my hips look a mile wide."

"Mom, you're a size four." Which might have raised some eyebrows in Hollywood, but in the real world, where she and her mom lived, that was tiny. "But if you feel that way, it's the wrong dress." She plucked a short halter dress in a color somewhere between peach and pink. "Try this."

After Jolene had zipped up the back of the dress, her mother turned this way and that in front of the mirror. "You don't think it's too short for a woman my age?"

"Very few women your age have legs like yours." Put her on ice skates and Gloria could have been a Rockette.

"It still feels inappropriate."

"I think it looks amazing. But, again, it's your wedding. It's important that you feel like a princess," Jolene said. "No—like a queen."

A dozen discarded dresses later, including a bright

pink one that had her mother comparing herself to
Barbie, Gloria was standing in front of the three-way
mirror, turning this way and that, studying every
view of a tea-length chiffon dress that was a wa-
tercolor wash of flowers that would look stunning
with the garden Amanda had helped Sarah Mannion
create behind the farmhouse. The twisted V neck-
line was low, but not immodest, with the back cut
to the same depth. Gloria took a few steps, causing
the flowered chiffon to flow around her legs, then
twirled. "I feel as if I'm floating on air."

"You look as if you are too. This is definitely *the*
dress. I don't know why we didn't think of it first
thing."

Gloria turned again in front of the triple mirrors,
taking in the deep back V. A natural redhead, she'd
always worn sunscreen, even here in the gray Pacific
Northwest, and her expanse of fair skin proved it.
When Jolene had first used her as a model for her
products for aging skin on Instagram, many of the
people commenting had accused her of photoshop-
ping the pictures. "It's also a beautiful dress to wear
to the gallery showing Michael is having in Santa
Barbara the week after the wedding."

They were spending their honeymoon in Italy and,
not wanting to be surrounded by tourists, Michael
had suggested a delayed honeymoon in September.
Part of which would be spent at his close friends
George and Amal Clooney's twenty-five room villa
on Lake Como. And hadn't that news set a record for
comments on the town's Facebook page?

"And by the way," Jolene said as they left the dressing room to show the others what her mom had chosen, "you look like a goddess."

"Aphrodite," Velvet said, turning from hanging summer tops on the wall. "Goddess of beauty, passion, love, and pleasure."

"It's perfect," Dottie exclaimed, clapping her hands.

"And since it fits perfectly, it won't need any alterations," the ever-practical Doris noted.

"It fits perfectly because it was meant for her," Velvet said. She held out her hand toward the sisters. "You each owe me ten bucks. They didn't think she'd pick that one." Velvet directed her explanation to Jolene while Gloria had found a freestanding mirror across the room and was standing there, seemingly transfixed by the image. "I was betting on the turquoise tiered one," Dottie said. "Or maybe the bright Barbie pink that's become such a popular color. Dorothy thought the champagne sheath with the three-quarter-length sleeves was more elegant and age appropriate."

"The champagne was elegant and lovely," Jolene said, not wanting to insult Doris by repeating her mom's insistence that she did not want to look like the mother of a bride or groom at her own wedding.

"But she chose the watercolored flowers because she's a romantic," Velvet said. "I noticed when she walked in that although she was obviously hesitant about choosing a gown, her aura was shimmering very pink, revealing that she's affectionate, romantic, and loves love for its own sake. And was probably already in love, which, admittedly was an easy guess since she was coming in for a wedding dress."

While Jolene wasn't all that sure about the aura deal—although it was tempting to ask what color Velvet saw when she looked at her—she couldn't deny that Velvet had described her mother to a tee.

"I think we should go out to celebrate," Gloria said, sounding and looking much more upbeat than when they'd gone into the shop. "What would you say to splurging on the tiramisu at Luca's?"

"With champagne," Jolene agreed. With her mom still floating on air, Jolene was relieved that Gloria seemed to have overcome any lingering doubts regarding her marriage. That, along with the perfect dress, was definitely deserving of champagne.

CHAPTER TEN

As SHE PACKED for the weekend trip to the coast, which was usually a place where she found an almost religious sense of peace, Amanda was feeling like Maggie the Cat, from *Cat on a Hot Tin Roof*, the old Elizabeth Taylor movie that had recently appeared on a streaming channel. A million thoughts were going through her mind. Had Quinn invited her just because they were friends? Or was this some sort of test, to see how well they got along together outside of work and her dinners at the pub. Or, maybe, he was simply as attracted to her as she was to him, and the weekend was simply about sex. After all, she'd heard the story of John Mannion cooking a seduction dinner for Sarah the night they'd arrived back in Washington—him from Nepal, her from Japan. And hadn't Lily Carpenter, now Mannion, told them about Burke having done the same thing when he'd returned home from New York?

She knew that the Mannion family tradition of seduction dinners at the coast house had been followed by proposals. Could this possibly be the reason he'd invited her to spend the night there? Could he possibly be planning to propose?

"Don't be ridiculous," she said as she closed her overnight bag with a burst of frustrated strength that risked breaking the zipper. Not knowing what to wear to a beerfest, she'd gone with a T-shirt, white clam-digger pants that stopped at the ankle (not that she intended to enter the razor clam digging competition she'd seen advertised online), and a pair of sneakers. "You haven't even had a date yet. Life doesn't work that way." *Especially not for you*, piped up the nagging voice in the back of her head that she'd managed to keep mostly silent until now.

"Shut up," she said. "You're not the boss of me anymore." The weekly, now monthly, visits to a Seattle therapist Caroline Harper had recommended had helped a great deal. Yet, there were still days, like now, when her past would come back to haunt her.

Except for having asked Caroline for the name of the therapist who, she'd claimed in casual conversation, had saved her marriage, Amanda never talked about her former life. She'd mostly locked it deep inside her, with the only other exception being the day she'd told Piper about her father being a professional gambler, only because she'd recognized a lonely wistfulness in the teen she'd so often felt herself growing up.

What she hadn't shared with anyone but Dr. Alicia Blake was that while he'd played well enough to go pro, their life was nothing like the glamorous one depicted in James Bond movies. In reality, the day-to-day life of most gamblers had nothing to do with private jets and spending nights in casinos on the

French Riviera. In her case, it was racing around the world, from Malta to Bangkok, to Vegas, to Vancouver, and everywhere in between as her dad chased the next game. The next win.

From the day her mother had left them when Amanda was eight, her life had revolved around a father she wouldn't see on any given day except briefly when she'd return home from whatever school she was enrolled in. Her breakfasts had mostly consisted of cold cereal and milk from the chest he'd refill with ice from the bins in front of gas station food marts. Sometimes the motel would have a continental breakfast that consisted of a stale cinnamon roll wrapped in plastic and a carton of milk.

If she was lucky, she had enough money for a school lunch ticket. Sometimes, an intuitive teacher, guessing at her circumstances from her outgrown clothes and shoes they'd find at Goodwill, would take pity on her and pay for her lunch. Other times, she'd go without, professing not to be hungry, making up stories about the towering stack of syrup-soaked pancakes and bacon her dad had fixed her before the bus had arrived to take her to school.

Dinner would mostly consist of more cold cereal or hot dogs from a local gas station. From time to time, when she'd complain about their nomadic life, he'd point out the people living in cars, or even on the sidewalks, and remind her that she'd never, not once, been forced to live without a solid roof over her head.

It was one of the few things he'd been right about. Plus, to be fair, there had been flashes of good times.

Like when he'd arrived back at two in the morning, having used part of his winnings to buy a huge red and white bucket of fried chicken, mashed potatoes, gravy, and biscuits. Of course, after wolfing it down, she'd spent the rest of the day sick to her stomach from gorging after going without.

And then there were those times they didn't stop at a motel at all. When they'd drive all night to make a game, or worse, when he was running from loan sharks. She'd once spent several hours in a police station after thug mob collectors in Hot Springs, Arkansas, had badly beaten her dad's leg while she'd been forced to watch. Next time, they'd warned, his little girl wouldn't get off so easily. One had even threatened trafficking. Amanda had seen enough warning signs on the inside of rest stop bathroom doors to know exactly what the jowly man with the face of a bulldog and shaved head had meant by that.

The policeman who'd taken her to the station had stopped at McDonalds and bought her a Happy Meal, as if that would give her anything to feel happy about. While sitting in a corner, eating slowly, waiting for them to hopefully take her to the hospital to see her dad, she'd nearly choked on her chocolate shake when she overheard two of the police officers talking about calling social services to put her into foster care. Before the second cop could make the call, the station was suddenly overtaken by the loud ruckus of a prostitution bust. Claiming a desperate need to go to the bathroom during the distraction, Amanda had escaped.

Unfortunately, she'd left the rest of her Happy Meal behind, but at least she was free. At the time, to her twelve-year-old mind, the idea of "going into the system" was as bad as it got. While on the road, she'd heard stories from kids who were treated like unpaid servants by their foster families, or worse, sexually. In one case, she'd heard firsthand from a girl who'd been impregnated in a group house by one of the parents' birth children. At age thirteen.

It was then, for the first and thankfully only time in her life, she'd become one of those people living on the street, like those her dad had pointed out to her. Fortunately, she'd come under the protection of an older woman who kept a baseball bat in her tent, its insides plastered with photos of celebrities torn from magazines she'd dug from recycle bins.

While the woman was obviously delusional, claiming to be Princess Di's mother—insisting she'd been stolen from her at birth and raised to marry into royalty—she'd been kind, and seemingly considered a sort of mascot of the street community, who'd bring her food obtained however they could. That generosity, along with the woman's black and tan Chihuahua, who was, in his own way, fearsome with a big dog attitude, had helped keep Amanda safe and fed.

One of the members of the community had talked a nurse who visited regularly to give vaccines and wellness checks into claiming to be a friend of her dad so she could learn when he was going to be released. Meanwhile, Amanda had been kept in hiding, because the consensus was that she was safer with them than she was in any foster system. Years later, whenever she'd think back on those days, Amanda still wasn't certain which would have been better. She'd mostly decided that just like her dad's former occupation, it had depended a lot on luck. On the social worker and the family you'd end up with. It had, however, changed what had earlier been sympathy for the homeless to empathy, having learned from individual stories, and discovering firsthand, how fragile some people's security can be.

Two days after she'd escaped the police department, two seemingly endless days her dad had spent in an ER hallway, he'd limped out of the hospital, his battered face and body looking as if he'd been run over by a truck. But that hadn't stopped him. He'd gone to the impound lot where the police had their car towed, and bailed it out with the cash he'd kept hidden beneath the trunk's carpeted floor liner. A place where those thugs hadn't thought to look.

"Guess things have gotten a little too hot for us here in Hot Springs," he'd said, proving that nearly getting killed and leaving his daughter an orphan hadn't dented his optimism nor sense of humor. Nor the generosity that had him stopping by the elderly lady's tent and handing her a paper-wrapped package of bills to share with the others to thank them for taking good care of his princess while he'd been incapacitated.

It was gestures like that, and the sweet sixteen birthday cake, pink roses, and tarnished necklace that she still kept in its box in her nightstand drawer, that had left her with feelings too complex to sort out.

As Dr. Blake had advised, even Mother Teresa had confessed to not having been a perfect person. Except for the truly evil among us, we all live our lives on a sliding scale that can change from day to day.

The therapist had spent a year in Japan, where she'd learned the Japanese concept of wabi-sabi, part of which she'd explained to Amanda, noting that all things in nature were in an imperfect state of flux, which meant all people, including Amanda and her father were impermanent, incomplete, and imperfect.

"One of the teachings of wabi-sabi philosophy is that since perfection is impossible, we must strive for excellence," Dr. Blake's words echoed in Amanda's memory. "Was your father perfect? Of course not. But, with all things being in flux—his broken marriage, his unstable career choice, his parenting—the stories you've shared about your good times together showed that he loved you, and was, in his own way, handling each imperfect experience the best he was able." She'd given Amanda a book to read about the philosophy, and flagged her need to strive for perfection, which she'd recognized years before going to therapy had been an attempt to control everything after having grown up with such a lack of stability. She realized that while everyone's situation was different, everyone around her, including Quinn, were all experiencing the same ebb and flow of nature. Of being human.

She wished she'd read that book decades earlier. Even during college, she'd kept to herself, giving the impression that she was antisocial, or perhaps just one of those nerds who lived in their own weird little world. She hadn't cared what anyone thought because she was solely focused on getting an education and achieving a more secure life than her parents had.

Living in Honeymoon Harbor had her beginning to look at life differently. Perhaps it was the slower pace that allowed her more time for contemplation, but she'd learned, that unlike what her twelve-year-old self had feared, there were good foster parents out in the world. Like Chelsea Mannion, the town librarian, who'd taken two children in as fosters, then adopted them with Quinn's brother, Gabe.

She'd also witnessed many romances bloom among her friends, and she recognized the relationships had eventually worked thanks to each person trying, in their own way, to be the best partner they could be. Which meant that if Quinn did have a deeper relationship than friendship in mind, she was going to have to open up and share the most private parts of herself. Possibly as soon as this weekend.

IT WAS JUST another beer competition, Quinn reminded himself as he drove in from his lake house to town. Winning wasn't everything. *The hell it isn't*, he remembered a much younger Burke telling him before the game when his brother had led the Honeymoon Harbor Pelicans to the state high school championship.

Quinn had suggested that if Burke hadn't been playing for the love of the game, he wouldn't have spent so many hours of his life throwing that ball through the tire his father had set up and studying televised college and pro games every weekend the way Quinn had prepped for the SAT. Which was when his brother had retorted that sure, he loved football, but winning made it a helluva lot more fun. And besides, losing sucked.

Which Quinn had discovered for himself during his law career. Mostly, he'd advised his high-end clients on how to legally become even wealthier, yet there'd been times when some of them would go rogue and land in court. That was when his job changed to getting them off the hook, which had reminded him of something his grandfather had told him while fishing when he'd been about eight years old.

Nothing they'd tried that morning had gotten so much as a bite. Not changing lures, or lines, or even locations. Then Quinn had been instructed to throw some chum—chopped up pieces of fish—into the water, and bingo, a flurry of younger, less canny fish came roaring toward the chum, only to be followed by the larger ones, who, while gobbling it all up to keep the smaller ones from getting any, surrendered the caution that had allowed them to live long enough to become the big fish in the pond.

"Never forget, fish are greedy," Quinn's pop had told him. "Because they never know where their next meal is coming from."

Many of his clients had been greedy like that. The difference was, they'd known where their next meal was coming from. Their accounts, scattered across various continents, assured they'd never go hungry.

But an innate greed kept them always fighting the little guys for every bite. And that greed had occasionally landed Quinn in court tying to defend what his inner sense of honor and integrity instilled by his parents had considered indefensible.

That was why he'd walked away from an offered partnership, big bonuses, and a waterfront view penthouse in a building that, when he'd left Seattle, had been ranked the third most expensive place to live in the country, in favor of coming home to brew beer.

After his Captain Jack Sparrow successful release, Quinn had admitted, only to himself, that he had more in common with his football-playing brother than he'd originally thought. As much as he enjoyed his work—strike that—*loved* creating that perfect blend of ingredients to make the best beer he could—winning all those competitions he'd entered over the past few years was a helluva lot more fun than losing.

Still, despite this weekend being centered around beer, and even knowing that this year's Surfin' USA had a good chance of topping his previous seasons' brews, Quinn's mind was focused on something—someone—else entirely. This weekend, he was risking a close friendship for something more. Because, as Brianna had so succinctly pointed out, if he didn't make his move to win the woman he loved, some other guy was going to.

"Which isn't going to happen," he vowed as he pulled up in front of her Victorian house that had been painted a deep gray with white gingerbread molding on the peaked roof and arch leading to the front porch. The dark of the gray had been brightened by the snow-white front doors and shutters on the front window. He was not surprised to see a variety of ferns hanging from the cedar roof of the porch and colorful bedding plants scattered about the porch floor in pots.

Suggesting that she'd been waiting for him, she opened the door before he could use the brass flower-shaped door knocker.

"Hi!" As bright as the sun gifting this summer morning, her smile caused a now all too familiar tug. He skimmed a look over her. Except for a bit of lipstick the color of a ripe peach that made him want to taste her, she wasn't wearing any makeup. Her silky brown hair had been twisted into the same braid she always wore while working, then pulled through the back of a white baseball cap.

"You're not wearing your Wheel and Barrow T-shirt," he said, inwardly cringing at what wasn't exactly a stellar opening line. "But you look great," he tacked on.

"I have enough business to keep me busy on this side of the peninsula," she said. "I figured I'd wear one of your Surfin' USA T-shirts from the Dancing Deer. Velvet said your Beach Boy–themed shirts sell very well in their touristy section. Though, according to them, they can't keep your Captain Jack Sparrow in stock."

"It makes sense pirates would beat surfers," he

said. "I would have given you one. You didn't have to buy it."

"I wanted to." She'd put on a pair of oversized sunglasses that made her look like photos he'd seen of Jackie Kennedy, or a movie star, and treated him to another one of those smiles that sent the too-familiar tug lower, beyond his belt. What was it about this woman that had him responding like a horny fifteen-year-old?

"So, what's the itinerary today?" she asked after she'd climbed into the passenger seat, having given him a view of her slender butt that, again, had him feeling as if he were back in middle school, hiding out with Burke, going through Quinn's stash of *Playboy*s.

"I hired a company that does all my setups. But I'll have to spend a lot of the day pitching beer to attendees." A thought hit like a hammer to the skull as he walked around the front of the SUV. "Damn," he said as he joined her. "I should've thought of that part. It leaves you on your own."

"No, it doesn't," she said. "Because I'll be helping in your booth. You can pitch and I'll pour."

When he looked a little skeptical, she added, "Don't worry. I worked as a bartender when I turned twenty-one my senior year in college to save up money to start a small nursery after graduation. I promise I know how to pour a beer without having the head overflow."

"I wasn't worried about that." Because it hadn't occurred to him.

"Good. And for the record, I didn't come here for the clam digging, the kite flying, sandcastle building contest, or musical acts. I came to escape for the weekend and spend time with you away from the pub. Also, I've heard wonderful things about your family's house, so I'm looking forward to finally seeing it."

"It was built in the 1800s."

"So I've heard. I've also heard about a special Mannion men's custom that takes place there." When he wasn't about to touch that statement, she let a long pause drag out as they drove down Water Street along the harbor. "So, I have a question," she said as he turned, headed toward the still snowcapped Olympic Mountains. "Are you planning on making me a seduction dinner?"

He glanced over at her. "That depends. Were you expecting a seduction dinner?"

He couldn't see her eyes through those Jackie O sunglasses, but he could sense a mix of laughter and seduction of her own in a flirtatious tone he'd never, ever imagined, even after all these months he'd fantasized about her.

"Surely you didn't think I accepted your invitation just to pour beer," she said. "And, by the way, this T-shirt isn't the only thing I bought at the Dancing Deer yesterday."

Yet more images from the glossy centerfolds of those old magazines flashed through his mind. "That sounds intriguing."

"I don't want to give anything away," she said. "It was supposed to be a surprise. So, all I'm going to say is that it's a good thing the twins and Velvet can keep a secret. Otherwise, we could break the Facebook page."

"You do realize that you're making it very difficult for me to concentrate on beer all day."

She leaned over and skimmed a finger, tipped in that peachy pink color that matched her lips, down his cheek and around his jaw. "They say—" her voice turned deep and sultry "—that patience is a virtue."

"So I've heard."

"I'm sure. But Ben Franklin, who was known for his libertine ways in Paris, also had his own take on it." Another of those pauses that had Quinn realizing that while he might be the one cooking the seduction dinner, she was demonstrating a surprising expertise of her own in the art of seduction. "He's quoted as saying that 'he that can have patience can have what he will.'"

UNLIKE THOSE FEW times he'd had to engage in courtroom litigation, Quinn always enjoyed brewery competitions. Whether from the West, Midwest, Texas (which was currently exploding with craft brews), or the East Coast, brewers were a convivial group, and like an artist community, they all supported each other and learned from one another, partly because they loved the variety of beers being produced, but also because they had a common enemy in the huge corporate industrial brewers. Whenever one of these events ended, as much as he was glad to be heading back home, there was always a thought in the back of his mind that he could have enjoyed just one more day.

Not today. The lines were steady, the compliments, from first tasters to longtime fans were also satisfying and, while it might not have been his initial career, it made him happy to have made the switch that still puzzled many of his former legal peers. But as the line continued to grow, even as the closing time drew near, and he'd won the best Taste of Summer yet again, he was wishing that the damn thing would be over so he could finally get a taste of Amanda.

CHAPTER ELEVEN

BECAUSE QUINN WANTED tonight to be perfect, and not a quick, frenzied rush to bed to satisfy the chemistry that had been building between them, on the drive to the coast house, he purposefully directed the conversation back to the events of the day, rather than what else he'd planned for the weekend. That seduction hadn't been mentioned again, though he knew it was on both their minds.

Amanda had surprised him with the easy way she'd chatted up event attendees as she poured the beer with professional expertise. He hadn't known that she'd bartended while in college. Thinking about it, he didn't even know where she'd gone to college. Or anything about her life until she'd ended up in Honeymoon Harbor.

"You had us selling out before closing," he said.

"It was the beer. You've developed quite a reputation. I was listening to the people in line having friendly banter about who was the first to discover you."

"That's nice to hear." He was too busy answering questions about ingredients, and how he'd gotten into brewing, and taking cards from reps from two of the nation's largest breweries, along with another from Colorado, wanting to talk to him about a deal that could be advantageous to both parties.

He'd politely said that he was quite happy just the way he was and ditched the cards as soon as they'd walked away. One of the reps had been a twenty-something blonde who looked as if her previous job might have been lounging across the hoods of a BMW or Ferrari at a car show while wearing a sprayed-on evening gown, or maybe a bikini. Apparently the company she was representing believed that old adage that sex sells.

As often happened, they were thinking along the same lines again when Amanda said, "That blonde rep was certainly obvious when she got into the part of her spiel about 'shared opportunities.'"

"I'm sure it was just her way of talking shop. It's a tricky slope," he said. "For both parts. The appeal of craft brews is that each one is unique and those who are into that world are always on the lookout for new ones. And when they find one they like, they enjoy talking about it. Google 'craft beers' and you'll come up with over thirty-seven million hits in less than a second."

"Surely not that many?"

"Try it," he suggested.

She took out her phone and typed in what he'd suggested. "Wow. You're right. I just got thirty-seven million, six-hundred thousand."

"That popularity is what makes the big guys want to buy them up. Individually, they're not big competition. But when you put them together, you've got a movement the major markets want a part of."

"Buying an established brand is certainly easier and faster than developing their own," she considered.

"That would be true."

"But let's say a company like yours becomes part of a conglomerate—doesn't it lose its mystique among the fan base?"

"Bingo. It's a dual edge sword. The suits in the tower window offices believe it's an easy solution. But not so much when sales start falling off. Because many of the craft drinkers accuse the craft brewer of selling out."

"So both lose," she pondered.

"It can happen," he agreed.

"Surely you've been approached by conglomerates before today. And, by the way, that woman may have been representing her company, but believe me, she had an entirely different shared advantage in mind."

"I got that. But I wasn't interested."

"A lot of men would be."

"Not me. Partly because she'll be playing the same card at the next competition with some other guy. But mostly because she couldn't hold a candle to you."

He glanced over to watch the rosy flush come into her cheeks again. Quinn liked that he could make her blush and imagined using his hands and mouth to cause that soft pink color to rise all over her body.

"Flatterer," she said.

"It's not flattery if it's true. To quote a movie I once watched on a date, 'You had me at hello.'"

Amanda glanced over at Quinn, surprised, but with his eyes on the twists and turns they were taking on the steep downgrade, she could only see his profile.

"I was married the day I first came into the pub."

"I was well aware of that. If you hadn't been, I'd have cooked you a seduction dinner a very long time ago."

"I don't know what to say to that," she admitted. Though it did cross her mind that forbidden temptations were often the most appealing.

"You don't have to say anything. I just thought you ought to know that this weekend wasn't spur-of-the-moment. I've been thinking about it for a very long time."

"Oh." Amanda knew him well enough to know that, unlike her former husband, he didn't have it in him to lie, but it was hard to wrap her mind around the idea of him having wanted her from when they'd first met.

Again, she was at a loss for words as she thought back on all the conversations they'd had over the past years. She'd later wondered if that special moment—which seemed frozen in time—had been more about her beginning her life anew. Had he been letting her know, in his own quietest of all the Mannions' ways, that he wanted to be part of that life?

"I thought I'd felt something," she murmured as a few raindrops from the coastal clouds gathering overhead began to dot the windshield. "A connection, that moment in the pub, after I'd gotten off the ferry." She'd been so sad. And drained. And unsure of so many things. At the time, the only thing she knew was right was saying goodbye to her husband. Forever. Which had left her emotions tangled in a complex knot of heartbreak and relief. "So I wasn't alone in experiencing that?"

"No. You weren't."

"But you didn't say or do anything."

"You weren't ready," he said. "Not that day, definitely. While I don't know the details, it was obvious, after all that happened, that you'd been through a lot. And, I imagined, as you'd tried to make your marriage work, you'd begun to lose yourself."

"I'm embarrassed to admit that's true." Except for Wheel and Barrow, so much else in her marriage had been like living through a constant series of hurricanes and tornados. But with Aiden's help, and that of friends she'd made, and her therapist, she'd managed to come through all those storms into the sunshine. Today, working with Quinn, there'd been times she'd thought that if she'd looked up at the sky overhead, it would have been filled with rainbows.

"There's no need to feel embarrassed. It happens to many of us. Though fortunately, most to lesser degrees."

As she gathered her thoughts, the wipers automatically came on, the only sounds in the SUV were the ping of the rain on the roof and the swish, swish, swish of the wipers, clearing the glass.

Finally, she turned toward him. "Yet, even having wanted me, for all that time, once I'd made the decision to break free of my marriage, you still didn't say anything."

He sighed. Heavily. "You weren't ready," he repeated. "You'd been through a traumatic, intensely public situation, and had a lot on your plate moving past that while keeping Wheel and Barrow going, all while finding yourself again. Who you were. What you truly wanted. If I'd said anything, it could have changed the equation. I didn't want you thinking about *us*. I wanted to give you time to concentrate on yourself. To be able to establish a new life that suited you, without having to worry about what anyone else might think about your choices…

"I've never been married, but there was this woman I'd spent some time with when I was in college. The first one I'd ever thought of having a future with."

"What happened?"

"She broke up with me. Accused me of being a small-town boy at heart, who'd never understand her ambition to live an adventurous life. At the time, my ego was wounded. Looking back on it, she did me a favor. As it turns out, I *am* a small-town guy. If we had gotten married, it would've been a disaster."

"Like my marriage."

He shrugged. "I don't know what all went on, and I'll always be angry at myself for not noticing what my brother was smart enough to see, but from what I could tell, your situation was pretty messy."

"We need to talk about it," she said. "It was messy, complex, and if we're going to have any kind of relationship beyond friends with benefits, you need to know who I was. About my screwed-up life before that day."

"Whatever you want to share," he said. "I'm here to listen. But know, going in, that nothing you can say is going to make a difference in how I feel about you. This definitely isn't the way I'd planned to tell you, and God knows I've thought about it a lot, but there's nothing complex about my feelings.

"I've been crazy about you even when I knew I shouldn't—couldn't—be. Your past, while it obviously has some bearing on where you are now, is in the past. It's where you are now, and your future—which I'm hoping will be with me—that I'm focused on."

Amanda considered that Brianna was right. When Quinn did say more than a couple sentences, it was well worth listening to.

"You make it sound so easy."

He shrugged, glanced over at her for a long moment on a rare straight stretch of road, and said, "It can be." Taking advantage of a view turnout, he pulled off the road, cut the engine, unhooked his seat belt, and turned toward her. "Will it be perfect? No. Because perfection is an illusion, something that people are always chasing, which allows them to never stop and enjoy the moment.

"But trust me on this—if you're willing to move beyond friends, we could have a lot of special moments together." He ran the back of his hand down the side of her cheek. Then leaned toward her, until his mouth was a whisper away from hers.

"Okay if I finally kiss you now?" he asked, his voice somehow managing to be both rough and soft at the same time. "I've been distracted all day by the need to taste you."

He wasn't alone. Amanda had fantasized kissing him since that moment, which had remained—as if preserved in amber—in her mind.

"Definitely okay." Her assent was merely a whisper, but heard easily over the light rain pattering on the roof.

Proving himself to be a man of contradictions, a man who had his own stories he'd kept to himself, his own past she'd wondered about for so long, the touch of his mouth to hers was soft yet sure.

He brushed his lips lightly against hers.

Once.

Twice.

A third time.

Then began tracing them with the tip of his tongue before nipping her moist bottom lip. As the light bite send shimmers of golden light flowing through her, she lifted her arms around his neck and parted her lips, inviting more.

He murmured her name, his deep voice vibrating through her like a tuning fork causing sensitive nerves in her lady bits to vibrate.

As his tongue glided in, deepening the kiss, wispy ribbons of fog rolled in from the coast, seeming to wrap them in their own private world. Sinking into the teasingly gentle, but oh, so seductive kiss, Amanda's whirling mind flashed back to a day when her father, who'd had a winning streak at a Seminole tribe casino in Hollywood, Florida, had treated her to a weekend at Key West, where she'd had her hand read by a fortune teller who'd been one of the street performers during the nightly sunset celebration.

"You will fall in love not once, but twice in your life," the old woman, who'd been wearing a caftan printed with astrological signs, said in a deep, husky voice. "The first will, unfortunately, bring you pain and heartbreak. The second will be your soulmate, and will be with you not only through your very long life line, but many shared lives throughout the ages."

At the time, being a cynical thirteen, Amanda had secretly scoffed at the idea of soulmates. Now, as she found herself lost in both the fog outside and the thicker one swirling in her mind, she had to wonder.

"Well," Quinn's voice broke into her thoughts as he ended the exquisite contact. "That was definitely worth waiting for."

"If that was your idea of the amuse-bouche part of your seduction dinner, I'm seriously looking forward to the main course," she said.

"Jarle, who's hooked on cooking shows, told me that amuse-bouche means one taste to please the mouth," he said as they continued down the tree-lined coast road. "And although I want to taste a lot more of you, that one definitely lived up to its definition."

She laughed, thinking how, although she'd heard him banter with his brothers all the time, she couldn't remember him joking with her. Not like this.

Was it possible that he'd been hiding his inner self as she so often did? Hadn't her therapist assured her that everyone tended to do that? What he'd shared about having had feelings for her all this time was definitely a surprise. As the warmth created by that brief kiss continued to flow through her veins, even as her nerves began to tangle again, Amanda was looking forward to discovering more of Quinn's well-hidden depths.

"SOMETHING'S BEEN PUZZLING ME," Jerome Harper said over dinner as Quinn and Amanda were driving to the coast. Although the house he and Harriet lived in had a small kitchenette, most nights they ate at the farmhouse. Not just for the meal, but for a long-held tradition of shared family dinner conversation.

"And what would that be?" Sarah asked, as she passed him a plate of horseradish- and herbed-panko-crusted halibut served with mashed potatoes and grilled asparagus.

"That girl Brianna and Seth brought to the barbecue. The one working at the pub."

"Piper?" Sarah said.

"Yeah. That's her. She reminded me of someone as soon as Brianna introduced her, but I couldn't figure out who."

"He's been fussing about it ever since," Harriet, his wife for the past half century, complained.

"I don't fuss," he returned. "I ponder. Think things through."

"And did you come up with an answer?" John

broke in to ask before the bickering began. His wife's parents had bickered for as long as he'd known them, which was nearly all his life, and he'd come to realize that it wasn't mean-spirited arguing, but a game they'd fallen into, perhaps going back to the beginning of their marriage.

Jerome nodded. "I sure enough did." He reached into the pocket of his plaid shirt and pulled out an old, faded photograph. "Digging through some old boxes, I found this photograph of Harriet's mother on her wedding day. Tell me that girl's not a dead ringer."

He handed the photo to Sarah, who was seated beside him. "Oh," she said. "I see the resemblance." She studied it a moment longer, and then handed it to John, who was seated at the head of the table.

"It's a faded black-and-white," he said "But the resemblance is there and your grandmother, Emmeline, had that copper hair as the girl does."

"I remember grandmother's bright hair," Sarah agreed. "Whether it came from the Celts or Vikings, she once told me that redheads in our family skipped every other generation, which made us special." She patted her own curls. "Of course, mine's lighter now that I started having Gloria add highlights."

"It was the same color as that girl's when you were her age," Jerome said. "Same as Emmeline's."

"Piper is British," John pointed out. "That country certainly has its share of gingers."

"Forget the dang hair then," Jerome said. "If you had a picture of that girl and put it side by side with this one, they could be the same person. Their eyes, nose, lips. All are the same."

"They say everyone has a doppelgänger," Sarah mused. "Even more than one."

"That's the word I was looking for," Jerome said. "I had a bit of a start when I first saw her."

"Well, grandmother was lovely, as is her daughter," Sarah said with a smile toward her mother, whose hair had turned from chestnut to silver over the years. "And Piper's certainly very pretty."

"And polite," Harriet said. "Though I did notice her sneaking off with that boy from Gabe's boat shop."

"They weren't sneaking off," Sarah said. "They were merely having lunch together. I imagine it wasn't easy being the only ones their age. They were surrounded by adults and noisy children. And since they're both new to Honeymoon Harbor, it makes sense they'd want to be able to talk away from the crowd."

"Sneaking off seems to be a teenage thing," Jerome said. "The way you two used to do."

John, who'd been lifting a piece of flaky halibut to his mouth, paused, leaving the fork in midair. "You knew?"

"That you and my daughter spent an awful lot of time riding that dang ferry and never going anywhere? How stupid did you think her mother and I were?"

"I never considered you stupid," John said.

"You two were so crazy about each other, we didn't want to push you into doing anything even more rebellious," Harriet said. "Like running off together. So we taught you about the risks of having unprotected sex and held our breaths."

"Your mother, who nearly wore out her rosary beads during that time, was relieved when you went off to Japan, and John went to Nepal," Jerome revealed to Sarah. "Nothing personal," he assured John. "It's just that she had big ambitions for our girl."

"I wasn't the only one," Harriet shot back. "You threatened to chop your own son-in-law into minnow-sized pieces and throw him in the harbor for crab bait if he got our Sarah in trouble."

"He wasn't my son-in-law yet," Jerome muttered.

"But it all worked out in the end," John, always the peacemaker, pointed out.

"That it did," Jerome agreed. "And while I still contend that you two were too young to be carrying on like you were, you've been a decent husband to my girl and a good father to our grandchildren."

"As much as we love Gabe and Chelsea's daughters, John and I wouldn't mind another grandchild or two to spoil," Sarah said. "It's not as if we're getting any younger."

"Funny you should mention that." Brianna exchanged a look with Seth. "We have a photo of our own to share." She got up from the table, went over to the sideboard, where she'd left her purse, and pulled out a black-and-white photo of her own, which she handed to her mother. "Ask and ye shall receive."

"Oh!" Sarah's free hand flew to the breast over her heart. "You're having a baby!" Tears welled up in her eyes. "Look, John," she said, handing the photo to her husband. "We're going to have a new little Mannion."

"Who'll be half Harper," Jerome pointed out as he studied the photo that had been passed down the table to him. "I can't tell if it's a boy or a girl."

"It's too early," Brianna said. "There's something called a nub theory that sort of lets you guess, but we decided we don't want to know."

"Like the old-fashioned way," Harriet said, snatching the photo from her husband, who appeared to look as if he was prepared to hold on to it forever. "It's sucking its thumb."

"The doctor says you can see fingerprints at this stage," Seth said, finally entering into the conversation. "But it was turned the wrong way, so we couldn't see them. But it's still a miracle."

There was a brief moment of silence as his words of a miracle brought up the memory of him having created a nursery for the child he'd hoped to have with his first wife, Zoe, who'd been killed while serving as an army nurse in Afghanistan.

"Babies are always a miracle," Sarah said, bringing the mood in the room back up. "Fortunately, Mother must've been prescient, because she brought over her famous celebratory lemon, blueberry, and buttermilk cake with the meringue buttercream frosting for dessert. Why don't you help your grandmother and me cut and plate it while the men clear the table?" she asked Brianna.

The kitchen began bustling with activity, conversations flowing back and forth, so that by the time everyone have moved out onto the deck for dessert, the bittersweet moment of Seth's loss had passed, and the conversation had turned to what to name the upcoming addition to the Harper/Mannion family.

CHAPTER TWELVE

THE COAST HOUSE that had been in the Mannion family for generations had originally been built for a whaling captain. "There's still a widow's walk around the top," Quinn told Amanda after they'd crossed the bridge over a small creek that he'd told her would often flood during spring thaw flowing off the Olympic Mountains, thus the reason for the bridge, which had been built by his dad later.

"When we were kids, Brianna used to make up romantic stories about the captain's wife standing up there for hours, pacing, watching for her husband to come home. Which, of course, being the romantic that she was—"

"Still is, from what I can tell," Amanda said.

"She certainly has been with Seth. I've always suspected that in the beginning she stayed away for so long because it was too hard to see him with Zoe, despite the three of them having been close friends. And as tragic as Zoe's death was, they both seem to have gotten the happily-ever-after she used to end all her stories with."

"They seem like the perfect couple," she said.

"You'd never guess there had been a feud between the Mannions and the Harpers."

"Mom and Dad's marriage pretty much did away with that," Quinn said. "By the time Brianna and Seth got married, the feud was ancient history. The story about it having started when Nathaniel Harper voted against the town's name change isn't true, by the way. Gram insists it was over a woman."

"That's not what it says in the town museum."

Quinn shrugged as he stopped for a fawn who'd frozen in front of them, seeming unsure of which way to go. "I suppose that sounds better than the truth. The supposed reason was that Nathaniel Harper and Gabriel Mannion were both courting the same woman—Edna Mae Kline. Nathaniel was fairly wealthy at the time, having constructed most of the buildings in the town. But Gabriel was also doing well, being not only the head of the bank, but mayor."

"I've seen their names on the courthouse's cornerstone," Amanda said. Quinn, having kept his law license, had represented her during her divorce while Brianna had gone to the courthouse with her for emotional support.

A doe and a second fawn came out of the curtain of trees alongside the driveway. The doe gave the fawn, who'd begun to lose its spots, a nudge with her velvety dark nose and the little family crossed, disappearing into one of the last remaining old-growth forests on the other side.

"Anyway, the Harpers had long memories that kept the feud going for a few generations."

"The name change argument definitely makes for a better historical story because it brings Theodore Roosevelt and a royal family into the mix."

"That's how I look at it."

He pulled up in front of a house covered in cedar siding that had been stained a silvery blue hue the color of the ocean at twilight. Amanda looked up at the high roof and the widow's walk with its bright white railing that had inspired a younger Brianna's stories. "How did the captain's wife get all the way up there?"

"There's a trapdoor and ladder in the attic. Aiden, doing his best to be the Mannion bad boy back then, would always change the endings to Bri's tales, having a violent Pacific storm blow in from the sea and capsize the whaling boat in the turbulent waters, causing the ship, captain, and crew to sink to the bottom of the sea to spend eternity in Davy Jones's locker. In one of his more graphic versions, the suddenly widowed woman, who'd witnessed the sinking, unable to imagine a life without her husband, threw herself off the cliff into the sea."

"Well, that's certainly tragic."

"It gets worse. One version had her swallowed up by a great white shark."

"I shouldn't laugh," Amanda said, even as she did exactly that. "But the Aiden I know, the one who may well have saved my life, is about as far away from a bad boy as you can get."

"Life changes people," Quinn said simply as he cut the engine.

"You're not going to get any argument from me

about that," Amanda said, thinking how much she had changed. And, as this weekend proved, was still evolving. She'd had a grand time at the beerfest. But there was still one serious hurdle to overcome before she could embrace the woman she'd come to believe she deserved to be.

Although the traditional Mannion seduction meal included steak, having noticed that she'd never ordered steak at the pub, Quinn had suggested grilled Dungeness crab, which she'd immediately agreed to. Obviously wanting this night to be as pressure-free as possible for her, he'd given her the choice of bedrooms, in case she changed her mind about the seduction part of the weekend.

"Whichever one you're going to be sleeping in," They both knew why they were here, so why play coy?

"Excellent answer," he said as he carried both overnight bags into the master bedroom which had a glorious view of the sea. The house had been built back from the edge of the cliff for safety, as sea and land were in a constant battle here in the Pacific Northwest.

One of the things that had fascinated Amanda when she'd first moved to Washington were the sea stacks—magnificent, towering parts of the continental coastline that had broken away, and were now standing out there alone in the surging surf, providing resting spots and even nesting locations for the millions of migrating birds who visited every year.

After leaving the suitcases, he went out to get the

cooler of items he'd brought for dinner, leaving her alone in the bedroom with its adjoining bath, which featured a deep, free-standing lion-footed copper tub like one that might have been included by the house's builder to warm the captain after months on that icy Pacific sea.

Or, Amanda thought, as naughty images flashed through her mind, perhaps for the captain and his wife to warm each other as they made up for all that time apart. There was also a shower large enough for a basketball team with a long, tiled bench that had other erotic thoughts flashing through her mind.

Although she'd only brought a minimal amount of clothing for the weekend, after a lifetime of never taking time to unpack as she and her father moved from place to place, there was something satisfying about putting all her new, sexy lingerie and day clothes for tomorrow in the knotty pine chest of drawers.

Then she went downstairs to where Quinn was taking ingredients out of a red metal cooler. "I'll admit to cheating a bit on the dinner," he said. "Jarle made the coleslaw and I picked up some crusty bread from Desiree's to sop up the butter from the crab. I am capable of grilling it though."

"It all sounds delicious. And this way, we'll have more time to sit and talk."

He paused in pulling out a bottle of wine from the cooler. That same Maison de Madeline chardonnay he'd had her try that day. The same she ordered every time she came into the pub. "That sounds serious."

She shrugged, feeling foolish, but there was something he needed to know. Otherwise, there was a chance this fantasy seduction weekend could end in disaster.

"Be open with him," Dr. Blake had advised. "He sounds like a good man—"

"A wonderful man," she'd said.

"Then he'll understand."

Even as Amanda knew the therapist was right, she didn't know exactly how to start. Or how long it would take.

"The crab is already cooked," he said. "I just have to grill it for a few minutes in the garlic butter sauce. So, why don't we sit outside, unwind, and watch the sun set?"

There were times, and this was one of them, that Amanda considered that Quinn was out of reach because he was too good for her. A thought the therapist had firmly shut down. But that didn't mean that insecurity and fear didn't sometimes hover in the far reaches of her mind, preparing to make an appearance, like those monsters that would jump out in haunted houses. Which, to Amanda, had never been fun.

Five minutes later, they were seated side by side on a cushioned double chair, watching streaks of color begin to fill the sky. The wine bottle sat on the table in front of them, and he'd poured them each a glass of the Oregon Willamette Valley wine.

"I'm embarrassed to be asking you this," she said, looking out over the water to where a red and white fishing boat was chugging along the horizon, heading back to harbor before dark.

"You can ask me anything."

She turned toward him. "I know it sounds foolish, but I need you to be patient with me."

"I thought I had been."

"You have. More than I'd even imagined. But I have this thing."

"A thing."

"Yes. It's hard to explain unless I start at the beginning."

"I've always found that's the best place to start."

"True. But it's—well, it's complicated. And why are you smiling?"

"That's what Burke always told me when I asked about him and Lily. And Aiden and Jolene. Gabe and Chelsea. Seth and Brianna. And you've heard my parents' story. I've come to the conclusion that most relationships are complicated. Why should ours be any different? Which, may I point out, it already has been. At least on my side."

"Mine too." She blew out a breath, took a sip of wine, and gathered her thoughts as a pod of pelicans flew along the coastline in perfect winged formation. She'd practiced this in her mind so many times. But this time was real. So, she decided to just dive right in.

"My mother was a cocktail waitress at a Reno casino. She always wanted to be a showgirl, and she was stunning and dramatic enough to have been one, but at five foot-eight, she was too short."

"That sounds tall to me."

"It is, in the real world. But showgirls have to be really tall. Five ten is the minimum, going up to six two. Which was how she ended up a cocktail waitress instead. She was stunningly beautiful, and, like I said, dramatic, which earned her lots of tips."

She remembered times her mother would come home and toss what seemed like a small mountain of bills all over the bed. Whenever that happened, her parents would send her outside to play, or to her room, and it was only later, when she'd been watching *Bonnie and Clyde* on a late night movie, she'd realized that, like those infamous outlaws, her parents had probably had sex on all that money. Which had made her want to wash out her eyes with bleach.

"She ran off with a dealer when I was eight."

"I'm sorry."

Amanda shrugged. "She wasn't home that much anyway. She worked nights—the tips are better during that shift because the heavy drinkers have been downing free drinks all day and winners love to tip big to show off—so she was usually asleep when I came home from school."

She'd loved watching her mother get ready for work later in the afternoon. The pots and bottles, and the triple layers of oversized false eyelashes had made her look more glamorous than any movie star. The makeup had been off-limits, but there'd been one day, when she was eight and her mother was still sleeping after the bus had dropped her off from school, she'd gone into the bathroom and tried to duplicate the artistry her mother had created.

Remembering back, she'd ended up looking like a clown, and had been afraid her mother was going to scream at her, the way she was always yelling at Amanda's dad, but instead, she'd laughed, taken some tissues and wiped off the mess, then pulled up a chair next to the satin-padded stool Amanda was sitting on and, with those brushes and sponge pads, creams, and bottles, she'd created magic.

Amanda could still recall looking in the mirror, stunned at the reflection that had made her look like a miniature adult. She'd been wondering if she could keep it on overnight, to show off at school the next morning, when her father walked in, said she looked like a slut, and asked what her mother was trying to do, get every pedophile in the city after her?

"The only reason I remember the words were that my dad told the story a lot as an example of what a bad mother she'd been and how we were better off without her," she told Quinn.

A flashback of that day, being eight years old, not understanding what had angered her father, or the meaning of the words he'd used, tears streaming down her face, the lines of color washing off it like a chalk sidewalk drawing in the rain flashed like a video in her mind.

She'd never, not even for her own wedding, "glammed up," as her mother had put it, again. Until Jolene had done all the hair and makeup for Kylee and Mai's wedding attendants. Not wanting to make a fuss on her friends' special day, she'd allowed the makeover. When Jolene had finished, she hadn't looked overly dramatic, like her mother. But she had, she realized, with not a little surprise, looked pretty.

"My dad was a professional gambler. He never made it to the level where he'd play with movie stars on TV." Although it was hard, and made her childhood feel so inadequate compared to the Mannions', she shared a bit of her nomadic life. And how he'd finally hit it big, only to be killed by a drunk driver while bringing her the check that ended up paying for her college.

"I'm sorry you had such a tough life." He took the hand that wasn't holding her glass, linked their fingers together and brought them to his lips. "But it sounds as if, in his own way, he loved you."

"I always knew he did." She shared the story of her sixteenth birthday celebration. "But I've come to realize that that roller coaster life I'd lived was why I stayed with my husband too long. And it's why I need to tell you about my marriage," she said.

"You don't *need* to tell me anything."

She found herself drowning in those Mannion blue eyes, as so often had happened. Even that first night she'd had dinner at the pub. Her response to him had been so immediate, so strong, that she'd been afraid Eric would have picked up on it. Fortunately, he was too busy focusing on himself to notice.

"I know that. But I want to. I need to explain before we, well, you know…"

"Make love."

The words sent a warmth flowing through her

veins. But beneath the warmth lurked a lingering fear. "Yes."

She dragged her eyes back to the sea, where seagulls were whirling and diving for their dinner. One overly confident gull had come out of the surf with a fish too large to handle. It fell to the sand, only to immediately be set upon by other, more opportunistic birds.

"All right. Take your time. We're not in any hurry."

He was back to his short responses, a familiarity that made it easier on her.

"Because of always moving, and the places my dad and I stayed in, I never had friends away from school, the kind you have playdates and sleepovers with. So, my only understanding of what families were like was from TV, which I knew wasn't real, and my parents, who were always fighting, then my nomadic life with my dad.

"Of course, since very little about our marriage is a secret in this town, you know Eric was bipolar. We met when I was updating landscaping at a California restaurant where he ate every day while working at Lawrence Livermore National Laboratory. His job was so top secret, we'd dated a month before he even admitted he worked there. The place itself was so secret that I had to Google it.

"I'll admit I was surprised to learn of the connection to nuclear weapons development. Although he seemed bashful, he was sweet and funny in a nerdy kind of way. He wasn't at all the type of person I imagined would be working with weapons of war. Not that I'd ever thought about it all that much, but I'll admit to realizing that I had a stereotypical view of scientists.

"Which is ironic, given that while studying for my degree in landscape architecture, I had to take a lot of lab classes in biology, botany, and environmentalism. I realize that most people think of me as a gardener with a degree, but landscape architects have to learn applications of technology in order to design and create outdoor spaces.

"We're also taught to think analytically about historical and contemporary theories of landscapes and gardens..." She blushed. "I'm sorry. I get carried away about my work, and digressed. I'm also probably boring you."

"First thing you need to know, sweetheart, is that you could never bore me. And secondly, you have passion for your work, which I admire. I left law because I wasn't passionate about it, and growing up with my parents, watching how much they loved their work—all of us learned by example the importance of loving what you do.

"I could probably bore you to death with details about brewing. And I've watched you work all over town. It's obvious that you're not just sticking plants in the ground to pretty up the place, but rather to increase the quality of public life by creating spaces that are meaningful, relevant, and sustainable."

"Where were you when I was writing my sales brochure for Wheel and Barrow?"

"Here in Washington. Waiting for you to show up."

It could have been a line. With some men, it

might've been. But not Quinn Mannion. While he was known to be a man of few words, she'd realized early on that it wasn't because he was reticent. Just that he chose his words carefully. At first, she'd thought it to be a skill he'd developed while practicing law. As she'd gotten to know him better, she realized it was merely his nature. As much as she'd enjoyed their conversations over the past year and a half, the quiet moments were also lovely.

"In the beginning, when he was taking his meds regularly, everything was fine. It wasn't until after we married that he even told me he was bipolar. I hadn't suspected a thing. Then, gradually, things began to fall apart when he was having problems with a vital point in an equation, and although I didn't know it at the time, he came to believe that the meds that stabilized him were taking away the edge that had always made him so brilliant. So, he quit taking them, which is when he began growing impatient toward me. It started with sarcasm, demeaning my work compared to the brilliance of his. Then he began to reveal a temper he'd never had when we'd been dating."

She paused and appreciated it when Quinn remained silent. Letting her get through this her own way. In her own time. "One day, I got hung up at the nursery waiting for a delivery of azaleas and was late getting home, so dinner wasn't ready on time. That was the first time he hit me."

She lifted her hand to her cheek, remembering the pain as if it were moments ago. She felt the fear returning and resolutely stamped it back down, needing to finish what had to be said if she were to truly move on with her life.

"I was stunned. And didn't know what to do. But he immediately apologized and promised me he'd never, ever hurt me again. That the pressure at work was too much, that it was breaking him. He told me that he'd quit that day, but I later found out that he'd been fired.

"I supported us until he found another job as a propulsion engineer, building rockets to send spy satellites into space. I don't know what happened, but he got fired from there too. As the cycle continued for eight years, the logical part of my mind knew I should leave. But there was an equally strong part of me that still loved him.

"Or, as my therapist has pointed out, perhaps I just loved the idea of us being a romance between two very opposite people. I'd had a crazy mad middle school girl crush on Heath Ledger's brooding, misunderstood loner Patrick Verona, who was always getting into trouble in the movie *Ten Things I Hate About You*. I loved that movie so much that when we left town, I purposely didn't remind Dad that we needed to return the VHS tape to Blockbuster. Which was my first and only act of theft."

"As an attorney, I can assure you that the statute of limitations has run out on that crime, so you don't have to worry about Aiden showing up at your door to arrest you. Besides, the only Blockbuster left is in Bend, Oregon, and I doubt, even if you did still have it, they would want it back."

"How do you know that? About there being a Block-buster in Oregon?"

"There are thirty craft breweries in the town that dedicate the month of November as the annual Bend Ale Trail. I have friends there. Maybe we should take some time before the holidays get busy and take a trip over there. Do you ski?"

"I've never lived anywhere to take it up."

"Central Oregon has some great skiing, including at Mount Bachelor, near Bend. We could add that to a bucket list."

Never having thought of the idea of careening down the side of a mountain on two skinny sticks all that appealing, Amanda, realizing that they'd gotten off track, merely said, "That's something to consider." Then took a deep breath and forged on,

"Getting back to my story, I've come to realize that, as illogical as it sounds, not having any real-life examples of how healthy relationships worked, I'd layered much of Ledger's fictional character onto my husband. I'd hoped, when he wasn't cycling between depression and mania, that we'd be able to make it work. That we'd get our happily-ever-after ending like Kat and Patrick."

"Brianna had us all watch that when it was her turn to choose the movie on family movie night," Quinn said. "Ledger nailed that part so well, I suspect most teen girls had a crush on his character."

"Yet, Brianna was smart enough when she grew up to marry someone entirely different. She and Seth seem perfect together."

"They are. But as you've pointed out, she had two generations of families as role models. From what you said, you didn't want the life your parents had, so you found another ideal."

"A fictional one." And a terrible mistake.

"Has that therapist suggested that you give yourself a break? You were a young girl essentially living on your own. The fact that you've turned out so well—perfectly in my opinion—just goes to show how strong you are to transcend such a difficult upbringing."

She lifted a brow. "That's pretty much the same thing my therapist said. Although she used the term, *overcome*."

"I grew up with a mom who taught English. Also, I became an attorney, where the wrong word in a contract could cost a client millions. So, I had no choice but to know all the best words."

She laughed, as he'd meant her to. And felt a bit of her anxiety ease. Enough that she almost felt as if she were telling a story of someone else. In a sense, she was. Because she'd moved far past that girl she'd once been. Once again, he was right. She'd transcended.

"Unfortunately, as those events grew more frequent, I honestly didn't know which husband I was going to wake up to. All those days and nights were like walking on eggshells."

"That must've been very tough."

"Toward the end, it was more like walking a tightrope blindfolded, while juggling flaming torches." While she'd been talking, the sky had turned brilliant with red, orange, pink, and purple streaks that again brought back that night in Key West and the brilliant orange sun as it sank into the water, making it look as if the surf was ablaze. Seeking the comfort he was offering, she laid her head on his shoulder, soothed by the easy way he put his arm around her shoulder. "I couldn't count the times I'd decided to leave. But then he'd cry and promise to do better, and stay on his meds, which he would for a time, and life would be, while not perfect, somewhat calm."

"The calm before the storm."

"Exactly," she agreed.

Quinn's mind went back to those bruises she'd explained away as part of her work until Aiden had set him straight and told him that he'd hidden her away in a safe house because her life could be in danger. "But he continued to be abusive."

"Yes." Her gaze drifted out to the water. Later, the sea would have a silver path lighted by the moon, but at this moment, it was beginning to look as dark and deep as their topic, which was not, Quinn considered, what he'd planned for his seduction dinner. But he also realized that she had to free herself of the last vestiges of the past before she could allow herself to be free with him.

"I'd finally decided to file for divorce when he told me he wanted to move here because his brilliance was being held back by all those government types who'd been programmed not to think outside the box. He literally got down on his knees and promised me that he'd stay on the meds. That things would be better in a smaller, quieter place where he could feel at peace. He showed me Honeymoon Harbor's website and it looked like a wonderful place for both of us. And for a while, it was."

Her eyes moistened. "But then he grew quiet again, and I could feel the storm brewing. Since moving to the Pacific Northwest, I began to liken his bipolar illness to the heat building up beneath Mount Baker or Rainier's ice and snow crowns, where there was always the possibility of an eruption."

Like Saint Helens had done. Quinn decided her analogy fit, given that her husband's emotional explosion had ended up in a manhunt that made the national news.

"That day I came into the pub from the ferry was the worst day of my life," Amanda confessed. "When I'd gone to see Eric at the hospital. After all the drama and his arrest, I'd finally accepted the fact that I'd become more caretaker than wife. And that things were never going to get better. And that even if they did, it was no longer my job to make it so. That Eric was going to have to do that on his own."

"And if he does get better?"

It was a question that, as hard as Quinn had tried to ignore it, had teased at the back of his mind from time to time. Amanda was a natural born nurturer. The same way she'd nurtured her gardens. Seasonal blooms she'd planted around the snow-white gazebo in the center of town were always showing up on Instagram and Pinterest, posted by brides, from not only the peninsula, but all over the country, adding to Honeymoon Harbor's reputation as a wedding destination.

"He won't." Her fingers were making little circles on his thigh as they talked. And although this conversation may be one of the most important ones he'd ever have, although he was a grown-ass man, edging toward forty, his body was reverting back to sixteen when he spent seemingly his entire junior year of high school with a semi hard-on.

"He'd promised, so many times. And when things were calm, I could tell how hard he was trying," Amanda said. "But that day at the hospital, he'd finally accepted, and admitted, that he'd probably never entirely change. Maybe with the court-ordered therapy, he'll get better. But having grown up with a father who was addicted to gambling, I know that it'll be difficult for him to not chase the highs. His sister told me that there was a history of suicide in his family."

It hadn't been her husband's life Quinn had been worried about. It had been those mysterious bruises. And Aiden's frustration about not being able to do anything about it when Amanda had, understandably, as many victims did, lied about the reason for the tell-tale signs of domestic abuse.

"You knew I'd been there," she murmured. "To the hospital. At the time, I didn't say a word about it, but of course, news travels fast in Honeymoon Harbor, so I knew that you knew. But you didn't ask any questions. Not about what had happened, or even how I felt. Because you also knew that if you'd asked how

I was doing, I would've humiliated myself by breaking down and crying right there in the pub."

"It wouldn't have been the first time someone cried in the pub." Brides, he'd found, could be very temperamental. Especially the one last week who'd caught her maid of honor in bed at the inn with the about-to-be groom.

The sun had finally disappeared, causing the water to turn as deep and dark as the story she'd been telling.

"There's one more thing," she said. "Which is why I shared all this."

"Okay." Again there wasn't anything else she could have told him that would change his feelings. She could even admit to an affair, or even multiples, and he would understand that she'd only been seeking comfort from a dangerously chaotic marriage.

She lifted her head off his shoulder and met his eyes. "I sometimes have these flashbacks. Of those times."

He should have seen that coming. "Like PTSD."

She nodded. "Mostly it's in dreams. But occasionally, I'll be planting a hydrangea, or watering the nursery plants, and it'll all come back, like a scene from a movie. And as much as I want to make love to you, I don't want to freak you out."

Which was how she'd told him, without saying the words, that striking her hadn't been the only violence she'd suffered from her husband.

"You asked me to be patient," he reminded her. "We don't have to—"

"No." She touched her fingers to his lips, cutting

off his words. "I want to. You're not the only one who's been dreaming and thinking of us together. The seduction meal sounds delicious. But that's not the only thing that I came for. The problem is, there were times when Eric would get jealous, for no reason, such as when I landscaped the house for the tech guy that Gabe, Chelsea, and the girls now live in. And he'd feel the need to, as he put it, claim me and remind me who I belonged to."

Quinn felt a rare temper flare at the thought of her being defiled in that way. And decided the rocket scientist rapist was damn lucky to be locked away in a federal prison where he couldn't get to him.

"Later, as the mania grew more and more out of control, he lost interest in sex for months. So I haven't tried, well, you know, doing anything with anyone for quite a long time. I honestly don't know what'll happen."

"I do." He stroked her hair, which was misted from the sea, then thread his fingers through the silken strands that framed her face. "Do you trust me?"

"Absolutely," she said. "But it's me that I'm not sure of."

"I'll be patient. And if, for any reason, you need me to stop, I promise I will." He touched his lips to hers again, this time with a feathery touch, not to savor, but to soothe. "But you don't have to worry. Because I recognized you the minute I saw you. And knew we'd be perfect together."

"You'd didn't know me."

He smiled. And softly took her mouth again, licking, lingering, until he felt her relax enough to sink into it. "One of these days, let me tell you about a relative of mine, a horse breeder named Kate Sullivan, known throughout County Clare as having Second Sight, who'd be arguing that point about that having been our first meeting," he said, after finally breaking the exquisite contact.

At first her eyes widened. Then she surprised him by laughing. "I want to hear that story," she said. "Over dinner. And then *I'll* tell you about Madame Sybil, who told my fortune during a carnival in Key West."

"This sounds promising."

She laughed again, the sultry sound banishing the last of the dark mood. "You've no idea."

CHAPTER THIRTEEN

"It's true," Amanda said over the dinner Quinn had refused to let her help with. "You Mannion males have many talents, but I have to rank seduction meals up there at the top of the list."

He'd prepared the Dungeness crab in a garlic butter sauce in a cast iron pan on the grill. Beneath their crispy, bright orange shells, the meat was sweet, juicy, and rich. "And although I realize that you dislike being referred to as the 'perfect' brother, this definitely tops a grilled steak."

He'd put down newspaper on the table, and there was something intensely sensual about breaking apart the butter-drenched crab and eating it with her hands. It was, she thought, definitely a meal meant to seduce. Not that she needed any seducing. As she touched her napkin to the corner of her mouth to remove a bit of melted butter, she watched his eyes darken to the hue of the sea.

"I'll bet its proven effective over the years." She regretted that comment the moment it had escaped directly from her head to her lips without any filtering. Although she'd only had a single glass of wine,

...he food, the night, the man, all had her feeling a bit tipsy.

"I wouldn't know." His usually matter-of-fact voice was deeper, more intimate than she'd ever heard it. "I've never cooked it, or any other meal, for any other woman."

That had her heart skipping a beat. As she felt the heat rise in her cheeks, she was grateful for the darkness that was only lit by a trio of fat white candles in glass jars on the table. "I wouldn't imagine you'd need to add cooking to your bag of seduction tricks," she said, dragging her gaze from his while she dug a bit of crab meat out of a leg with a claw. Rather than the teasing tone she'd tried for, her voice gave away a knee-jerk insecurity.

He set down his glass and put a finger beneath her chin to tip her face back up. "I've never cooked for anyone before because it's definitely not in my skill set and wanted tonight, with you, to be special. Jarle assured me I could pull off the meal part and said that he was leaving the seduction part up to me."

"So he knew?"

His smile was slow, sexy, and though a cool, misty fog had begun to drift over them, it sent heat flowing through her veins. "I hate to be the one to break the news to you, but apparently we've been providing entertainment for some time. Both Bri and Magnus told me that if I didn't make my move soon, someone else was going to come in and sweep you off your feet."

At first, the idea of everyone in Honeymoon Harbor knowing about their mutual attraction had her inwardly cringing. Then she remembered how she'd been rooting for Seth and Brianna. And, as hard as they tried to hide it, Jolene and Aiden's affair had become fodder for the town gossip mill too. There had even been bets on how long Gabe would be able to stay away from Chelsea and the girls after leaving Brianna and Seth's and Jolene and Aiden's double wedding reception, driving away in that limo to the chartered plane waiting at SeaTac to take him back to New York City.

"Small towns," she murmured.

"I was back a week when I realized that if I wanted any action, I'd have to buy my condoms online," he admitted. Then it was his turn to openly cringe. "Sorry. That was TMI."

"Don't apologize," she said, after a quick laugh. "It makes this seem more normal." More the way they usually talked without the huge subject of the night ending with the two of them naked and tangled together in bed hovering over them. "But better. More comfortable."

"I want us to be lovers," he said. "But equally important, I want us to stay friends. Best friends. Like my folks. And my grandparents."

Was he talking about forever? Before they'd even tested their sexual compatibility? As if that was going to be a problem. Which had another laugh escaping. When he arched a questioning brow at what was, admittedly, the wrong response to that statement, she shook her head.

"I'm sorry. It wasn't because of what you said. Just a random thought. I'll tell you later."

"Later," he agreed.

Meaning, they both knew, after sex. And why did she feel like the nervous teenager she'd once been, agonizing over whether to lose her virginity to a dark, intense bad boy one summer night in her junior year of high school. She'd foolishly imagined he'd end up having the tender heart of gold Heath Ledger had portrayed. But not only had he not called her the next day, she'd seen him kissing a cheerleader beneath the bleachers. That experience, she'd later realized, was another reason she'd given her heart to Eric, who'd seemed so shy. So nerdy. So safe. That mistake had not only left her heart broken, but shattered it into little pieces, like those bits of shell that washed up on the shore by the lighthouse.

The moon was rising and stars had begun to twinkle on, reminding her of the fairy lights Brianna and Sarah had put around the mirror behind the bar of the pub her first Christmas in town, shortly after Eric's arrest. The two had also coaxed her into attending the lighted boat festival, where, although she'd worried people would be staring at her after Eric's bizarre behavior and arrest, everyone had proven warm and welcoming, and the holiday spirit filling the air had her nerves finally loosening.

With the sun gone, the night was turning cooler and more fog was drifting in on the coastal breeze.

When she shivered, Quinn suggested going inside. And saving the dessert he'd brought for later.

"I'd like that," she said. "Also, if you don't mind, I'd like to take a shower. As much fun as I had today, I feel a little gritty from the salt air and sand."

"Of course I don't mind. Go warm up and I'll bring all this in, clean up, and join you in a bit."

As much as the idea of showering with him had all sorts of erotic possibilities flashing through her mind, if Amanda had to rank her fantasies in order, showing off her sexy new Dancing Deer purchase and letting him warm her up in other ways topped the list.

QUINN WAS OPERATING on autopilot as he cleared the table, deciding to keep the candles burning to bring into the bedroom. As he put the dishes in the dishwasher, he kept picturing Amanda in that large shower his parents had created when they'd had two of the upstairs bedrooms merged into a master suite. There'd been many years when it had been unusual for all five of their grown kids to fly back home to the nest, so they'd decided to utilize the space for themselves.

He carried the candles up the stairs on one of his mom's serving trays, balancing it in one hand as he knocked on the door. He'd heard the water in the shower stop running a few minutes ago, and she hadn't seemed like a woman who'd spend a lot of time fixing up just to get mussed again.

"Come in." There was a waver in her voice. From

anticipation or nerves, he wasn't sure. God only knew that he was experiencing both. Anticipation of finally showing her how he felt, pleasuring her, and nerves that, after what she'd told him, he'd screw it up. And risk losing her forever.

He stopped in the open doorway, looking at her standing beside the bed. Which had been turned down. Megan had sent a crew from her Clean Team out here yesterday to rid the house of any dust that had accumulated since the last time a family member had used it, and to change the sheets and towels.

Even knowing that the Dancing Deer had added a sexy lingerie section to their popular inventory, Quinn had been expecting something sinfully black or a flaming scarlet. But what she'd chosen was an unadorned silk gown that slid down the length of her body like water, like a beautiful, pure clean slate. Or would have been if the bridal-white material hadn't been spun so sheer that, backlit by moonlight, she appeared nearly naked.

She was holding her hands together behind her in a way that arched her back just a little, causing the tips of her breasts to press against the silk. As his gaze slowly moved over her, his body instinctively hardened at the shadow between her thighs. He'd imagined this moment so many times, dreamed of it, fantasized in the shower as the hot water streamed over him and his hand proved a poor but necessary imitation of the real thing. He hadn't been with another woman since she'd returned back to town after leaving her husband. And if there was one thing waiting for this moment had taught him, it was that celibacy sucked.

"You're so beautiful," he said, his gaze moving up again, drawn to the creamy flesh of her bare shoulders. Shoulders he yearned to nip.

"I'm glad you approve."

Oh, he approved of everything, including that soft pink flush that rose everywhere his gaze touched. "How could I not?"

"I was concerned it wasn't sexy enough," she admitted. For a woman so independent, so intelligent, so talented, Quinn found it near criminal that her ex had left her sexually insecure. Amanda had not only been in his head all this time, she'd been in his blood. And he intended to spend the rest of their lives proving how amazing she was.

"FYI, sweetheart," he said, as he put the tray down on the dresser, lit the candles, and moved toward her, "I find you just as sexy in mud-stained jeans and a T-shirt. It doesn't matter what you're wearing…" He skipped a beat for emphasis as he took another, longer tour of her body clad in that barely there silk. "Or not wearing."

The soft pink deepened to the center of one of those erotic flowers, causing him to want to touch her in that shadowed place beneath the silk. Taste her. Bury himself deep in her.

"Velvet had suggested a black corset, G-string, garter belt, black fishnet stockings, and skyscraper stilettos."

"That sounds intriguing. But I like this."

"Maybe some other time," she said, a wicked glint he'd never witnessed before lighting up her eyes. "I was thinking maybe tomorrow night."

And didn't that have him nearly swallowing his tongue? "You bought it?"

Her smile was slow and seductive, like one of those movie stars from old black-and-white movies his parents liked to stream. Without showing nudity, some were, in their own way, hotter than the graphic porn DVDs his college roommate, who worked part-time at a Seattle adult fetish store, would bring to their room after work.

"Velvet's very persuasive," she said. Her luscious lips turned down. "Though there is one problem."

"And that is?"

"She taught me how to lace myself in. But taking it off is much more difficult."

"You're trying to seduce me."

Sure, it was a line stolen from *The Graduate*, but there was a reason screenwriters wrote movies and he made beer. They were better at writing, and he'd bet he was a helluva lot better at making beer than any Hollywood screenwriter would be.

"I'm surprised you've seen *The Graduate*."

"It was one of Brianna's choices for family movie night. She'd insisted that since she was the only girl with four brothers, she should get to choose a romance for every Western or bloody Tarantino movie we inevitably chose."

She tilted her head. Chewed thoughtfully on the tip of a nail that he'd noticed earlier had been painted a soft pink instead of the natural look he was used to seeing her wear. "Well, to answer your question, yes, Quinn Mannion, I am most definitely trying to seduce you."

She reached up and slipped the gown's thin straps off her shoulders, allowing the creamy silk to slide down her body to pool at her bare feet, leaving just her toes, their nails painted the same pink as her fingernails, showing. "Is it working?"

When he'd first entered the room, he'd been thinking that he'd spend the night treating her carefully, like a skittish fawn. Now, unexpectedly, by standing there in front of him as nude as the day she was born, the candlelight playing over her body, Amanda had changed the game plan.

"You tell me." He closed the distance between them, took her hand and held it against his groin.

"I think," she said, on a low, throaty purr, "that, having fantasized about this moment for a very long time, I'm going to do my best not to disappoint."

Damn. There it was again. He saw the faint shadow flit across her remarkable eyes, which lowered. "Amanda. Look at me. Please."

She lifted her gaze.

"How many people are in this room?" he asked.

"Two," she said softly.

"And who's going to spend the best night of his life making love to you?"

"You." She blew out a breath. "I'm sorry, I warned—"

"He's not here," Quinn said. "We're not going to let him in this room. With us, tonight. Or any other time we make love. So, whenever he tries to break in, you need to let me know. Because he's out of your life. Forever. Right now. Right here."

He ran his palms over her shoulders, down her arms, took her hands in his, and lifted them to his lips. Opening her stiff, closed fingers, he lifted her palms, one at a time, to press a kiss at the center. And felt her pulse leap in response.

"Only you," he said. "Only me... Are we okay with that now?"

She blew out a long, deep breath. And treated him to a smile that wasn't the seductive one she'd flashed his way earlier, but which made its way straight to the center of his heart.

"Better than okay." He'd released her hands, allowing her to comb her fingers through his hair as she kissed him. The kiss, while quick, was hot, and once again, had that too-familiar heat shoot straight to his groin.

"Take me to bed, Quinn. Make love to me." When she pressed her nude body against his, he was surprised his clothes didn't burst into flame. "You did after all, make me a seduction dinner. It would be a shame for you not to follow through."

He was out of his clothes faster than Superman could shed his Clark Kent suit, and wanting to give Amanda whatever she desired, forever and ever, he did as she'd asked and took her to bed. Where he spent the rest of the night living up to his part of the Mannion male seduction dinner.

CHAPTER FOURTEEN

PIPER HAD GIVEN IN, as she suspected Jamal had
known she would. He hadn't acted like a player, more
like a nice guy who'd made sure she knew they'd not
be alone out at the lake. Of course, that didn't mean
that a group party couldn't turn into trouble. There'd
been more than a few times during her teens when
she'd climbed out of her bedroom window at her
grandparents' house, once she'd heard her grandfather snoring away, to join friends at a beach party.

During the day, the sand and pebble beach had
filled with families, but once the lifeguards left for
the evening, there'd be barbecues in the designated
area, while impromptu parties popped up along the
long strand of beaches connecting the various towns.
She'd gone, as always, with girlfriends, but as often
happened, they'd broken up, drawn to one boy or
another, only to share and giggle over stories later.
One summer night, when she'd been sixteen, a boy
with long, black hair, eyes as dark as midnight, full
tattooed sleeves displayed by a black T-shirt which
appeared to have been sprayed on, and tight, ripped-
at-the-thighs jeans, had sauntered up to her and offered her a drink from a flask. He'd been like no

other boy Piper had ever met, exactly the kind of rebel her parents, always so bloody concerned about appearances, never would have approved of. Which, of course, at that age, had made him all the more appealing. Also, he'd radiated a powerful vibe, as if daring her to take a drink, that had made him impossible to resist.

She'd never had liquor before and the gin had tasted like the juniper berries her grandmother would make into a sauce for salmon and groupers. She would have spit it out, but he'd been mocking her with those flashing, wicked eyes, so she swallowed, feeling the burn scorch its way down her throat. Taking the flask back, he'd chugged. There'd been a waning moon that night, but the lights from the pier had allowed her to watch his Adam's apple bob. Which, already feeling a little floaty, she'd found incredibly male and hot. Those dangerous eyes had met hers as he swallowed, and when he lowered the bottle, he'd smiled, as if having read her mind. Then he reached out, his hand curving at the back of her neck, and kissed her. A hard, deep kiss that neither teased nor tempted, but devoured.

Piper had not been entirely innocent. She'd kissed boys before, even kisses that included some tongue tangling. She'd also let an Italian boy—with an accent that caused goose bumps to rise on her skin—touch her breasts beneath her jumper. Two weeks later, when her Swedish roommate was on a boarding school excursion to Wembley Stadium for a football game, she'd sneaked him into her room where he'd

charmed her with words and touch as he slowly, one
at a time, unbuttoned her uniform blouse. Then, pulling his shirt over his head, they'd been skin to skin
and although they'd only touched each other above
the waist, she'd felt his need pressing against her in
a way that had left her dizzy. And wanting.

After many late night discussions with her roommate, who'd gone all the way a year earlier with a
smooth-talking French boy, and then others, Piper
had decided that Allessandro Ricci would be her first
lover. But before they'd had an opportunity to act
on her decision, his parents had been transferred to
the Italian embassy in Belgium, ending their brief
school romance. A romance that had triggered needs
in her that finally had her understanding the passion
in those racy novels she'd hidden away from her parents and school staff.

Unlike her kisses with Allessandro, that night
on the beach there'd been no seduction. No finesse.
While the boy claimed her mouth, the hand not holding her neck roamed over her breasts, squeezing hard
enough that even if she could have cried out, she
never would've been heard over the music, laughter,
and the low roar of the tide.

"You liked that, didn't you, Princess?"

When she couldn't answer, his hand had roamed
lower, down the stomach of the daring red tankini
she'd bought for that summer.

"I've been watching you for the past week," he'd
said. "You're one of those posh summer birds, here

in Cromer to walk on the dangerous side with us low types."

"I'm not posh." How dare he kiss her like that, then insult her? "And my family has been here for generations."

"Yeah. So I've heard. Your grandfather sacked me last Christmas after he caught me shagging a server in the walk-in fridge. But *you're* not local. I've heard all about you. Your parents are some kind of bigwigs in the government. I'll bet you've never been with a guy like me."

Technically, she'd never been with any guy, at least not in the way she took him to mean. But she hadn't wanted to admit that. Because even as her head had been warning her that he was behaving abominably, other, needier parts of her body, which had only ever climaxed in the lone, secret darkness of her bedroom at night, had been saying just the opposite.

He'd handed the bottle back to her. Annoyed at him, and even more annoyed at herself for not telling him to shove off, she'd taken a longer drink, determined to prove she wasn't a posh *princess*, which, from the scorn in his tone, had not been a compliment.

Holding her gaze, his lips had quirked, as if he'd known exactly what she was doing. After shoving the crotch of her suit aside, his fingers had slid over her. "You're wet." His voice had been a rough, satisfied growl. "Wet and ready to rock and roll."

Which was how Piper had ended the night drunk

and losing her virginity in the dark shadows beneath the looming beach cliffs.

"You weren't that bad," he'd said as he collapsed on her after a brief period of grunting and painful plunging that had been nothing like she'd imagined making love to Allessandro would have been. He stood and yanked up his ripped jeans, which he hadn't even bothered to take off all the way, while she'd somehow ended up naked on the sand.

"By the end of summer, I'll have you all broken in for one or your rich lads when you go back to school. Meet me back here tomorrow night. Same time. I'll bring some weed. You'll be looser and more into it when you're high."

Without bothering to help her up, he'd strode away, leaving her to struggle back into the tankini she swore never to wear again. He hadn't looked back.

The next morning, her grandmother, who'd found her throwing up in the toilet, had brought her tea and toast and told her to take the day off. "You must have caught a bug," she'd said. "Who knows what all these tourists might be carrying. Don't worry darling," she'd soothed. "We can handle things today. You just rest and get better. I'll bring you some chicken broth later."

Piper had never told a soul. When her girlfriends had asked her where she'd disappeared to, sharing their own stories of innocently making out, she'd lied and said she'd gotten a headache and had returned home.

How could she had done anything so stupid, she'd asked herself over and over again for the next two weeks as she'd barely slept, unable to remember whether or not he'd bothered to wear a condom. Even having been told the story of how her mother had supposedly gotten pregnant after a one-night stand with a stranger, altering Fiona Jones Lowell's life's plan forever, she'd gone and taken the exact same risk.

Her mind racing, Piper had spent those weeks mixing up so many orders even her grandfather had noticed. When he'd asked her if something was on her mind, after she'd delivered an order of crab to a vegan who'd started shouting about murdering innocent animals, she'd lied and told him she was just worried about her parents, as she often legitimately was.

Even after her period came, Piper had stayed away from the beach for the rest of the summer. She hadn't even gone wandering through the quaint shops where every year she'd buy some little souvenirs for her dad and mum. Her grandfather had chided that there were far better ways for a pretty, young girl to be spending her summer than working and staying inside, even on her days off, but her grandmother had told him to leave the girl be, that if she enjoyed reading, then let her spend her school holiday her own way.

After that night, Piper had never kissed another boy. She also hadn't gone on any dates except the occasional safe group ones she'd be talked into by friends. But Jamal Washington was different. He was smart. Intriguing. Fun. Easy to talk to. And, as he'd pointed out while they'd eaten barbecue beneath that tree, they had a lot in common. Just maybe, she considered, as she climbed into the passenger seat of his car, since this was the first summer of the next act of her life, it was time for a summer boyfriend.

"We've got a clear night," he said as they drove out of town. "You never know about the weather here. It must be my lucky day because I'm out on my second date with the prettiest girl in town."

"It's technically our first date. Because we were surrounded by people at the barbecue."

"I asked you to go sit on the bench with me. You agreed. We talked about our lives. We had a distinct connection, even while surrounded by people. So, I'm counting this as our second. Because I have this rule against kissing a girl on the first date."

"You're expecting me to kiss you?" It'd be dark. Just like it had been on Cromer Beach, which had also been crowded with night partiers.

"No. I'm planning to ask you if I can kiss you. Later. When I take you back to your apartment at the pub. And I'm hopeful you'll say yes and kiss me back. Because I've been thinking about you all week." He glanced over at her, his brown eyes warm and friendly. She had nothing to be afraid of, Piper assured herself. "Have you been thinking about me?" he asked.

"Yes." She paused. "Are you always so direct?"

"I guess I am. It's easier that way, don't you think?"

The question brought up the guilty thought that

she still hadn't told Quinn what she was doing here in Honeymoon Harbor. The problem was, she'd been living in Procrastination Land and the longer she put it off, the more difficult it was becoming.

"I suppose so," she said, determining to tell him. Soon. Maybe tomorrow. "But my parents are diplomats, so I've been taught that, sometimes, diplomacy doesn't mean being entirely honest. Such as, if I were to tell you that I hate your shirt, my statement might be direct, but it could hurt your feelings and take away from your enjoyment of the evening."

"You hate my shirt?" He glanced down at the navy Henley he was wearing with a pair of medium wash jeans and white-soled black trainers.

"That was just an example. I do like your shirt. It looks great on you."

"Well, that's one hurdle passed," he said. "I like yours too. It's like we're in sync again, with matching colors."

She'd bought the navy boat-necked tee, which was one of her fallback colors that didn't wash out her fair skin, yesterday at the Dancing Deer. "Great minds," she murmured.

"I was in Louisiana for a while," he said after they'd driven past a herd of deer grazing on the side of the road. "Working for a luthier—that's what you call a guy who makes guitars. Your multilingual mom would probably recognize it coming from the French word for *lute*."

"I'm guessing since you continued on across the country, it wasn't your thing."

"No, but it was a great experience. There's more that goes into the process than you can imagine. Especially the neck, which is the next to hardest part."

"What's the hardest?"

"Hands down, the finish. Because the gravity of a finish is greater than bare wood, it dampens vibrations, which filters out unwanted frequencies. But there are a lot of arguments about how it affects tone. Not being that good a musician, I couldn't tell you who's right, but some guitarists like lacquer, because it goes on thinner and allows the wood to age, which gives you a purer tone. Poly has become popular these days, but since it's sprayed on, it ends up thicker, which some claim mutes the tone too much.

"Anyway, I was able to build one in six weeks, while I was also doing cleanup work, sweeping, sharpening tools, sometimes even sanding, stuff like that. But I didn't get to touch the ones people were willing to wait six to eight months for."

"You're a musician?"

"If plunking out a few simple chords makes me a musician, I guess I am. But as Elijah the luthier pointed out, playing a guitar for money probably wasn't going to get me any bliss because I'd be starving…

"The thing is, while I was there, I met this friend of his who ran a take-out joint. Best jambalaya I've ever tasted. She claimed to be a distant relative of Marie Laveau, a Creole New Orleans Voodoo queen back in the eighteen hundreds. This woman didn't practice voodoo herself, but did some card reading for people. She had a lot of theories about life, and one that's stuck with me is that when we die, since everything in the universe is made of energy, we turn into stars. And that whenever you see a falling star, it's a new soul falling back to Earth to be reborn. Which, since nobody knows what actually happens to us, is probably as good a theory as any. And my point, which I'm getting to, is that she also told me that I'd fall in love with my soulmate on a night when the stars were falling."

Piper folded her arms. "That has to be a line."

"Nope." He crossed the fingers of his right hand over his heart. "I swear to God, that's exactly what she said. Now, I'm not predicting that you're going to fall madly in love with me tonight. But hey—" he shrugged as he pulled up next to a line of cars belonging to people who'd already arrived to see the meteor shower "—I'm willing to keep an open mind."

As they got out of the car, she saw he'd also brought along a duffle bag. "I've got two blankets," he said. "One for sitting on, another to cover up with because it's going to get cold by the time the showers start. I only have one camp chair and should've thought ahead and gotten a second. But this way is better because we can sit closer."

"So you can make a move?"

"No." His quick smile caused butterflies in her stomach. "So we can share body heat."

"That's got to be a line."

"Maybe more of a suggestion." He flashed another grin that caused tingles. Oh, yeah. She was really in trouble. "But I figured it was worth a try. And I really do only have the one chair. My only excuse is that we've been working overtime to get a project done for this guy down in Newport, so I honestly didn't think about the logistics. I should be working tonight, but when Gabe heard I wanted to take you to watch the showers, he gave me some time off."

Piper believed him. Partly because she had become familiar enough with the Mannions, who seemed to have taken her under their collective wings, that she was pretty sure one of them would've warned her if he was the kind of guy she needed to stay away from.

She lifted a small bag of her own. "I brought a thermos of cocoa. And not the mix kind, either. Jarle taught me the recipe." The cook had also become like family. In so many ways, working at the pub felt like being back in Cromer. Before the town, which had always felt like home, had been ruined for her.

"See," he said, taking her hand as they began walking toward the beach. "Together we make a great team."

He wasn't lying about them being with a group of people. Not that she'd really believed he had, but he almost seemed too good to be true. After that night, when girlfriends would ooh and aah over cute boys, both ones they knew and movie stars and singers, especially the hot K-pop boys, she'd pretend to go along, even though the part of her that could feel sexual attraction had shut down. Until now. It had stirred the day of the barbecue, and now it was suddenly roaring back.

Reminding herself that rushing into things could only lead to trouble, she smiled and chatted as he introduced friends he'd met from the college. All seemed nice and normal, and, as she was used to in America, people commented on her accent. Fortunately, the responses were always positive and if there was an American her age who hadn't watched the Harry Potter movies, she'd yet to meet one.

There were also workers from the boat shop, but they were from the carpentry team, whose part of the project was already done. Jamal had cheerfully endured some kidding digs about him being Gabe Mannion's favorite, given that he'd been given valuable time off.

"He's a space enthusiast," Jamal had responded. "And, surprised I'd never seen a meteor shower before, he didn't want me to miss this one."

"If you decide Jamal's not your type, I just want to let you know that I'm available," said Trey Blaine, a cute twentysomething guy who looked like a young Ryan Gosling. When introduced, she'd learned he'd spent two years in the Coast Guard, then used the G.I. Bill to attend a Great Lakes boatbuilding school, graduating just as Gabe had expanded the business into restoration.

"I love the history of old boats," he told her. "They all have a story. The one our team is working on now is a hundred-year-old fishing boat. Jamal's overhauling the mechanics, while I'm discovering all the different ways boats were put together back in those days." He grinned. "Once I get it done, I'd be happy to take you out on the Sound. Maybe even down the coast on her second maiden sail."

"Not if you can't get it to run," Jamal said. "Which might never happen if you continue to hit on my girl."

"Sorry." He looked over at Piper. "Since I haven't seen you at the shop, I figured this was just a date. I didn't realize you two were a couple."

"I've been super busy working at Mannion's," she said. She looked over at Jamal, who she could tell was waiting for her answer every bit as much as his friend was. "And yes, I guess you could call us that." For now anyway, she thought, with that pesky little business about how long she'd be able to stay in Honeymoon Harbor still up in the air.

The night turned out to be magical, making her realize that there'd been nothing wrong with her after Cromer. Apparently, her years of sexual apathy were more due to having not met the right person, rather than that night of her big mistake.

"I like what you confirmed to Trey," Jamal said, after they were seated side by side on the blanket on the grass a bit away from the sandy beach, beneath the other blanket because, as he'd predicted, the temperature seemed to be dropping by the minute. "About us being a couple."

"It just felt like the right thing to say at the moment. I didn't want to encourage him."

"So, was that the only reason?"

"No." She shook her head, causing a curl she'd clipped back to come loose and fall across her cheek. "As I said before, I've been thinking of you. A lot."

"Right. Yet another thing we have in common. I'm looking forward to tonight." He reached out and pushed the curl away from her cheek, behind her ear, then framed her face in his hands. "You know how I said I was going to ask if I could kiss you when we got back to the pub?"

"That's not exactly something a girl would forget." The romantic she'd discovered lurking inside her had secretly been hoping it would be sooner.

"What would you say if I suggested changing that timeline?" His eyes drifted from her eyes to her lips. When he rubbed the lower one with the pad of his thumb, they parted ever so slightly in anticipation.

"I'd say yes." Piper's voice was close to a whisper as she breathed in the scent of his soap, which was rich and spicy, as if he'd spent the day walking in the woods.

This time, his slow, satisfied smile sent golden warmth streaming through her veins. He glanced up at the star-studded ebony sky. "Thank you, God." Then he bent his head, his mouth brushing against hers, the kiss as soft as milkweed fluff.

"Nice," he murmured. He took his time, gently kissing the corners of her lips before moving up her cheek to her temple. As leisurely and delicate as it was, it caused her heart to race, and as physically impossible as she knew it to be, she could have sworn her bones were melting.

Piper had never been kissed like this. Except for Allessandro. Before that night, the boys she'd been with had been single-minded, focused on their own needs, their own pleasure, without taking time to think about hers. But even her school boyfriend's kisses hadn't made her want so desperately as she wanted now.

"Jamal." Her voice was ragged. Needy. "Please."

"Shhh," he whispered against her temple. She could feel his smile against her skin, which was heating up even as the night air cooled. "There's no hurry."

Easy for him to say. Her brain was shutting down, muddling her thoughts, yet somehow, unruly needs she'd manage to keep tightly reined in for so long were coming alive.

As if they had all the time in the world, he continued to beguile, his lips brushing across her forehead, then moving back down the other cheek until returning to hers again and finally(!) lingering. But, even then, he was achingly patient, slowly savoring, drawing her deeper and deeper into the mists.

Then, as her lips parted, he drank deeply, stealing her breath, fogging her mind. She wound her arms around his neck, kissing him back, tongues tangling, blood rising.

"There's one!" A shout rang out, followed by more. And more. And all around them, the shouts echoed in a darkness lit by a bright, falling flare.

"Talk about timing," Jamal murmured against her mouth. Breaking the exquisite kiss, he pressed his forehead against hers, even as his fingers continued to stroke the back of her neck.

"It's probably just as well," she said as she looked around to see if anyone could see them. "Before we end up getting arrested by Quinn's brother for indecent exposure."

"I'd never let that happen." He trailed the back of his other hand down the cheek his lips had warmed, then curled his fingers beneath her chin and lifted her gaze back to his. "Kissing you could become a habit." His voice was husky with the same erotic need still simmering in her. "We'll take it slow and easy. Get to know one another better, because I'm thinking we've maybe got ourselves more than a summer fling going on."

"That's all I can do." She would not, Piper reminded herself firmly, follow in her mother's footsteps, letting herself be distracted by first sex, then marriage, which had taken Fiona Jones Lowell off her planned career track.

"Then we'll give that a try. I'm not going anywhere. So, it's ultimately on you to decide how far to take this thing we have going on." His smile was slow and irresistibly charming. "Meanwhile, maybe you can pour us some of that cocoa you went to the trouble of making, and we'll just sit here, side by side, enjoying each other's company while we watch the stars fall."

CHAPTER FIFTEEN

SINCE RETURNING HOME from the beerfest weekend, Quinn had been spending every night at Amanda's small, tidy rental house in town. Tonight, given that his log house was on the lake, they'd decided to watch the meteor shower together from there. It had taken some negotiation to talk her into spending the entire night, rather than her driving back to town in the dark. He'd been leaving her house before dawn. Her idea, not his, but at this early stage in their newly changed relationship, he'd reined in his impatience and had decided to play it her way.

"People are going to talk," she said, as they sat on a teak wood couch covered with deep blue marine cloth cushions beneath a tall patio cover boasting skylights. When he'd first moved into the house, his mother, hearing that he'd been planning to put out some folding camping chairs, had immediately gone shopping and come up with a look that he had to admit was stylish and comfortable. He also had a fire pit, which he wasn't using tonight, because the light from the flames would dull the showers. Since the temperature was dropping, he'd brought out a blanket to cover them. Not that his mind wasn't on other ways to keep warm.

"Sweetheart, they've been talking about us ever since the guys at Cops and Coffee caught me kissing you when you got off the ferry the other day." They'd even made the Facebook page in a not-so-blind statement suggesting one local plant enthusiast had been seen sharing a PDA with a popular local brewer at the ferry dock.

"I love those guys, especially the way they built their business on a stereotype about cops, coffee, and donuts," she said. "But now they're living up to the saying about guys gossiping just as much, if not more, than women." Quinn took the fact that she didn't sound overly upset as a positive.

"Aiden wasn't the only former cop worried about you," Quinn revealed. "They'd talked to him about their suspicions. Not because they were gossiping. But because they were worried about your safety. And now, even though you're safe, they still care about you and want you to be happy."

"I know. And that's sweet of them. And you do make me happy." She leaned over and touched her lips to his.

"Ditto."

She laughed. "Well, that was romantic."

"You want romantic? We can go inside and I can get down with that." He leaned over and nipped her lip, which had her putting her arms around his neck.

"But then we'd miss the meteor shower," she said against his mouth.

"We've got a while yet. The darker it is, the easier it is to see them. We'll be able to hear the shouts when they start."

"Or," she said, "we could just stay out here and make out."

"You're not worried about providing entertainment for all the folks on their boats?"

"We're all covered up." She slid a hand beneath the blanket and his shirt and trailed her fingers down his chest. "No one's going to see us."

Her mouth was still on his and he could feel her smile. "I never realized you had a rebellious streak."

"Neither did I." Her hand moved lower, leaving a trail of sparks until she ran into the barrier of his belt buckle. "Until you." She unfastened it, then, ducking beneath the blanket, moved on to the five buttons of his Levis. "Though did you ever consider changing to jeans with a zipper?"

"No. Because I'm a man who likes tradition. I've been wearing this brand since high school. They're iconic, going back to the original Levi Strauss ones. Why fix something that's not broken?" He didn't mention that the idea of some woman getting frisky enough to yank down a zipper could end up being painful.

"Amanda—" As her fingers got busy on those buttons, all the blood in his head flowed downward, following her touch.

"Trust me," she echoed what he'd told her at the coast house. "I promise to be gentle."

He laughed at that, even as she dispatched more

buttons. Even without her yet touching him, he was so close. "I can't promise not to be quick."

She undid the last one, folded back the denim and reached into the fly of his boxer briefs, freeing him. And as she teased him with smooth strokes of her fingers and flicks of her tongue before taking him into her mouth, she proved him right.

It was Monday, and before taking Amanda out on his boat for a planned day on the water and love-making in a hidden cove, Quinn was taking inventory in the pub's kitchen with Jarle and Piper when there was a knock at the door. Thinking it was the delivery of live Dungeness crabs he'd ordered from Kira's Fish Market, and wondering why it was coming in the front and not the side alley door, he went and opened it.

And then felt as if he'd been hit with a meat cleaver in his chest. He could've sworn his heart stopped before it began hammering like the damn woodpecker who'd take up residence on his roof every spring and begin pecking at his rain gutter.

"Hello, Quinn," the woman said, sounding much more like a BBC newsreader than that accent that had urged him on during sex with an impressive repertoire of dirty Welsh words he'd never be able to pronounce, but had no problem figuring out their meaning.

"Fiona?" His brain was having trouble keeping up with his body, which had chilled to the iciness of Hurricane Ridge during a winter blizzard, and he could hear a roaring sound, like the sea pounding against the cliffs below his family's beach house. "What are you doing here?"

"Mum?" Through the roaring in his ears, Quinn heard the now familiar voice and looked over his shoulder at Piper who'd come in from the kitchen, apparently having overheard them. Her young face was as white as the ghost that every kid in town had been told reportedly haunted Herons Landing.

"It's been a long time," Fiona Jones said.

"We need to talk." As if watching himself from some detached state, like a near death experience, he turned toward Jarle, who was standing in the kitchen doorway and appeared to be going through the same mental gymnastics as Quinn was.

What were the odds of a British teenager who'd walked into the pub, seemingly out of the blue, coincidentally turning out to be the daughter of a woman he'd had a brief, hot, summertime fling with? Quinn had always been good at math. Which was why he'd been assigned clients needing complex financial advice early in his career. Piper was eighteen. He'd been in Barcelona with Fiona Jones—damn—even rounding the numbers, he came up with eighteen years, nine months ago.

"Indeed, we do." She appeared as uncomfortable as he was with the situation. But, dammit, she wasn't surprised. Because she'd *known*. For over eighteen effing years, she'd known that he was the father of her child. A child who had somehow ended up in

Honeymoon Harbor, working in his pub. Living in his former apartment. Sleeping in his old bed.

Atypical anger flared through his veins, like a fiery lava flow from Mount Baker, which rose in the distance over the town.

"But not here." He turned toward Piper, forcing his voice to something that sounded more normal and far calmer than he felt. She wasn't to blame, he reminded himself. She was only a teenager. Her showing up in Honeymoon Harbor couldn't have been a coincidence. Or, as she'd claimed, the universe sending her to town. And to his pub. She'd known from the beginning that he was her father, but hadn't been honest with him. Though, he considered through the storm of unwelcome emotions roaring through his mind, who could blame her? He was an adult who'd kept from sharing the truth of his feelings with the woman he'd loved for a very long time. How could she have been expected to greet a total adult stranger with "Hi, Dad. I'm Piper, your biological daughter my mother neglected to tell you about."

Eighteen years. He uncurled his hand, which ached from having clenched into a fist at his side. "Don't worry. You're not in any trouble and we'll work this out. You wait here. I've got to make a call."

Piper's blue eyes swam in that too-pale face and as if any words were choked back in her throat, she only nodded. Her knuckles, he noted, were even paler than the rest of her complexion as she twisted her hands together.

It was still early enough that he had the sidewalk

to himself as he called the one person he knew he could count on to handle this situation. His sister, who his mother used to jokingly say could have been his twin if there hadn't been those years between them.

"Hi," she said. "What's up?"

"Are you busy?" Stupid question. She was always busy. Running a bed-and-breakfast could be, especially during tourist season, a 24/7 job.

"Actually, I'm sitting out here on the deck with Seth, watching a blue heron feeding her baby fresh-caught fish. All our guests have gone out whale watching, so we have a rare, entire day to ourselves."

Guilt hit at interrupting their rare time alone, especially with her being pregnant, and had Quinn considering his mom as a second choice. But grown men did not go running to their mothers when their nice, steady, predictable lives were suddenly turned upside down.

"Quinn?" With that so-called shared ability to read minds, Brianna asked, "What's wrong?"

"I have a situation. It's complicated." And wasn't that the understatement of the damn day? Month. Year. Eighteen damn years. "I just found out I have a daughter."

"Ah." She did not sound surprised. "Piper told you?"

"No." Another shock hit his system. "Did she tell *you*?" He couldn't imagine his sister keeping such a secret from him. Even if Piper had asked her to.

"Of course not. If she had, I would have told you right away," she echoed his thoughts. "But I've been wondering. There have been a few small things. Like the way she puts her thumb in the dent of her chin and her brow wrinkles when she's thinking through a problem."

"Lots of people do that." Both of Quinn's professions had taught him to read faces well. "There are even emojis for them." Not that he was one to use emojis. But both Brianna and his mother did. Almost excessively, in his opinion, not that either had ever asked.

"True. But Gramps noticed a similarity to Gram's mother and dug out an old wedding photo. The resemblance is remarkable. Although the photo's black-and-white, apparently she and Piper have the exact same color hair. And the curls Mom inherited."

"Well, Piper's mother, a woman I spent a week with in Barcelona during Easter break from Oxford, just showed up."

"At the pub?"

"Yeah. While we were doing inventory. Obviously, she and I need to have a tough discussion."

As a former attorney, he knew he should insist on a DNA test. And if it turned out he was Piper's father, which he knew he was, he'd unknowingly avoided years of child support Piper had been deserving of. Which then had him realizing that since Piper's last name was Lowell, not Jones, the guy Fiona had married must have adopted his daughter. Christ, what a mess. He dragged his hand through his hair. Something that each of his siblings and, he realized, Piper also did when stressed.

"Before you need to ask, of course bring Piper over here. Did she know her mother was coming?"

"Apparently not."

"Oh, dear. That poor girl. Even more reason to bring her here." Quinn heard Seth talking in the background. And Brianna answering him.

"Don't worry about her," Seth told Quinn, having apparently taken the phone from his wife. "We've got this. You stay there with her mother. Bri and I will come get her." From his matter-of-fact tone, it sounded as if Brianna had shared her thoughts with her husband. Of course she had. Because that's what married people did.

Unfortunately, his brief relationship with Fiona Jones had been based on no strings. Which had been just what both of them had wanted that Barcelona week. But if their agreement had been put in writing, he should've added an addendum regarding an unexpected pregnancy.

For not the first time, Quinn knew he'd made the right decision by leaving Seattle. He'd partly come back, as he'd always told people who'd ask, because he'd tired of his legal career. But, after returning home to Honeymoon Harbor, he'd realized that he'd been drawn back to this small out-of-the-way town he'd been born in because of his family. They were, as his mom's accident had proven, what truly mattered in life.

When Quinn went back inside, he heard Jarle, who was wisely staying out of this family drama, noisily moving around crates in the kitchen.

"It's going to be okay," he assured Piper, ignoring the woman he'd spent that whirlwind romance with in Barcelona. When, despite precautions, she'd gotten pregnant. *Eighteen years.* Those words kept tolling in his head like Saint Peter the Fisherman church's Sunday morning call to Mass bell.

The girl's pale face looked as if someone had run over her dog. Not that she had one but still… "You probably hate me."

"Not at all. Not even a little bit. Though you and I do need to sit down and talk, too. But later. After I speak with your mother. Bri and Seth are coming to pick you up and take you over to their place for a while."

"She's going to think I'm a terrible person," Piper wailed, sounding and looking a great deal younger than the eighteen-year-old who'd proven that she could run the front of the pub as if she'd been doing it all her life. Tourists and regular customers all loved her and she'd even managed to charm those who'd walked in and had to wait during the busiest of times, giving them buzzers and suggesting they go sit on the benches on the dock and enjoy the view and the region's glorious summer.

"There's no reason for my sister to think that. At all. You're wonderful, not just at your job, but as a person. Everyone loves you. Also, Bri wasn't surprised."

That caused her eyes to widen and forestalled the crying jag he'd feared was coming. The one his sister was undoubtedly going to have to deal with. "She knew?" Her thumb went to her chin and her brows furrowed, exactly as Bri had described.

"She wasn't sure. But she'd guessed. Apparently you and I share some unconscious habits. And, according to my parents and grandparents, you look just like our great-grandmother."

"Does everyone know?"

"Only Bri and Seth. The others just found it to be an interesting coincidence. I suspect my mom might have an inkling of an idea. Which means she'd have told my dad."

Looking younger than her eighteen years, Piper covered her face with her hands. "They're all going to hate me for showing up at their house for the barbecue, and lying about who I was."

"You didn't lie," he said, thankful for having moved back to a town so small it had only last year gotten its third stoplight, because Bri and Seth pulled up in front of the pub before Piper—his *daughter*—went into full meltdown mode. He went out to meet his sister while Seth stayed at the wheel.

"How is she?" Bri asked.

"Not good. Prepare for drama."

Despite the seriousness of the situation, she managed a smile. "Believe me, there's no way even a teenage girl in full drama mode can touch a lot of the adult behavior I've dealt with in my former career." She patted his arm. "We'll handle this. Then, once you deal with whatever you have to with her mother, come over and we'll have lunch. Or, better yet, if she's calmed down enough for you to assure her that everything's going to be all right, and that we all love her, I'll pack you a lunch and you two can have a picnic. Maybe at the lake. Or, for even more privacy, you might take her out on the boat.

Her boat suggestion led to another thought. Oh, damn. How could he have forgotten Amanda? As soon as Piper was on her way to Herons Landing, he'd have to call her and cancel their day. Fortunately, she was a forgiving woman and would understand his predicament. Which he was going to have to share with her. There'd already been too many secrets.

After he'd led Piper out to the SUV, Brianna put her arms around his daughter, giving her a consoling hug that was as natural to his sister as breathing. She was going to make a dynamite mother, Quinn thought. Which brought up another mother he still had to deal with. After watching the trio drive off, with Brianna in the back seat with Piper, their heads close together, he returned to the pub.

CHAPTER SIXTEEN

"THAT BEARDED GIANT with the interesting tattoo told me to tell you that he has the rest of tomorrow's prep work nearly done," Fiona told Quinn. "He was just going to marinate the wings."

"That giant is my business partner." His tone was lawyer brisk. "And one helluva cook, but you're not going to be staying around long enough to taste his food."

She sighed. "Now you sound like an American Western. Are you suggesting this town isn't big enough for the two of us?"

"You dislike—abhor—to use the word you preferred for your own Welsh birthplace—small towns. So, once you've said your piece and explained why you kept my daughter a secret from me for eighteen years, there's no more reason for you to stay."

"I hadn't intended to." Her tone was calm. One, he suspected, served her well at the UN.

"Is it true what she told me? That you and your husband work for the British government? And that you're currently a translator at the United Nations in New York?"

"Yes. That's true enough. Though I doubt she

would've used the term *translator*. A translator translates written material. An interpreter takes the context of words spoken in one language, and then repeats them in another. Which is what I do. But I digress... Piper has always been a truthful girl. She doesn't lie. Admittedly, she failed to tell you the entire truth, as I kept advising her to do—"

"You knew she was coming here?"

"Yes. Her father—" her creamy British complexion flushed a bit as she realized her slip in words "—my *husband* and I realized that we couldn't stop her once she found out who you were and decided to come west to meet you."

"We'll get to the guy she calls Dad later. Right now I want to talk about her. Did you actually expect a young girl, still in her teens, to come across the country by herself, then just breeze in and say, 'Hi, I'm applying for the job you've posted, and by the way, I'm the daughter my mum forgot to mention to you?'"

"Not exactly. She's well traveled, so I wasn't all that concerned about the trip itself."

"That's the least of what she was facing. It was *your* job to tell me as soon as you found out you were pregnant. And, for the moment, trying to focus on her and not what you did to me, you should have at least given me a heads-up when you learned she was going to do this. Unless she ran away?"

"No. She didn't run away." The color in her cheeks deepened. "Do you think I could have a drink? I have the feeling I'm going to need some alcohol to ease the pain of your legal grilling."

"I'm not going to grill you," he said. "I just want some damn answers."

"And I'm here to give them to you. Admittedly late—"

"You think?"

Another sigh rife with British coolness. "We need to come to an understanding. For Piper's sake."

She had not said "our daughter," he noted, trained, as he'd told Amanda, to pay close attention to word choice. Which made sense. Given that she'd chosen to allow some other man to play the father's role in their child's life.

Tamping down an unaccustomed temper and a jealousy he'd never before experienced, especially of someone he'd never met, Quinn went behind the bar. "Are you still drinking G&T?"

"I'm British," she reminded him. "Although trendier cocktails have caught on, as Winston Churchill is known to have said, 'gin and tonic has saved more Englishmen's lives, and minds, than all the doctors in the Empire.'"

"Spoken by a guy who should have known, given his own statements about heavy daily drinking," Quinn said as he filled a highball glass with ice, poured in some top-shelf gin, topped it with tonic and lightly stirred, so as not to disturb the carbonation. He finished it up by slicing a lime wheel he ran around the edge of the glass before dropping it in.

G&Ts weren't a popular drink in Honeymoon Harbor, but one thing he remembered about that boozy week they'd spent together was how to make them.

She lifted a blond brow. "That's rather a strong indictment coming from a man who runs a bar."

"It's a craft brewery and pub. Where I set limits on drinks," he said as he placed the glass in front of her on a coaster.

"So Piper told me when she first started working here. She also mentioned you're allowing her to live in an apartment over the store, so to speak."

"This is a tourist town. Like the one you and your husband sent her to every summer to live with her grandparents. Vacation town housing fills up fast. The apartment was empty since I've moved to a lake outside of town, so it was an obvious solution."

"I suppose that makes sense." She took a sip. "This is quite good." A second sip. "Actually excellent."

"I don't believe in doing anything halfway."

"So I remember." Her eyes drifted to the trophies and awards. "While it's not exactly the law career you'd set out to achieve, you seem to have done well for yourself."

"Thank you. I find it fulfilling."

"As is my career." She paused. Then sighed. "Hell, since we're being truthful, of course I'd rather be working at the World Court as I told you was my dream back then. But pregnancy sidetracked me, then being a single mother for two years took me off that track."

"You said you were on the pill."

"I was. But that was a crazy week and I somehow missed one." She paused. Took another, longer drink.

"Well, actually two. My cycle was always unpredictable, so I didn't immediately realize I was pregnant."

"And when you did, you decided not to notify me."

"We'd already discussed that," she said. "About what we both wanted out of life. You knew that I had plans far beyond small-town living."

"Seattle had nearly three million people at the time, so it hardly counts as a small town." He shook his head. "Sorry. I know. You were an adventurer who was going off to save the world. While I was a stick-in-the-mud lawyer."

"That wasn't what I was saying. I also remember that, at the time, you were trying to decide whether you wanted to defend unjustly arrested people, or put bad guys behind bars. It appears I wasn't the only one whose plans changed. From the online information about your career, you were, what do they call it? A 'rainmaker'? Due to make partner if I recall.

"I merely wanted to point out that we each had conflicting ideas of how we wanted to live our lives. Plans that would have been irreconcilable. Not telling you wasn't a spur-of-the-moment decision, Quinn. I gave it a great deal of thought, and, while I want all women to have the power to choose whether to be a mother or not, I came to the conclusion abortion wasn't for me."

"Did you consider marriage?"

She took another, longer drink. "I did. And knew you'd ask, out of a sense of honor—"

"You make that sound like a flaw."

She looked at him over the rim of the tall glass.

"I didn't mean it like that. Honor is a good thing. It's also in short supply in so many places around the world. So, I respected you for being one of those people who possess it. It's one of the things that attracted me to you."

"So, you slept with me because you thought I was honorable?"

"No. I slept with you because you were, and still are by the way, really hot. And, for the record, that week remains one of the best times of my life." She reached out, as if to touch his hand, then drew hers back. "But it wasn't our real lives, Quinn. We were living a fantasy. You're not the kind of guy who'd normally pick up a woman at a beach *chiringuito* and have her in bed ten minutes later."

Memories he'd put away years ago suddenly flashed through his mind. He'd dropped into one of the bar huts on Barcelona's Sant Sebastià Beach on the way back to his hotel, when he'd seen her up on the small stage, taking part in a noisy amateur flamenco contest that he'd later learned was a nightly attraction.

She hadn't had the best classical style, not that it mattered since her intensity, foot stomping on those tall red heels, clapping her hands, seductively and sinuously moving her arms while coquettishly swishing her scarlet skirt, had nearly every man in the place shouting out to be chosen to be her partner.

When their eyes had literally met across the small hut, she'd stalked haughtily to the front of the stage and placed her hands, tipped with nails painted a bright scarlet, on her hips. As she held his gaze, Quinn felt as if time had stopped.

Then she'd sent her skirt flying with a high kick of her leg, beckoning him forward with the crook of her finger and the crowd went wild. Caught up in the intensity of the moment, along with the rashness brought on by the beers he'd sampled as he'd made his way down the beach, he'd leaped onto the stage and, as the acoustical guitarist began building up to a blistering crescendo, he'd followed the lead of the other male dancers, stomping, scowling, spinning, and striking arrogant poses.

"It was twenty minutes," he said as he remembered lifting her up and taking her mouth like a conquering macho bullfighter. The music had abruptly stopped, but the crowd was still shouting when he finally released her, having to catch her as she nearly swayed off the stage. When the MC put his hand over each couple's heads for judging by applause, they'd won by a landslide. Scooping her up in his arms, the crowd parted as he carried her out of the *chiringuito* to his hotel, which was conveniently right next door, and claimed his prize. "Because you lured me up on that stage." That had led to a long, passionate night.

Then six more days and nights. They'd drunk, laughed, shared plans about their futures when the world had seemed like their oyster. They'd also spent a lot of time in bed because one thing neither of them had planned on was how much of the city would be shut down, being focused on Easter as a religious holiday, rather than a time to let loose.

"I'm sorry," she said, her voice softening from its earlier brisk, defensive tone.

The shared memory of that dance, and the intimacy of the week together, had cooled much of Quinn's initial anger. He'd never before in his life acted so out of character. In fact, until she'd shown up in the pub today, he'd put that sensual, drunken flamenco out of his mind.

"We were both young," he said. "We didn't really know each other—"

"Two ships passing in the night," she agreed. "When I discovered I was pregnant, I panicked. My first thought was to contact you, but we'd agreed. No commitment. No strings. Wanting to keep things simple, when she was old enough to ask, about her father, I told her you were a one-night stand and I'd forgotten your name. She never asked again, so that story worked until she recently found an old photo of us in Barcelona. And I knew I had to tell her the truth."

"I would've done strings," he insisted. "If you'd let me know. But you're right. A marriage would've been a disaster. We had nothing in common but chemistry. I doubt we'd have made it to Piper's first birthday. But I would've at least paid child support. I would have stepped up to my responsibility." And he'd have been able to have a relationship with his daughter, watching her grow up. They could have made it work.

"I know that now. But, to be perfectly honest, motherhood changed the course of my life enough that I was afraid that if I let you into it, I'd lose my dream entirely. At least now, while interpreting isn't what I'd initially intended to do, I still travel the world making a difference by connecting people through language. I'm not that crazy, sex-crazed girl you spent a holiday week with. I assist in making history and there's not a day when I'm not fully aware of the responsibility on my shoulders.

"Most of my free time is spent reading newspapers, books, watching regional newscasts, to try to understand all I can about a country and any political situations it might be facing. Because if we want the world to get along, then people have to be able to talk to one another. That's where an interpreter comes in. It's also admittedly stressful because even the smallest error in wording could have severe consequences in world politics."

"I never thought you were crazy." When she gave him a look, he shrugged and said, "Okay, we were probably both a little crazy. Letting off steam from having taken our studying so seriously. Also, you win."

"Win what?"

"Your job is more important than mine."

She shrugged as the tension gradually dissipated. "Piper has told me a great deal about this pub. You bring people together. Give them a place to congregate with friends, to celebrate, and somewhere to be when you're feeling lonely but can't bear to be alone. That's important to the community.

"She loves working here and said that although

you're a man of very few words, your actions speak louder than any words and that you're one of the kindest people she's ever known. And that's saying something because her father, I mean, my husband, is both honest and kind."

"She calls him her dad," Quinn said. "Which he is, having taken on that role when the two of you married. He sounds a lot like my dad. Who's the most honest, kindest man *I've* ever known. So—" he blew out a breath "—it sounds as if you did the best thing you could at the time."

Her eyes moistened again with tears. "Thank you… There's something else."

Quinn braced himself for yet another unwelcome surprise. "What?"

"She wants to stay here. In Honeymoon Harbor. Apparently she spoke with one of your brothers' wives, who works at a community college."

"That would be Lily. Burke's wife."

"Yes, the American football player. My husband is a fan."

"Your husband is not only honest and kind, he has good taste in quarterbacks."

She managed a smile at that. "He does. The thing is, she wants to cut her gap year short and enroll there next semester."

That came as a surprise. "It's a good school."

"It's very well ranked. I looked it up. There's more. After getting her AA, she intends to attend the University of Washington. Apparently it's a world-class center for international study, including international law."

Another thing Piper hadn't told him. Then again, why should she? Their agreement was that she'd work through the summer. As far as she'd let him know, he was merely her employer. Not her father. He wondered when—or if—she'd planned to tell him.

"Interesting that she'd have chosen a future that includes parts of what we'd both wanted when we were just a few years older than she is now," Quinn said.

"Isn't it? I suppose there could be some genetics involved."

"Does it bother you? That she wants to stay here with me?"

"No, to be honest. I feel it's only fair. I had her the first eighteen years of her life. What she's told me about you, and what I found online, was encouraging enough. But what was truly reassuring was that not only was your sister the first person you called, she and her husband came immediately to help with the situation. Which demonstrates a strong familial bond. I'm perfectly comfortable with Piper becoming part of your family. All of whom, by the way, appear to be quite the overachievers."

"We had good role models," he said.

"So it seems. David and I talked about it before I came here and we think she can benefit from experiencing her roots. It was obvious that she was always happiest when staying with his parents."

"She told me about summers with them. It's partly

what got her the job. And you can tell your husband that I've added his parents' crab recipe to my menu. But I'd still bet that our Dungeness crab could beat his Cromer crab any day."

This time, her laugh was bold and bright and reminded him of the girl he had, that day they'd gone their separate ways, momentarily considered making a life with. Now, it appeared, their lives would be entwined after all. Through the daughter he hadn't even known he had until today.

Then her expression sobered. "There *is* one thing that concerns me."

"Oh?"

"It's about a boy."

"A boy?"

"Well, not exactly a boy. He's twenty-one. And apparently works at your brother's boat-building company."

"Ah. You mean Jamal. Yeah, he's a good kid. You don't have anything to worry about."

"I've warned her about how pregnancy can drastically change a life plan—"

"You didn't put it that way, did you? Like it's her fault you're not saving the world?"

"Of course not. I'd never put that guilt on my own child. Because it isn't true, and, as it's turned out, I believe I'm better suited for the career I have now. But she's such a bright light, and has such lofty goals—I'd hate to see that diminished due to a mistake."

"You trusted her to know the truth when she finally nailed you down about my identity," Quinn reminded her.

"True."

"And trusted her to be mature enough to come here alone?"

"True yet again."

"And you trust me to care for her."

"Yes. I wasn't initially certain, but I am now."

"And you do know about my large family, with many uncles, including a chief of police, who'd set straight any guy who might look as if he's leading her toward trouble."

"You Mannions sound formidable."

"We built this town, along with my brother-in-law's family. It's not only still standing, but thriving. So, yeah, united as a group, we're pretty damn formidable. We'll do everything in our power to help guide Piper to reach her potential toward the life she's dreamed of. Or whatever one she might end up deciding on. Which I'm sure is what you and your husband want for her."

"Of course."

"Also, I'll work with you both on helping guide her or share advice when any one of us feels she needs it."

"This is admittedly surprising. I'd expected more *Sturm und Drang.*"

"I don't do drama," he said. "And there you go again, showing off your multilingualism." Quinn remembered how she could curse in multiple languages, but also possessed a remarkable number of sexy phrases.

"I had a filthy mouth in my youth," she admitted on a laugh. "I've become much more prudent in my personal language to avoid it slipping into my professional work. And you're right. I was showing off. To turn you on."

"It worked."

Her expression turned serious again. "Thank you for accepting this situation so well."

"You're welcome. After all, all three of us love her."

He'd come to, Quinn realized. He hadn't quite put that specific word to the feelings that had been developing yet, but now, hearing the words out loud, he realized they fit. So much so that if Lily hadn't beaten him to it, he'd planned to suggest she consider attending Clearwater Community College. Because he'd known he'd miss being with her every day if she left after the Labor Day crowds thinned out.

"I merely want her to be happy," Fiona said. "Whatever she ends up doing with her life."

"Oh, we'll make sure of that."

"So." She polished off her gin and tonic. "Since we're on a roll, as you Yanks say, there's one more thing I'd like to ask for."

"And that would be?"

"A glass of that Surfin' USA our daughter told me is winning prizes all over the place."

"You've got it." Quinn pulled out two pilsner glasses. "But there's a condition."

"And that is?"

"My mom's going to want you to come to the farm

for dinner so the family can meet the mother of their newest member."

"Oh." She paled a bit at that prospect. Then he watched her square her slender shoulders. "I've interpreted for UN peacekeeping forces in Cyprus, Kosovo, and Lebanon. I suppose I can handle whatever your family is going to think of me."

"I had no idea UN translators—interpreters," he corrected himself, "went to war zones."

"Peacekeeping zones," she clarified.

"If situations were already peaceful, there'd be no need for peacekeeping forces, so soldiers, and even interpreters, must occasionally be killed."

"That's a downside," she admitted. "It's also a professional risk for interpreters working for the military, news organizations, and companies doing business internationally."

"Now I'll admit to being glad we never got married, because if we had, and managed to make it work, I'd have spent the past eighteen years worrying about you." Which now, he would anyway, for fear of Piper losing her mother.

Because he was Irish enough to believe in jinxes, he locked that unpalatable thought away as he filled the two glasses from the tap. "You don't have to worry about meeting the family. They're already fond of Piper. They'll see that you and your husband are, in great part, why she's turned out to be such a special young lady."

She took a tentative sip of the beer. Remembering

her not being a beer drinker, Quinn folded his arms and waited.

"This, like your G&T, is quite excellent."

"Thank you."

"I'm also glad Piper found that photograph of us together and insisted I finally tell her the name of her birth father. And, although once she arrived here and started working for you, I urged her to tell you the truth right away, I've decided that it was better that you met her on her own terms. Without any parental feelings getting involved."

"Probably true," he agreed.

"And I'm very glad that I came here today."

Quinn realized that his mother was right over all the years she'd insisted that every cloud had a silver lining, if you waited long enough and looked closely enough to see it.

"Me, too," he said, lifting his glass to hers.

CHAPTER SEVENTEEN

QUINN'S FIRST CALL was to his sister, who assured him that Piper had calmed down and was sharing her plans to attend college here in town. She also suggested that rather than throw mother and daughter into a full family dinner, which could prove overwhelming, he should consider taking Fiona over to the farm himself, introduce her, and break the news about him having a daughter to his parents and grandparents.

Then later, after a few months, perhaps Fiona and her husband could join them for Thanksgiving, since they'd not only get to see how well their daughter was thriving—and Brianna had no doubt she would be—they could experience a holiday not celebrated in Great Britain.

Agreeing that was a better solution than his own first thought had been, Quinn's next call was to the farm, to ask his dad if he, his mom, and grandparents could be there in a half an hour or so. He had something he needed to discuss with them. His father agreed and said he looked forward to seeing him. In the background, he heard his mom ask if he wasn't taking Amanda out on the boat today. To which he told his dad to tell her that something had come up.

Last, but certainly not least, his third call was to
Amanda, while Fiona left to discreetly freshen up
in the restroom to give him privacy.

"I'm sorry," he said when she picked up on the
first ring, as if she'd been waiting for his call. Glancing down at his watch, he saw that he was already
late. "But I can't do lunch today. Something unexpectedly came up. A family thing."

"Is everyone all right?"

"Everyone's fine. It's complicated," he found himself saying what seemed to have become a Mannion
family mantra. "I'll tell you later. It's not bad," he
assured her. "I just need to go out to the farm and
talk with my folks about something."

"Okay. We can always have the boat picnic another day. I have a potential client that wanted an
estimate immediately anyway, as everyone always
seems to do, once they make up their mind to hire
a landscaper."

"Seth has said the same about renovations." It
felt good, for that brief moment, to have a normal
conversation. "I'll call you later this afternoon. Or
better yet, come over this evening, and fill you in."

"Take your time. I have pesto I made with fresh
basil from my garden and while it might not be as
sexy as crab grilled in butter, I can boil some store-
bought pasta and put together my own seduction dinner within minutes after you get here."

"That sounds perfect. Especially the seduction
part. But I can't promise anything right now," he
said, hating that he couldn't be more specific. Would

she think he was ghosting her, the way Lily had Burke, when she'd disappeared from New York City while he'd been away on a game road trip?

He hadn't thought past meeting with his folks. Would Fiona and Piper want to have dinner together? Would Piper still be upset at her mother and want to stay upstairs alone in the apartment? Which, although he had no knowledge of teenage girls other than memories of Brianna, who'd always been very even-keeled, being alone at a time like this didn't sound like the best idea after such an event as emotional as what Piper had experienced earlier.

Maybe she could stay at Brianna's into the evening? No. He'd already cost his sister and Seth their rare summer day together. The right thing, the *fatherly* thing to do, he thought, was perhaps for Piper and him to spend the evening together. Talk things through, make plans about her future for the next few months. Or years. And for him to reassure her that he was proud to be her father, even if it was happening eighteen years late.

Would she call him Dad? Wouldn't it be weird to refer to the two father figures in her life by the same name? No way did he want to be called anything as stuffy as Father. And she was too old for Daddy. Maybe, he considered, they should just stick to Quinn, which had been working well enough. Unlike Burke, who'd had to think on the fly when an entire defensive line was headed toward him, or Aiden, whose cop partner had been killed during that ambush gunfight when he'd been working with the feds in Los Angeles, Quinn had always preferred to think things through.

His mother had, fondly, called him her pondering son. Which was true. He preferred to gather all the facts, then put the pieces together until he had an entire picture of a situation. Just like that table they'd had in the family room with a jigsaw puzzle that would eventually get filled in as each person would sit down and spend some free time working on it. Even as video games became increasingly popular, the table had stayed, now with a new picture to fill in every few months, and grandchildren to keep the habit going.

This was only the second time in his life that Quinn had been faced with no clear answers for a problem. The first had been his mother's accident last summer, when his entire family had spent hours adrift, fearing that the woman who'd always been their anchor might not make it. But she had survived and he knew that, however surprised she might be by his situation, she'd handle the meeting with her newest grandchild's mother with her usual grace and charm.

One thing at a time, he decided, after Amanda had reassured him yet again that he should do whatever he needed to do, and they'd talk later.

"I think that's a lovely idea," Fiona said when Burke shared Brianna's suggestion about Thanksgiving as they drove over to Herons Landing. Although his sister had told him Piper was doing better than she would have expected, the first item on his agenda was to check on his daughter and assure her that everything was okay. That *they'd* be okay.

"I'll admit that the idea of breaking the news of you being Piper's father, me having kept her from you for nearly two decades, *and* trying to survive dinner with your entire family, who'll undoubtedly be very annoyed with me, was proving more unsettling than finding out I was being sent to Somalia a few years ago."

"You wouldn't have had to worry," Quinn assured her, even as his mind was shouting *Somalia? Seriously?* "Mom would have made sure of that. We all call her the velvet bulldozer. If she wants you to feel comfortable, and she will, everyone will fall in line."

"Oh, this is lovely," Fiona said as he pulled up in front of Herons Landing. "I'd tried to book a room online, but there weren't any openings. David and I are currently staying in Seattle."

"He came with you?"

"Well, not to Honeymoon Harbor, which, by the way, is such a quaint name. I read the history of the town's name change online. We decided things were going to be uncomfortable enough for you and Piper, so he stayed at the hotel and I drove the rental car here. Maybe next time," she considered. "At Thanksgiving."

"That works. Brianna can hold the tower suite open for that weekend."

She stayed in the car while he talked to Seth, who was in the workshop he'd built on the property, sanding a chest of drawers he'd made for the nursery.

Seth told him Bri and Piper were in the guest room, soon to be nursery. Quinn entered the gatehouse, followed the sound of female conversation, and found his sister and daughter going through a pile of fabric.

He knocked on the open door frame and immediately that light in Piper's face went out, like a candle snuffed out by a coastal wind. Her eyes, the Mannion blue of his father, brothers, and his own, he belatedly realized, turned from laughter to worry.

"Where's Mum?" she asked.

"She's waiting outside. I just came by to tell you that we're on our way to the farm, so she can meet my parents and grandparents. Everything's going to work out," he assured his daughter. A definition that had him feeling grateful and terrified at the same time. "I hadn't realized that you were planning to stay here and go to CCC."

"I'd just decided. Lily and I talked for a few minutes about it at the barbecue, so Jamal drove me out there and Lily gave me a tour. I think it'd be a good fit. And I could stay here in Honeymoon Harbor. If that's okay with you."

"I'm your father and since we have a lot of catching up to do, of course it's okay. Better than okay. And the apartment is yours, for as long as you want it. Though," he said, "I've got a home outside of town on the lake. If you'd like to stay there with me—"

"The apartment's great," she said quickly. "I'm old enough to be on my own."

That stung a bit. Not that she didn't want to live

with him, but the reminder that he'd missed all the years before.

"Of course you are," Brianna jumped in to fill the sudden all-too-obvious gap in conversation. "Quinn and I thought perhaps your mother and—" she paused, as if seeking the right word "—dad—" she'd decided on after an apologetic glance toward Quinn "—might come visit during Thanksgiving."

Piper's brow furrowed, and once again, that slender thumb touched her chin. "Have you brought it up with Mum? What did she say?"

"That she's looking forward to it." Quinn wasn't certain he was all that eager to meet the guy who'd taken on his role, but November was still months away and he'd already made progress wrapping his head around this new dramatic change in his life. Since they'd be sharing his daughter for the rest of their lives, he was determined to make this work.

"What are you two doing?" he asked, looking at the pieces of fabric scattered all over the bed.

"We're making a quilt for the crib," Brianna told him. "I'm gathering material from pieces of all our family members' clothing." She smiled at Piper. "And I'm glad I'm just starting, because now I can add my newly found niece to it."

"Cool. I didn't know you sewed."

"I don't. But mom took a special interest class at the college a few years ago. She gave me a block pattern she assured me would be beginner easy."

"I'm giving her a square from the dress I wore to the barbecue," Piper said. "Brianna tried to talk me out of cutting it apart because it's so pretty, but it's what I was wearing the first time I met my new family, so I want my baby cousin to have a piece of it."

Her words about wanting to share in a family gift for her not-yet-born cousin had something stirring in Quinn's heart, bringing to mind a moment in the book his mom had read to them every Christmas Eve. When the Grinch's heart had grown three sizes.

"That'd be perfect," he said. "And it *was* a pretty dress."

Piper shrugged. "I can always buy another one with the money I'll be saving living rent-free." Although all the sudden drama in his family was centered around her, she seemed a great deal less troubled than when her mother had walked into the pub.

Part of that was probably due to Brianna's natural ability to calm seemingly any situation. Another could be due to her age. Doing the math, yet again, he realized that he and Fiona had been only two years older than Piper was now that week in Barcelona. And while they'd had long-range plans for their lives, as his daughter did, they'd certainly spent most of those days and nights living in the moment. One of those moments had created their daughter. And, despite all the pitfalls he suspected might still lie ahead, hadn't that been a surprise gift from the universe?

After telling them he was taking Fiona out to the farm to explain the situation to his folks, who, he assured Piper, would be surprised, but thrilled to have a new granddaughter, he promised to return to pick her up as soon as possible.

"No hurry," she said, again with the ability of youth to move on, as she plucked a piece of plaid material he recognized from one of his grandfather's shirts, unknowingly putting it next to a square from one of his grandmother's aprons.

He left them as they busily moved fabric around like pieces on a chessboard, but Brianna caught up with him at the front door. "She's going to be fine," she said. "Better than fine. Fortunately, her life, moving from place to place, being shuffled back and forth between her parents, boarding schools, and her grandparents' home, has made her remarkably resilient." She went up on her toes and kissed his cheek. "So, don't worry. I'm looking forward to meeting her mother. She sounds quite remarkable. And, despite a demanding career, she's managed to raise a lovely daughter."

As angry as his initial response had been, that was one point Quinn couldn't argue.

"How is she?" Fiona asked as they left Herons Landing, headed out of town to the farm.

"She seems okay. Brianna has her helping put together pieces of material for a quilt for her upcoming child."

"How domestic. That's a trait I lack."

"My sister's never made a quilt before. I suspect part of why she's working on it now is to give Piper something other than our situation to occupy her mind. Brianna used to be a high-end concierge who catered to the ultrarich, famous, and pampered. She's had years of professional experience calming emotional storms."

"Just as you've had a lifetime of experience being the brother who fixes things and offers sage advice to his younger siblings."

He glanced over at her. "Yeah. I guess you hit that pretty close."

"I've spent many years reading personalities," she said. "Especially during one-on-one conversations, which are my favorite. When I'm working at the UN, I'm in a booth, listening to speeches in earphones while I simultaneously interpret.

"Two-person talks usually begin more casually, with each side discussing nonpolitical matters, like families, and weddings, the personal things you might talk about with someone you've just met. It's much easier to interpret when you've gotten a handle on people. You're the eldest of five. Which means that you either had a lot put on your shoulders at a young age, helping take care of your younger siblings, or, more likely, took that role upon yourself."

"My mother would, and has, agreed with that assessment," he admitted.

"Also, you were an attorney. Which means that you're detail oriented and consider all sides of an issue before coming to a conclusion. It wouldn't have mattered if you'd become a prosecutor or a defense attorney, both choices you talked about back then, or advising international corporations and wealthy individuals, as you ended up doing for several years. They all require the same skill set… I'm an only child."

"And the first in your family to go to college. Which placed a lot of pressure on you, much of it probably self-induced, to succeed."

"You remembered."

"I remember everything," he said. "And, coincidentally, I was thinking about you the other day."

"Oh?"

"Yeah. There's this woman."

"The one you broke the date with. I'm sorry about that."

"That's her. And it's okay. She's an understanding person. And we were friends before things got serious."

"Ah." She glanced over at him. "As in marriage serious?"

"I'd say so. But the thing is, her first marriage was pretty much a disaster, so I've been taking my time, staying in the friend zone."

"And how has that been working for you?"

"Driving me crazy. But I want her to be sure. Because I'm all in. I want a lifetime."

"That's wonderful. David and I have that. So, I take it you were comparing our whirlwind week with your longer courtship?"

"In a way. But only because, back when you were walking down that Jetway to board the plane back to Cambridge, I thought, just maybe, I'd found the person I wanted to spend the rest of my life with."

She smiled. "As I said, we would've been a disaster trying for long-term. But although our backgrounds and goals were very different, I think we clicked on more than just chemical attraction. That could've burned out the first day or so. Since nothing was open, and we couldn't have sex all the time, we spent a lot of time talking, and having studied personality types for my work, looking back, I believe that with you growing up as an eldest and me as an only we had more in common that we realized at the time. Enough, I'm hoping, that someday, when you've forgiven me, we can co-parent as friends."

"Except for Amanda's—she's the woman I want to spend the rest of my life with—I never handled divorces," Quinn said. "Especially ones involving custody. Whenever one of my clients' marriages broke up, I'd turn the case over to one of the family law attorneys."

"Because divorces can be messy. Especially, I'd imagine, when you're talking about children and/or a lot of money."

"That would be true."

"And also because you prefer orderly to messy."

He laughed at that. "You really must be good at your job."

"I'm extremely excellent. And in high demand," she said, making it sound more like fact than bragging. "Which, unfortunately, didn't mesh as well with motherhood as I would have liked. It sounds as if our daughter might have been better off growing up with your family,"

"In some ways, maybe. But then she wouldn't have had her eyes opened to the rest of the world. Which has made her passionate about saving it."

"That's how she sees it," Fiona murmured. "I'm afraid she'll be disappointed when she realizes the magnitude and impossibility of achieving that goal."

"Amanda told me about the Japanese philosophy of wabi-sabi. One of the tenets is that, since perfection is impossible, we must strive for excellence."

"What a good way of looking at it. And now that you've mentioned it, it's often the goal of diplomacy. I believe I've noticed it occur more often when I'm interpreting during negotiations with Japanese delegates."

"You speak Japanese too?"

"It's one of my more recent languages," she said. "I learned it when talks of Brexit began building steam. Although it doesn't get much media attention, the UK and Japan have long been diplomatic allies with a bilateral trade relationship valued in the billions. There was fear that Brexit would disrupt the links, but many politicians view Tokyo as an essential link to Britain's new Asia-Pacific strategy.

"I stay out of politics as much as possible, and never allow personal feelings into my work, especially in economic discussions where my husband might also be working to deepen trade relationships, but I will admit to enjoying visiting a country where I don't have to worry about being assassinated when I get off the plane."

"That assassination potential has to concern Piper."

"I downplay any dangers as much as possible. But yes, she has mentioned it. More so in recent years.

But, as I remind her, in my own way, I'm working for the same goal that she's aiming for. Bringing peace, stability, and equality to the world."

"As impossible as it may be, it's still a noble goal," Quinn allowed. "Do you ever get discouraged?"

"Of course. Quite often. Then I make a cup of tea, listen to Lennon's 'Imagine,' and remind myself that I'm not the only dreamer. And carry on toward the goal of, as he stated so beautifully, 'the world living as one.'"

"On one level, I'm still angry at you," Quinn said.

"Totally understandable," Fiona agreed.

"On another, I like and admire your optimism. The same way I did back then."

"I still like and admire you too," she said.

"But we wouldn't have worked out," they said together.

"We're going to make *this* work," Quinn said. Because despite what Fiona had already admitted was a betrayal, they still had a vitally important connection.

"Absolutely," she agreed. Then added a caveat. "What about Amanda? How do you think she'll take this news of your sudden parenthood?"

"She'll embrace it." That was one thing Quinn had not a doubt about. "They've already become friends. Piper helped her plant the herbs at the pub." A thought occurred to him. "Perhaps the two of you should meet before you leave town."

"I was planning to drive back to Seattle after meeting your parents, and spending some time with

Piper to assure her that you and I are united in wanting only the best for her."

"Why not spend the night?"

"Where?"

"The apartment has a queen bed. We'll pick up Piper at my sister's, then the two of you can spend the rest of the day together. Have a sleepover. In the morning, Jarle will cook you the best breakfast you've ever had. Well, maybe short of Brianna's. She has a repertoire of over eighty-five different breakfast dishes at the bed-and-breakfast. Not that she serves them all at the same time."

"Definitely overachievers," she murmured.

"Hey pot," Quinn said. "This is kettle."

She laughed, although the closer they got to the tree farm, the more Quinn could feel her tensing up. "It'll be okay," he said.

She looked out the passenger window. "They'll hate me."

"I have the feeling they already know."

"Your sister told them?"

"No, actually it was my mom who brought the resemblance up to Bri. Apparently it was the topic of a dinner conversation one night."

"This is definitely worse than Somalia." The words were muted due to her having buried her face in her hands.

"Look at it this way. Since it appears I won't exactly be dropping a bombshell on them, it'll be easier for you to meet them. They're not the enemy, Fiona. They're Piper's grandparents and great-grandparents.

And, despite them undoubtedly being disappointed they've missed out on her early years, they'll treat you with respect. Because you're her mother."

"If I ever screwed up my job as badly as I've done my personal life, the world would've been embroiled in World War III long ago," she muttered.

"I'll accept that you're an excellent interpreter. But I seriously doubt you have that much power when it comes to world diplomacy," he said as he drove through the open red gate.

"Piper kept telling me about all the trees," she said as they made their way down the long driveway. "They're truly magnificent."

"You won't get any argument from me," Quinn said.

"They remind me of my home town in Betws-y-Coed."

"The Welsh one that was too small for you."

"True, though I look at it differently now that I'm older. It's a beautiful Victorian town, and a wonderful place to get away to. It has Douglas fir forests like these, alpine lakes, and snowcapped mountains, just like here. My parents passed a few years ago, but I inherited the house and mostly use it as a lease property, though we occasionally manage to carve out time for a holiday there.

"Oh!" she said as they passed the big red barn. "Your family has a theater?"

"It's a summer deal they added a few years ago to bring in tourism dollars since the Christmas trees only pay out for the month between Thanksgiving and Christmas Eve."

"That's very special. I was in a school play in year eleven of my secondary school. It was *Taming of the Shrew.*"

"Let me guess. You were Kate."

She smiled. "I was, indeed. I developed a mad crush on my co-star that lasted the length of the rehearsals, which broke my heart for a few weeks when he asked the actress playing Kate's 'ideal' sister to go to the May Day festival with him. But I'll admit to enjoying the applause."

"Burke always said that a cheering crowd was one of the best things about being a high school quarterback."

"The hometown hero," she said.

"Especially on Friday nights and then Saturdays after winning the game," Quinn agreed.

"It's ironic that the career I chose not only doesn't involve spotlights and applause, but I'm required to be as invisible as possible."

"I seriously doubt you could ever be invisible," he said. Although he wasn't attracted to her in the way he had been that week, there was no denying that she was still a beautiful woman.

"I'm going to take that as a compliment."

"It was intended as one. I see a great deal of you in Piper."

"There is a resemblance. Though she's the only redhead in our family line—that we know of. She definitely inherited your blue eyes and is left-handed, as are you."

Quinn still found it staggering that he had a

daughter who'd inherited not just the part of his DNA that made up her hair and eye color, and his left-hand dominance, but also his mannerisms. And although she'd been right there, spending nearly every day with him, it had been his grandfather who'd noticed the similarities.

"Oh." She drew in a breath as she took in the two-story white clapboard farmhouse with the apple-red door. "Your family's home is absolutely charming."

"It was built in the early 1900s. But it's been updated over the years. Although Mom insisted it wasn't necessary, Burke used his signing bonus to have the kitchen remodeled and expanded. It was always the heart of the house, but now it's a state-of-the-art place that fits the entire family and guests for dinner."

He pulled up in front of the house and cut the engine. "I'll go in and tell them about us, and Piper, then come out and get you so you can meet them."

"You're protecting me from their initial reaction."

"Just easing into things," he said. "It's not going to be easy for them, and my grandfather had a TIA—"

"Transient ischemic attack," she murmured. "My father had two of those. Before he died."

"Of a stroke?"

"No. Lung cancer. He smoked like a chimney. Always said he was safe because it was a pipe, not cigarettes. We told him that the tobacco in pipes contained the same nicotine and the same carcinogens as cigarettes, but he was stubborn and refused to listen."

"I'm sorry."

"Thank you. I was too. I lost my mom a year to the date later. I firmly believe that she just didn't want to live without him. Hopefully they're together somewhere. Wherever we end up." She shook her head, as if shaking off a sadness she didn't want to be carrying on a day that was difficult enough, "You'd better get in there, before they come out to us."

"Good point."

No one was looking out the window yet, but he suspected that was because his mom wouldn't let them. Which had him thinking about the close bond between his parents. The type that Fiona's parents had apparently shared, which was another thing they had in common.

He knocked once, then, knowing they left the door open whenever everyone was home, walked in and found them gathered around one end of the enormous table Burke had built by an Oregon craftsman who charged exorbitant prices for furniture made from reclaimed wood. The aromas of fresh-brewed coffee and the just-baked shortbread cookies that were currently sitting on a plate on the table filled the air.

He sat down, took the mug of black coffee his mother offered, then, because he'd never been one to beat around the bush, told them about Fiona, a PG version of their time in Barcelona, and the news that Piper Lowell was his and Fiona's daughter. He also explained, as best as he could, Fiona's reasoning for having kept her secret for all those years.

"I knew it," Jerome said. "Soon as I saw that

photo, it clicked. Your mother," he told Harriet, "was a looker. And the girl's a dead ringer for her."

"The girl's name is Piper," Quinn said. "And I know you didn't mean anything untoward, but I have a problem with you describing my teenage daughter as a looker."

"He didn't mean it the way it might have sounded," his mom jumped in to defend her father.

"You've never had any filters," Harriet complained to Jerome. "Though you're right about my mother having been a beauty."

"She was. But she couldn't hold a candle to her daughter," Jerome said, proving himself an expert at finessing his wife's annoyance after half a century together. "And her great-granddaughter's on her way to being a beauty too. That's all I was saying."

"Let me get this straight," John Mannion, who was seated at the end of the table as if heading a meeting of the town council, said. "You met this Fiona Lowell—"

"Her maiden name was Jones," Quinn said.

"Okay. So, you met this woman, Fiona Jones, and you spent your Oxford Easter week in Barcelona with her. And fathered her child."

"I just found out today, so there hasn't been any DNA testing, but yes, I firmly believe that Piper is my daughter."

"Brianna noticed the similarity too," his mom said. "And there's no reason for her mother to have lied once the girl found that photo of the two of you. She could have simply said she'd forgotten your name."

"That was basically the story Piper had always been told. That it had been a one-night-stand and it wasn't until much later, when Fiona discovered she was pregnant, that she couldn't remember my name. Or where I came from."

"Was your name on the photo?"

"No. At least, not according to Fiona."

"Yet she chose to tell the truth when asked."

"That's what she says. She and her husband had discussed it, and although Piper hadn't asked any questions about her birth father when she'd been younger—he'd adopted her after he and Fiona married when she was a toddler—it was only in her teens she began to ask questions. At the time, Fiona didn't want to have to admit to having lied. So she stuck to her story until that photo surfaced."

"How did this woman's husband adopt a child without you relinquishing custody?" John asked.

"Good question. I had a client with that situation. He was trying to gain custody of a child he'd had with a woman he'd been dating at the time. The way it works in the UK, if you're not listed as the father on the birth certificate, which it turns out he wasn't, you have no right to custody, visitation, or ever being made to pay child support.

"To establish legal rights to a child, it's required that you establish paternity. Fiona listed Piper's father as 'unknown,' giving her sole custody. She had no legal obligation to notify me, and after she married David Lowell, there was no legal impediment to him adopting her."

"You're sure about that?" John asked.

"Like I said, I went through this with a client. Well, I didn't personally. I turned him over to a family law specialist at the firm, but since I handled his considerable portfolio, I followed the case closely."

"Well, it sounds as if she hasn't come here for your money," Harriet said. "From what you say, if she'd wanted that, all she'd have had to do was name you on the girl's birth certificate."

Quinn decided it wouldn't help this situation if he'd pointed out that he'd been a struggling student who hadn't had any money at the time they'd been together. Which was how he'd ended up in a low-rent hotel just one step above a youth hostel.

"And you could've fought it if you had questions about paternity," Jerome added.

"I wouldn't have because the timing is right. She and I have discussed her reasoning. She knew I'd offer to marry her, which she didn't want. She had important goals in life and didn't want to be tied down, so she chose freedom over whatever child support she would have received."

"Costing her daughter a family," Harriet said. The sharp edge to her tone verified Quinn's expectation that she'd prove the hardest for Fiona to win over. From the stories he'd heard over the years, she'd proven a powerful adversary while doing her best to keep his parents apart when they'd been young.

"She had grandparents," Quinn said. "Fiona's Welsh mother and father until recently. And she spent summers on England's North Sea coast, working in the seafood restaurant that's been in Fiona's husband's family for generations."

"Yes, she mentioned her grandparents' restaurant at the barbecue," Sarah remembered.

"Her *paternal* grandparents are biologically my daughter and son-in-law," Harriet pointed out. "She should have been spending those summers here. On the farm."

"Mother," Sarah said gently. "What's done is done. And from our admittedly brief discussions, it appears Piper's mother and her husband raised a lovely young woman."

Harriet folded her arms. "Just saying… So, this girl—"

"Piper," Quinn corrected.

"So, *Piper*," his grandmother said on a tone as brisk as a winter wind coming off the Olympic Mountains, "came all the way to Honeymoon Harbor from New York City to find you. Not only that, she's been working for you all these weeks without telling you who she really is. It sounds as if truth isn't a very strong trait in that family."

"She's eighteen, Mother," Sarah chided. "She had every right to be curious. Having that job at the pub drop in her lap was a fortunate coincidence. Almost like an act of fate."

"Brianna said the same thing," Quinn said, not mentioning that he was beginning to believe that, as well.

"And once she serendipitously got the job, the longer she kept quiet about who she was, the harder it would have been to tell Quinn," John offered. "It was obvious at the barbecue that she's happy here. She might have been afraid that Quinn would fire her—"

"I'd never have done that," Quinn argued.

"You know that and I know that, along with everyone else here. But she'd have no way of knowing for certain. Do you know if she was in contact with her mother during this time?"

"She was. And, apparently, Fiona kept advising her to tell me."

"Humph. Seems the mother should've been the one to do that," Harriett said. "Not leave such an important announcement to a young girl, as you all keep reminding me she is."

"You liked her, Mother," Sarah reminded Harriet. "You told me yourself what a polite young woman she is."

"That was before I knew about the lying. Or, at least, her sin of omission."

"Harriet." His grandfather's tone was not their usual game of bickering, but one that Quinn had only heard directed at Aiden, after that long-ago teenage beer truck theft. "Give it up. She seems like a very sweet girl, everyone who met her at the barbecue liked her, Quinn's told us that she's a hard worker who's great with customers, and most important, she's both a Mannion and a Harper. Despite whatever happened in the past, that's what counts. She's one of us and we're all damn well going to welcome her into our family with open hearts and arms.

"And," he said, holding up a hand as his wife

opened her mouth to speak, "you're going to be respectful to her mother. Because, despite what I'll admit was a serious lack in judgment, the woman was young, and like I said, it's in the past. It's obvious by how well the girl turned out that she was a good mother. Plus, if you're rude to the mother, the girl might take her side. Then we'll risk losing her, just as we've found her. Is that what you really want?"

Silence settled over the room. Quinn was certain that after all their years together, his grandparents must have had a few serious arguments, but he'd certainly never witnessed this dynamic of their marriage.

"You're right." Harriett let out a long sigh. "The same as you were right when you told me that 'that cocky Mannion boy' would be a good husband for our Sarah. But—" she argued, "I'd like to point out that I certainly wasn't the only one who wanted a better life for our daughter than we had back when you were off risking your life fishing, leaving me at home trying to make do with what little money we had. I even took in washing and ironing for grocery money while raising our daughter alone for months at a time."

"That's true. And as it turned out, our Sarah got herself that easier life we'd wanted for her with John. So, in that way, we're damn lucky the two crazy kids ignored us. Because we'd have missed out on our five wonderful grandchildren."

"And a new great-grandchild," Quinn pointed out.

"She was great with Gabe and Chelsea's girls," Jerome said.

"Sweet as pie," Harriet agreed. Quinn suspected he wasn't the only one breathing a silent sigh of relief as his grandparents were back in sync.

"Go out and bring her in," Sarah said. "I'll put the kettle on for tea."

CHAPTER EIGHTEEN

THE MEETING WENT far better than Quinn could have hoped for. Over tea and the buttery shortbread cookies Sarah had made after Quinn's call, Fiona apologized to his parents and grandparents, even getting teary at times, which had Sarah fetching a box of tissues. Gratefully, even his grandmother behaved, stating how pleased she was that her mother's coppery red hair had continued in Piper's DNA.

"The resemblance is remarkable," Fiona said, looking down at the photo Sarah showed her. She glanced up at Quinn. "There's no chance of you denying parentage."

Although her tone was the teasing one he remembered, he nevertheless felt the need to respond for the record. "I haven't any intention of trying."

"I am so sorry." Fiona's eyes moistened yet again as she reached for another tissue. Her face was red and blotchy from the tears she'd already shed. It was if a dam that had been holding back all those years of keeping her secret had burst, allowing her emotions to flow free. "You're all behaving so kindly, after what I did cost you so many years. While Quinn was inside talking to his sister and Piper, I was thinking about how much she enjoyed spending summers at my husband's parents' seaside home. And how, thanks to acting on my own self-interests, she lost the opportunity to spend time here, on your farm with all of you."

"That is regretful," Sarah said. "Because she's a delightful girl and we already love her. But we all make mistakes when we're young." She looked over at Quinn's father and linked her fingers with his. "I'd loved John for as long as I can remember. Going back to childhood. We were best friends and by the time we were in high school, we'd become secret sweethearts. Well, we thought we were secret at the time, anyway," she said. "Because of a foolish feud that had divided the Harper and Mannion families for over a century, I went back East to college while John stayed here in Washington and attended UW. But whenever he could scrounge up extra money, he'd fly back East to see me."

"The last time I was there, I screwed up a carefully planned proposal," his father picked up the story. "But as we toured her campus and met her friends, I realized that Sarah was bound for great things, and I was returning home to Honeymoon Harbor. So, I decided—although I had a ring in my pocket—that if I really loved her, which I did, the only right thing to do would be to get out of her way and let her move up to the bigger, better life she deserved."

"So, he dumped me," Sarah said.

"I did not." It was an argument Quinn had heard

before. "I merely suggested we take a time-out while you were in England."

"That was just your clumsy male attempt to ease into the situation. You broke up with me."

"For your sake," he insisted, swiping a hand through his hair. "I knew that if I proposed, you'd accept and come back here with me. I was afraid you'd either spend the rest of our marriage regretting all the opportunities you'd given up, or eventually leave Honeymoon Harbor. And me."

Fiona exchanged a glance with Quinn, as if sharing the thought of how close their relationship had echoed that of his parents.

"So," John said, "while Sarah was achieving her MA in English lit at Oxford, then teaching a course on Jane Austen in Japan, I was a world away in Nepal, training farmers on better ways of agriculture."

"Then, after two years apart, we ended up at LAX on the same flight back to Seattle," Sarah said. "If fate hadn't stepped in, we might never have gotten back together, because I'd been accepted into the PhD program at Oxford and was only planning to stay a few days to visit my folks before returning to England."

She exchanged a warm smile with Quinn's dad, one Brianna had once described as them appearing to have little hearts circling around their heads. When he and his brothers were young, they'd make a big deal out of gagging whenever their parents got mushy. Now, looking at them, Quinn considered yet again how theirs was the connection he wanted with the woman he'd be spending his life with. Which was why he'd waited the longest of all his siblings to get married. And, why, as hard as it had been, he'd been willing to wait for Amanda.

After a bit more discussion, arrangements were made for Fiona—and her husband, which Quinn wasn't exactly thrilled about, but it sounded as if the guy had been a good father, so it wasn't that he had any grounds to object—to spend Thanksgiving in Honeymoon Harbor.

"The day after is the start of our Christmas holiday, so we may put you to work," Harriett warned.

"She's not kidding," Sarah said. "We bake and freeze all the cookies and make the cider ahead of time, then first thing Friday, we start putting up the wreaths and swags, and get out the wagon for the sleigh rides."

"The running family joke is that my parents had five kids so they'd have unpaid labor," Quinn said.

"I neither confirm nor deny that accusation," Sarah quipped back. "However, I will admit that once you all flew the nest, we did have to hire additional seasonal workers."

"I'd enjoy helping with the celebration," Fiona said. "And I'm certain Piper will, as well. We were going to take her to a Christmas tree farm in Scotland once, when she was young. Unfortunately, she missed it because I was interpreting during the breakout of a civil war that a team of negotiators had been attempting to prevent in South Sudan."

"She's mentioned missing that trip," Quinn said. "But didn't say anything about a civil war."

"That's because she didn't know. My husband and I have often been vague about our assignments. Partly for security reasons, but also to keep the more perilous aspects of our careers from her as much as possible. She knew, of course, that we were occasionally sent to places where families weren't allowed. And, as she got older, she'd come to realize why that policy existed those times she was sent to a boarding school for the children of diplomats, or to her grandparents." The word *grandparents* had Quinn holding his breath as Fiona turned toward Harriet. "Again, although I speak four languages fluently, I don't have enough words for a proper apology."

"What's done is done," Harriet said briskly. "But I might suggest you consider a safer line of work in order to live long enough to spoil your own grandchildren someday."

"I'll take that under consideration," Fiona said diplomatically. "Meanwhile, let's all hope my daughter doesn't give us an occasion to celebrate another grandchild anytime soon."

"Amen to that," Harriet said, having finally found something to agree with Fiona about, ending the visit on a congenial note.

Sarah walked out with them. "My mother can be brisk," she told Fiona. "But inside that crusty exterior is a marshmallow-soft heart. I assure you that she'll treat your daughter with the kindness and love that she shows her other great-granddaughters, who happen to be adopted, which doesn't make them any less Mannions."

"Thank you," Fiona said. "You've all been much more gracious than I could have hoped for."

"It's obvious that you and your husband raised an exemplary child, under what sounds like difficult circumstances," Sarah said. "Rather than dwell on what might have been, I prefer to view Piper as an unexpected gift. And I promise you that every member of our family will feel the same way, because she's one of ours now."

And that, Quinn knew, for the family he'd been fortunate to grow up in, meant everything.

"WELL," FIONA SAID, dabbing at tears that had started up again after his mother's private words to her, "that went much better than I'd feared."

"I told you," he said. "I think we all mostly took how fortunate we were to have grown up in such a close-knit family for granted. It wasn't until we'd grown up and left home, and especially last year when Mom was in what could have been a fatal accident, that we fully realized that she's always been the heart of the Mannion clan."

"She's very different from her mother."

"As you Brits would say, they're as different as chalk and cheese. But Gram sincerely does have a good heart. And, as Mom said, she'll treat Piper like family. Because our daughter is now officially one of us."

"Will all five siblings, spouses, and children be coming to Thanksgiving dinner?"

"Yep. Along with my dad's Uncle Mike, who's engaged to Gloria Wells. She's the mother of Jolene, who's married to my brother Aiden, who's chief of police. He usually doesn't stay all that long, because a lot of people tend to over imbibe on holidays, so he's out there with his officers, watching for drunk drivers. And, of course, it wouldn't be Thanksgiving without all the holiday orphans, people who might be spending the holiday alone, that Mom rounds up. Plus your occasional family arguments over football games or politics that require some outside diplomatic intervention."

He glanced over at her. "Hey, maybe you should do a ride-along with Aiden. He spent some time as a police negotiator. You've probably learned a lot about negotiation in all your years as an interpreter. You two could share stories."

"You are joking about the ride-along, right?"

"Yeah. But it's a fun idea. I'll bet your accent would stop people from shouting at each other. Or hey, maybe you could speak in Japanese. That'd be something to watch."

He turned onto the road leading back to town. At the crossroads where his mother could have lost her life, he wondered how long it'd take before he'd quit having that knee-jerk flash dread. "Last year, when Burke came home, was the first time we were all together. And this year, you and your husband will be part of the crowd."

"Is that going to bother you?" she asked. "Having David here?"

"He's the only father Piper's known. Of course he needs to share in the family celebration. Besides, he and my dad will probably get along great."

"He makes a delicious holiday mince pie with brandy butter we could bring if you'd allow him to use your pub kitchen."

"Sure. We're closed on Thanksgiving, so staff can be with their families. So, the guy bakes, too?"

"He not only bakes, having grown up working in his family's restaurant, he's our usual cook," Fiona said.

"Lucky you."

"Lucky me," she agreed, and the warmth in her tone told Quinn that their marriage wasn't just one of similar interests, but of love. Which meant that while his daughter's life growing up would have been the polar opposite of the childhood he'd known, she'd been well loved. And for that, he was reluctantly grateful to David Lowell.

"It's going to work out," he said. "This shared custody thing. For all of us."

She met his eyes for the brief moment he took his off the road. "I hadn't believed that when I got on the plane at La Guardia. Or landed at SeaTac. And, all the way driving here from Seattle, I was expecting a battle royal."

"I told you, I don't do drama."

"But you could have frozen me out. And I couldn't have blamed you."

When the first of the three traffic lights in town turned red, he looked over at her. "You and I made a child together, Fiona. A beautiful, intelligent, kind, generous, sweet girl who's everything anyone could want in a child. You and your husband raised her, but just like on those ancestry search TV shows, our genes came together that week and created a girl named Piper. You could not have given me a more wonderful gift. Albeit a bit late," he tacked on as she began to tear up again. "But I remember, during those few times we'd actually be able to get a reservation for dinner, your sense of time always had us running late."

"I've improved," she assured him.

"Good thing. These days, you spending that extra twenty minutes putting hot rollers in your hair could have the power to bring down governments."

She laughed, as he'd meant her to. "It's going to work out," she repeated what he'd stated.

"Absolutely," he agreed. "And this Thanksgiving, there'll be even more for all of us to be grateful for."

This time, they went into the gatehouse together. By now, Quinn suspected, Seth was there to stand by his wife in case anything got out of hand between Fiona and Brianna or even mother and daughter. Either they'd finished their quilt arranging or taken a break because all were sitting in the cozy living room.

After introducing Fiona to his sister and brother-in-law, Quinn turned to Piper, who, while appearing nervous to have them all together, was no longer looking as she had in the pub earlier, when it looked as if they could be approaching full teenage meltdown.

"Everything went well," Quinn told her. "You're now an official member of the Mannion family, which everyone is happy about."

"And you're still a Lowell," Fiona said. Brianna, who'd been sitting beside Piper on a love seat, had moved over to the couch beside Seth so mother and daughter could sit beside each other. "I've decided that your idea about going to school here is a good idea. And although I know you're more capable than most people your age, I'll have to admit that your father—" she paused and looked at Quinn, who gave her a continue-on move of his hand "—and I'll feel more comfortable knowing that you'll have so many people, family members, to watch out for you."

Piper, who'd hadn't missed the silent exchange between the two turned to Quinn. "It feels strange asking this, because most kids of divorce know who their parents are, but what do I call you?"

"Whatever feels the most comfortable," he said. "I was wondering the same thing myself, and decided that you've had the same dad for sixteen some years, so it only makes sense to stick with that. Because he's earned it." Because he was trying to stay positive about all this, Quinn didn't mention that he would have, too, if he'd been given the opportunity. "We've been doing pretty well with you calling me by my name, so what would you say to sticking with that?"

Watching her brow furrow as she put a thumb to her chin again while pondering that, Quinn exchanged a quick look with Brianna, who'd nailed it. "That works for me." Another thought occurred to her. "Is everyone going to know you're my birth father?"

"That's up to you. The family will keep it quiet, if you'd prefer. But, as you've already figured out, once anyone outside the immediate circle finds out, it'll be all over town."

"Would you mind?"

"Although I didn't have anything to do with the young woman you've grown up to be—" this look he exchanged with Fiona "—I'd be happy for people to know that you're my daughter."

Her brow cleared and she smiled. "I'd be happy, too," she said. "I've wondered about you for as long as I can remember, even made up stories about who you might be. And now that I finally found you and have gotten to know you, and the rest of the family, you're all even better than any of my fictional families." She turned toward Fiona and put her hand on hers. "But I'm also happy to be a Lowell, Mum. Because you've both been an inspiration to me."

"Well." Fiona was tearing up yet again. "That's a wonderful thing to hear. Especially when I was expecting you to tell me you hated me."

"I might have, when I was younger," Piper said honestly. "When all I could focus on would be the lie you told that changed my life. And I'll never know how things would have turned out if you had told Quinn the truth, and maybe you'd have gotten married, or worked out some sort of joint custody deal, but if I hadn't traveled the world with you and Dad,

I might not have found my life's calling. So, I guess everything worked out as it was supposed to."

She turned back to Quinn. "But I still wish that I hadn't missed all those years with you and your family."

"We've plenty of time to catch up," Quinn assured her. "Have you ever been to Nepal?"

"No."

"My dad was there for the Peace Corps after college. He has a lot of great stories he loves to share. And he's often talked about going back some day. Especially to show my mom—your other grandmother—the village he lived in for two years. Maybe we should plan a family trip there."

Her Mannion blue eyes widened. "Really?"

It was an impulsive idea, which wasn't at all typical for him, but as soon as he'd said it, Quinn realized it had been tickling at the back of his mind since their visit to the farm when his mom and dad had been sharing their story.

"That would be brilliant!"

Watching her face light up with pleasure, Quinn realized that, if he'd had to miss out on his daughter's early years, at least he'd been gifted this time, when she was on the brink of becoming a woman. He had a feeling the next two years, while she attended CCC, could be both fascinating and frightening and was grateful that he'd have his mom, sister, and Amanda for backup and insight into the female mind.

After it was settled that Fiona and Piper would be spending the rest of the day and night before Fiona had to head back to Seattle for her return to New York, Quinn dropped them off at the pub, then, with one more thing to take care of in a seemingly endless day, he called Amanda to let her know that he was on his way to her house.

CHAPTER NINETEEN

ALTHOUGH QUINN FELT as if he'd just gone ten rounds with Evander Holyfield in the boxer's prime, he dragged himself up to Amanda's front door. It had been a brutal day, and he'd managed to tamp down all his conflicting feelings in order to not make the situation worse for Piper.

But now, myriad churning emotions—shock, anger, fear of not knowing how to be a father, frustration that he'd lost all those years, and guilt that if he'd only stayed in contact with Fiona after that week, she might have told him about her pregnancy—had him feeling on the verge of imploding, like a skyscraper collapsing in on itself.

From their conversation, rationally, he realized that even if he had proposed marriage, Fiona would have turned him down, but he still could have been in his daughter's life. Piper could have visited the farm some of those times her parents had been in danger zones. She would have had grandparents, great-grandparents, uncles, and an aunt. A large family that would have embraced her as their own. As his parents, grandparents, sister, and brother-in-law had already done. And he knew the others would too.

But she was on the verge of womanhood, so surely the parental dynamics would be entirely different, wouldn't they? It wasn't as if he was going to have pretend tea parties like he did with Kylee and Mai's Emma. Or the way he played board games with Hailey and had Hannah beating him at chess, because it turned out that making money and building boats wasn't the only thing Gabe was an expert at. He'd started teaching his teenage daughter chess back when he and Chelsea were first dating and now she played like a grand master Quinn had yet to beat.

"Hi!" Amanda's warm, welcoming smile faded as she saw his face after opening the door. Apparently he looked as beat-up as he felt.

"What's wrong?" She put her arm around him and led him into the house she'd rented after leaving her former husband. It looked as if it had been furnished from Goodwill castoffs, or that Seattle furniture warehouse whose commercials always came blaring onto the TV during breaks in sportscasts. A desk in a corner of the room held a tidy stack of manila folders, and a jar of mechanical pencils. He'd learned, while she'd been drawing up his patio plan, that she preferred doing it the old-fashioned way, putting her vision on paper, rather than defaulting to the computer.

What brought the room to life, Quinn considered, were all the plants on every flat space, taller ones standing in pots, others hanging from wall brackets, their green leaves trailing. Here and there flowers added color to the boring wall color that couldn't decide if it was gray or beige. Taupe, he remembered his mother calling it, as she'd whipped through paint color chips while redecorating the house he'd bought when he'd been ready to move from the pub apartment. Where Piper—his daughter!—was currently living.

"You said it was a family thing. Is someone hurt?"

"No." He shoved his hands through his hair, then suddenly thought of all the times Piper had combed her left hand through her coppery curls. "Everyone's fine." Effing dandy. He drew in a deep, painful breath. "Do you have anything to drink?"

"I have wine I bought to go with the pesto pasta. It's my special chardonnay you first served me. But you look as if you need something stronger. I do have a bottle of what I'm told is excellent whiskey one of my wealthier clients gave me after I finished the landscaping at his house."

"That'll do."

"Good." Her eyes revealed concern. "I haven't opened it, but I'll get it. Why don't you sit down and relax from whatever it is you've been through today."

"Thanks." He sank down onto her rental sofa with its lumpy cushions, and tried to pull himself out of the dark cloud of miasma that had crashed down on him once he'd left Piper and Fiona at the pub.

Despite knowing that it was the right thing to do and he'd gone along with the idea, Quinn damn sure wasn't looking forward to Thanksgiving, when Piper would be united with her dad again. Like they were all one big happy family. Despite staying here to go to school, that didn't mean that they'd automatically manage to bond as father and daughter as Gabe had with his and Chelsea's adopted children, because this was very different.

Hailey and Hannah were younger and hadn't had any other father figure—especially one who just happened to be an international trade ambassador—standing in the way. Claiming a right that could have—*should* have—been his.

"Shit," he muttered, just as Amanda returned with a tray holding two coasters, a wine bottle, two glasses—one for wine, and another that looked like a juice glass—a container of ice, and the bottle of Kentucky bourbon she'd been gifted, which he recognized as one that went for over a hundred dollars retail. He never stocked it because even buying wholesale, he'd have to price it above most Honeymoon Harbor budgets.

"I'm sorry. Don't you like it?"

"No, *I'm* sorry. It's great. I was thinking of something else." He blew out a breath. "It's just been a helluva day."

"I'm sorry," she repeated. "Do you want to talk about it?"

"No." What he'd like to do is take her to bed and lose himself in her smooth, silky body. And stay there forever. "But we need to."

"Okay." She opened the bottle. "I didn't know if you like ice or not."

"I'll take it neat."

"Okay." She poured three fingers into the glass, then, after he'd lifted his hand, holding up a space between his thumb and index finger, added another. "If you still want dinner, it can wait," she said. "As I said when you called, the pesto's made. I also tossed a salad, and boiling the boxed pasta only takes a few minutes. However, if you're not hungry—"

"It sounds perfect. I think I will wait awhile, though, if you don't mind. I've got a pretty big emotional Band-Aid to yank off."

"Okay." Now it was her who was sticking to short responses. He wondered what she'd say when she heard the whole story of that week with another woman. Not the whole story, he decided. He'd better leave out the flamenco-dancing part.

"It turns out I have a daughter."

"Okay," she repeated, then waved her hand, as if brushing the response away. "I'm sorry, I seem stuck on that word because you've caught me off guard and I'm not sure of the best thing to say. How old is she?"

"Eighteen."

"Wow. That must have been a surprise." Then before he could answer, her eyes widened. "Oh my God. Don't tell me your surprise daughter is Piper?"

"Got it in one." Even knowing that all the work and time that had gone into making the top-shelf whisky she'd served him deserved serious and thoughtful sipping, he tossed it back and held out his glass. Although she looked concerned, she poured a bit more in. "I'm not going to get drunk and pass out on you," he assured her.

"I'm not thinking you would," she said. Though she didn't look all that certain. Which made two of them.

"Did Piper tell you?"

"No. Her mother showed up at the pub."

"Oh." She took a sip of the chardonnay. "The British UN interpreter?"

"That would be her. How did you know?"

"Piper and I talked about her life a bit as we planted the herbs."

"When I knew her, we were both going to school. I was studying abroad at University College, Oxford, and she was at Cambridge. We met in Barcelona during Easter break."

"And had a holiday affair." She stared down into the straw-colored wine, then took another, longer drink before meeting his eyes. "Was she the one? The woman you thought you might have a future with?"

"Yeah." He put the glass down, deciding that he was risking enough here. Getting drunk while talking about a woman from his past, one who'd given birth to his secret child, wouldn't help make his case that in contrast to her ex, he'd be a good and steady husband. "Like I said, and she and I both agreed today, any marriage wouldn't have lasted a year. We each wanted a different life and even if one of us had compromised, neither would've been happy."

"But you wouldn't have had to marry her to be in your daughter's life."

"Once again, you and I are in total agreement. She had her reasons, that I'm willing—or better yet, forced—to accept, because I don't have a choice. Or a time machine... And why are you smiling?"

"You've no idea how many times I've wished I had one of those."

Quinn thought back on what she'd told him about her early life. Compared it to his growing up. And worse, how she'd survived a dangerous hellscape of a marriage. "Damn, I'm sorry. I'm being selfishly narcissistic."

"You're being human. And, I suppose, angry."

"I am." Quinn had experienced true anger very few times in his life. When one of his high school debate teammates cheated during the state finals, which had gotten the entire team disqualified, putting Quinn's much-needed scholarship at risk; when that same guy had taken Brianna's Halloween candy; when Seth had broken Bri's heart by breaking up with her; and, more recently, whenever he thought about those bruises on Amanda's soft flesh. Today's revelation had been added to that list.

She smoothed her hand over his shoulder, her long, slender fingers massaging muscles that had bunched into boulders. "Yet you didn't let it out because you didn't want to hurt Piper. Because you wouldn't want her to think that you were at all unhappy to learn that she was your daughter."

"Bull's-eye." He rubbed the heels of his hands against his eyes. Just a few hours ago, he'd been filled with energy and anticipation of a day on the water. Now he felt not just angry, but drained. The conflicting emotions battering away at him were proving exhausting.

"I have an idea," she said quietly.

He lowered his hands to his lap, resisted picking up that glass again, and met her gaze, which revealed both caring and concern. She was, he thought, like an anchor in the midst of the emotional storm that had swept him off his moorings.

"Why don't you tell me the entire story from the start? Or, as much as you wish, without sharing personal details about that week in Barcelona I'd honestly prefer not knowing." She paused. "Unless you still have strong feelings for her?"

"None." He shook his head. "We talked about it and decided that although we'd both moved on, for Piper's sake, we need to work out some sort of friendship. But if you're wondering if I'm the least bit attracted to her, the answer would be a definite no. Why would I be, when I'm head-over-heels in love with you?"

She looked down into her wineglass for another long moment. Then lifted her gaze. "You just said the L-word."

"Yeah. I did. It's been something I've wanted to say for a very long time. Does it scare you?"

"Not at all. On the contrary, I'm vastly relieved. Because I didn't want to pressure you by being the first to bring it up. Because I've been so hesitant, Brianna and Chelsea both advised me to spring it on you while you were loose and well sated from some hot sex. But that seemed as if I'd be taking advantage of you. As if you'd feel the need to say it back."

Quinn barked a short laugh, surprising himself with the ability to find some humor on a day when his well-planned, comfortable life had, out of the blue, turned upside down. "Sweetheart, feel free to take advantage of me anytime you want."

Her smile lit up her eyes in a way that had those dark clouds that had been looming in his mind disintegrating like morning fog beneath a summer sun. "I originally had every intention of doing that," she said. "After dinner." She snuggled up against him, lifting her face to his. "But I'm thinking that perhaps, since it only takes a few minutes to prepare and it's still early, we could have dessert first again. Like we did at the coast house."

"Sweetheart, you just saved my day." Lowering his mouth to hers, he savored the sweet taste of wine and this generous, exceptional woman he loved.

She stood up, took his hand, and led him into her bedroom. The first time she'd invited him in here, he'd noticed a distinct difference from the living room/office. The walls were a soft and soothing sea glass blue-green, much like his mother had used in Jolene and Gloria's Thairapy, where he got his hair cut.

There were white candles in cut crystal jars, and large framed photos of flowers, some downright erotic. What he knew to be an original by his uncle Mike, who had a habit of giving his art away to friends, was an oversized painting of the Sequim lavender fields above a lacey white iron four-poster bed covered in varying shades of white, along with an array of those throw pillows women seemed addicted to.

In the corner of the room was a full-length mirror,

the white iron frame matching the bed. The dresser was a lightly finished knotty pine, as was the low chest at the end of the bed, and a white iron chandelier in the center of the room dripped with crystals and held lamps that looked like candles. This room was where the strong, capable woman who worked all day alongside brawny men digging in the loam and dirt of the area's soil, carrying heavy pots of plants and even trees, stacking stone walls, had embraced her most feminine side. Knowing that she'd moved into the rental after leaving her husband, Quinn realized that he'd been the first—and hopefully the last—man to have been invited into her private sanctuary.

And that's exactly what it felt like tonight. A sanctuary, a world separate from the outside, where someone from your past could show up from out of the blue and throw a grenade into your well-ordered life. A haven that smelled like the lavender fields hanging on the wall. The first time he'd been in here, he'd carried her in and laid her on the bed, then he'd gone around the room, igniting the candles with the lighter atop the dresser.

"Stay right here," she said, stopping beside the bed. This time it was she who lit the candles. Then she returned to him, twined her arms around his neck and kissed him, her lips warm and silky as she fit her slender curves against him. Despite her toned muscles, she was soft in all the right places. As her breasts pressed against his chest, he wanted to touch. To taste. To lose himself in her.

"Let it go," she murmured against his mouth, as if reading his mind. "Let me love you."

She began unbuttoning his shirt, first touching a kiss, then licking each new bit of skin she revealed. When she got to the buckle of his leather belt, he reached for her, but she placed a hand on his chest. "Don't move," she instructed, her voice throaty, but firm. "For now, I just want you to feel, to concentrate on yourself for a change."

At this moment, in this room fragrant with the scent of flowers, there was nothing she could ask of him that he would not do. Memories of the events of the day seemed to fade as anticipation rose.

She tugged the shirt free of his jeans, finished off the last buttons, touching her lips and tongue to his skin. Then pushed the shirt off his shoulders, where it landed on her slate gray wood plank floor. Then she unbuckled his belt and, leaving it open, knelt down in front of him.

"Those shoes have to go." He sensed where she was going with this, and thought how he'd never, in his thirty-plus years, been buck-assed naked in front of a woman, who was, so far, still fully clothed. He did as instructed, stepping out of the boat shoes he'd worn for the trip they'd never gotten to.

"Have you ever had your toes sucked?" she asked as she pulled his jeans down his legs, her lips following the trail of denim the same way they had while taking off his shirt.

"No." He'd done it on occasion to women who'd gotten off on it during foot rubs, but never experienced a role reversal like the one she was treating him to.

"Hmm," she murmured against the inside of his thigh after having had him step out of his jeans, "It'd be a first for me too. But maybe we'll try it. Later." She rocked back on her heels, looking up at him in a pair of red boxer briefs. "Looks as if you had a hot date in mind when you got dressed this morning."

They'd been one of a multicolored set he'd bought online and the first pair he'd grabbed that morning, but a hot date had, indeed, been foremost in his mind. Until Fiona Jones had blown his plans to spend the day enjoying some hot boat sex.

"I like them." She leaned forward, pressed her mouth against the cotton placket of the briefs and softly blew. Quinn's resultant groan was a mix of pleasure and painful need.

"You're not allowed to touch," she said as she dispensed with them. "Not yet."

Quinn was accustomed to being in control. Not just in life and his career, but in bed. Even when women were on top, they'd always encouraged him to set the pace. Amanda was like no other woman he'd ever been with and as her hands and mouth worked their way back up to his lips, bypassing the erection that was aching for her touch, kissing his abs, circling his nipples—which he'd never before given much thought to—with her tongue, before nipping at his jaw—he'd never needed a woman more.

She rose, evading his attempt to touch, tossed the

pillows onto the floor and turned back the snowy coverlet. "Lie down," she said. "On your stomach."

His erection was now as stiff and erect as a flag pole. "You do realize that I could break something we're both going to regret," he said, nevertheless following her instructions. The sheets were fresh and scented with that mix of sunshine and saltwater that came from having been dried outdoors.

"I wouldn't let you do that," she said. "It would be the metaphorical equivalent of cutting off my nose to spite my face. I'm only asking you to trust me to pleasure you the way I trusted you at the coast house. I promise you'll feel better afterward."

"I'm feeling pretty damn good now. Maybe we could just—"

"Not yet," she said on a light laugh that let him know that she was well aware he was ready to finish this round off. More than ready. "Close your eyes."

He closed them, which didn't help, because memories of their other lovemaking sessions were flashing through his mind, increasing the ache. He heard the rustling of clothing, followed by bare feet moving across the floor and a soft new age instrumental began playing from hidden speakers.

And then she was back, straddling him, rubbing an oil she'd warmed with her hands across his back.

"What's that scent?" He was going to smell like flowers, but Quinn decided having her sit on him that way was worth it.

"Jasmine. It's one of Jolene's oils. It alleviates stress and anxiety, which helps your body to unwind." He moaned a complaint as she climbed off him, so she could run the oil over the backs of his thighs, his calves, and massage his feet. "It's also an aphrodisiac, heightening sexual desire."

"I sure as hell don't need any flower to heighten my sexual desire for you." And although she may have eased his stress, he now had another more pressing need. "I don't know how much longer I can last if you keep this up."

"So much for your famous reputation for control," she teased, skimming her tongue from his butt up his spine. "I promise to keep this our secret." She went up on her knees. "You can turn over again."

He didn't waste any time following those instructions.

Sometime, when his eyes had been closed, she'd taken a condom from the bedside table drawer and with agonizing slowness, she rolled it over his erection. With her knees on either side of his thighs, she climbed on top, demonstrating a boldness that showed that she'd moved far past her initial fears. Rising up enough for him to once again admire those well-toned legs, she slowly, teasingly, lowered herself onto Quinn, revealing that she'd been close to the brink herself as a shuddering sigh of pleasure escaped those succulent lips he knew he'd never get enough of.

Her head fell back, tawny brown hair tumbling down her back as she began to ride him. Her skin flushed a rosy tone, and her nipples darkened to the hue of ripened berries. As he cupped her pert breasts with his hands, he decided that, having remained atypically submissive, he was entitled to one request. No, he decided, one demand.

"Amanda."

She paused. Her eyes, which had been closed, immediately flew open. There was a flash of nerves, come and gone so quickly, if he hadn't been watching her closely, he wouldn't have noticed. "Keep your eyes on mine," he said quietly. Reassuringly. "I want to share everything with you when we come. Together."

She bit her lip. Then nodded. "Me too," she agreed on a murmur.

She began to move again, her breath becoming short and ragged as she neared orgasm. Grasping her hips, he thrust upward as she came down, matching her movements, their bodies coming together as one, hers contracted around his. When he felt her on the precipice, he flicked his thumb over her swollen nub and was rewarded by her gasps. A second later, she cried out with the force of her climax, as Quinn gave into his own release.

She collapsed onto him, breathing heavily. "Oh. Wow. I may never move again,"

He stroked a hand down her damp back with one hand, while the other played in her hair. "That works for me. Just give me a second." Loathe to leave the bed, he went into the adjoining bath, disposed of the condom, then returned to bed, and drew her close, one leg over hers, so their bodies were still touching, chest to thigh. "I love you, Amanda."

More than he'd ever thought possible. He was aware that some couples were fortunate enough to have that lifetime soulmate bond. He'd just never been all that certain it was in the cards for him. He'd joked about having all the best words, but there were not enough words to describe how he felt at this moment.

"I love you too." She snuggled closer.

He knew that to be true. Yet he also knew that even with therapy, PTSD was like a virus once it got in your head. He couldn't expect her to not have moments when she'd find herself back in her past. And though he'd given her time, he decided it was time to move to the next stage of his plan.

"I want you to think about moving in with me," he said.

She lifted her head. "Move in with you? At the lake?"

"Call me selfish, but I want more time." They needed more than just a few hours and one full day a week. "Right now, we're just dating. Which, don't get me wrong, is great. I love it. But I want to go to sleep with you. Wake up with you. I want to welcome you when you get home from work."

"Which is your busiest time," she pointed out.

"Okay. You've got me there. But when I was trying to get up the nerve to ask you out, Bri told me to quit acting like high school. That I was too old to give you my class ring and go steady. It dawned on me today, after leaving the chaos that my life has become, that I don't know what I would've done without you to come to."

"I'll always be there for you," she said softly, framing his face and pressing her lips against his.

"I know that. But we're still living separate lives."

"So do people living together. Even your father and mother have separate lives outside their marriage and home."

"That's my point. They have a home." He purposefully left out the part about marriage, not sure she'd reached that point yet.

"I want to be ready," she said. "Seriously. But this—" she waved here hand around the room "—is the first time in many years I've had my own space. Been able to discover who I am. And what I want. And I know I want *you*, but—"

"I'm not asking you to marry me, Amanda. Not yet, anyway. I get your reasons for not being ready, or perhaps you'll never want to. But I want us to be a couple. And, as for this—" it was his turn for a wave to encompass the ultrafeminine room "—we can create a sanctuary for you at the lake. You can even put a sign on the door: No Boys Allowed."

Despite the seriousness of the topic, she laughed. "Like that treehouse you told me you and your brothers built with the No Girls Allowed sign Brianna made you take down?"

He smiled back at her. "Like that… Here's a suggestion. You've got to go to that conference tomorrow, right?"

She nodded. "In DC. I'm speaking on planning native landscapes and public places during a period of climate change."

"This wouldn't be a good time to change beds for me, either. Because Seth is doing some remodeling for me and the place is filled with workmen and noise. I just wanted to put the idea on the table. Why don't you give it some thought, even though I understand that you won't have a lot of time while you're concentrating on teaching people ways to save the planet. Because I love you and want more than nights and Mondays. As good as those are."

She was returning Sunday night. He'd pick her up at SeaTac and bring her back to her house. The next day, they'd be taking a ferry ride to Victoria's Butchart Gardens, ranked by many—including the *National Geographic*—as one of the top display gardens in the world.

"I promise that I'll do that," she agreed. "It's not that I don't want to be with you—"

"I get it," he assured her. Having spoken at length with Aiden about his own former bouts with PTSD, Quinn really did. As much as anyone not plagued with it could. She'd created a safe place. He could understand her reluctance to leave it. "And if you decide you want to stay here, that'll work for me too."

Because it would be pressure she wouldn't need, he didn't mention that rents were skyrocketing in the state, even in this part, now that so many people were working from home, and since she didn't have a lease, she could find herself out on the street if the development company that had scooped up a bunch of houses on the peninsula at discount prices had someone willing to pay more. Besides, he wouldn't

want her to move in with him because she had to.
But because she wanted to.

Soon. He promised himself.

CHAPTER TWENTY

QUINN MISSED HER. And not just at night, but during the day, when he knew that at any moment he could walk down to her nursery, or drop by a jobsite with one of the mocha lattes she liked from Cops and Coffee. There had been times when he'd been able to steal her away for a late lunch break on one of the town's beaches. He'd even gone to Leaf for dinner and eaten a grilled mushroom that he'd been promised could rival that steak he'd been thinking about all day. Newsflash: no mushroom could top a dry-aged, well-marbled grilled rib eye.

If that hadn't been bad enough, Mildred Mayhew had been seated at the next table and a photo of him eating a salad garnished with peppery-tasting orange flowers Amanda had told him were nasturtiums had accompanied Mildred's lead story in her "Seen Around Town" column. Suggesting that only love could have the same man who had tourists and locals alike lining up for his baby back ribs giving up red meat for posies was costing him a shitload of ragging from his brothers and brother-in-law, who were seated at the bar, plowing through orders of wings and ribs with coleslaw and fries.

"The last Mannion is finally falling," Gabe said.

"Eating flowers in public is a sure sign he's down for the count," Burke agreed.

"Oh, he's long past that," Seth said. Then began filling them in on the work Quinn had him doing on his lake house.

"That's supposed to be a damn secret," Quinn growled.

"Chelsea said Amanda's out of town," Gabe pointed out. "Your secret is safe with us."

"She's in Washington, DC, not Mars." Quinn looked around for Mable or some other loud-mouthed local, and except for Magnus, who was in his usual spot at the end of the bar enjoying his daily draft, and Piper, who'd come over with a bar ticket for the party at a four-top, the only people in the place were tourists.

"It's going to be so cool!" Piper said. "There's no way that won't win her over." She clipped the meal tickets in Jarle's window. "I had the strangest thought this morning," she said, as he poured a pinot gris and a summery rosé into two wine glasses.

"What's that?" he asked as he drew two drafts—one Surfin' Safari and a Surfin' USA.

"When you two get married, Amanda's going to be my stepmum."

"I suppose that's true," he said.

"Do you think she'll think of it that way? Or will I just be the kid whose birth dad married her?"

"We haven't discussed marriage yet," he said. "But I know she'd love being your stepmom."

Her young face cleared. "That's great. Because

I really, really like her." Quinn watched her eyes brighten. "Then she'll be a Mannion too."

"Like I said, the topic hasn't come up." Instead of having her deliver the drinks, Quinn grabbed the tray and headed over to the table to escape the conversation that was getting far too personal for his liking.

When he was back, the topic had changed to the game on TV, and whether the Mariners were going to break a seven–seven tie against the Yankees. Since they were in the seventh inning stretch, the conversation then switched to the worst and best Mariners promotions. "I'm still going for potting soil night as the worst," Seth said.

"Amanda would probably disagree with that," Quinn answered as he took an appetizer order from the window for Piper to deliver to one of the riser tables.

"Gotta be that green knit hat with the weird beard attached," Burke argued.

"You're both wrong," Gabe said. "It was the Edgar Martinez Chia Head giveaway a few years ago to celebrate him getting inducted into the Baseball Hall of Fame."

"For the win," Magnus called from down the bar. "Though, I gave mine to my great-grandkid, who thought it was cool. Until his cat ate it and cost his parents a trip to the vet because apparently those chia seeds really swell up."

The conversation, as ridiculous as it was, sure beat his previous life spent reviewing pages and pages of documents. Then suffering through countless boring hours in meetings and on the phone talking about those documents. Finally filing the papers related to the documents. The way Quinn saw it, if they ever made a TV show about what lawyers really did for a living, all those people who went to law school to be like Bull, or the characters on *Suits*, or *Law & Order*, or, for the more socially conscious, Atticus Finch, would immediately change their majors. It crossed his mind that he should've paid more attention to *Cheers*.

That night, instead of going over to Amanda's house after closing, he went home. He'd never before noticed how lonely it could be. The place, he thought, as he turned on some Thelonious Monk while checking out the progress Seth's crew had made that day, was as lonely as a mausoleum.

If he were at Amanda's house tonight, he'd tell her about the promo conversation, which would make her laugh, and surely defend potting soil night. She'd show him plants for a new project, flipping through photos of the ones she was using, and describing others; he'd nod at everything, not knowing what half the plants she was talking about were, but it was just hearing her talk, watching her hands move with her words, looking forward to later, when he'd feel those graceful hands moving over his body, that he missed.

The next morning, in his admittedly extravagant bathroom, he imagined himself in her much smaller one and could've sworn he could smell her shampoo, foamy body soap, and that fragrant green gel that she'd once, going down on her knees in front of him beneath the stream of hot water, having him expect something entirely different, rubbed into his thighs, laughing when he complained how it felt like sandpaper on his skin.

"It's exfoliating gel," she said, still laughing as she'd stood back up, then wrapped her arms around his neck. "You have no idea how much trouble we women go to for you men."

"For us men? Did you not use that before we got together?" He knew she had because the first night he'd been in her shower, he'd noticed the jar was half empty.

"I did." She'd pressed against him, chest to chest, thigh to thigh, and those achy, needy parts in between. "But it's a lot better having someone to appreciate it."

She'd backed up and there'd been a gleam in her eyes as she followed the dusting of dark hair bisecting his torso. Calling it his happy trail, she'd kissed and licked her way down until giving him a BJ that nearly brought him to his knees. Laughing again, she'd stood back up, brushed her lips against his, and told him that maybe next time she could introduce him to body waxing.

He'd laughed more since they'd been together than he could remember laughing for a very long time. He'd had better sex with Amanda than he'd known was possible. Sex that made his time in Barcelona seem like fumbling around in a car's back seat in high school. Which, admittedly, he'd done his share of. But this was different. Even if Fiona was right about them connecting in more ways than merely sex, their hearts hadn't been involved. If hers had been, she would have called him. If *his* heart had been, he would've called her. Or visited. They'd been, after all, only about an hour and a half apart. While his father had managed to fly cross-country to be with his mom at that same age. Because their hearts had entwined when they'd been young and nothing and no one on earth could ever break that bond.

Which was what Quinn had known he'd always wanted. And now that Amanda was not just in his thoughts, but imbedded deep in his heart, he was feeling hopeful. After getting dressed and checking out the work that was nearly completed, he blew out a long breath. She loved him. She knew he loved her. But, he worried, would love be enough?

Recently, while over at Gabe and Chelsea's, his brother and eldest chess-hustling niece, Hannah, had talked him into playing *Elden Ring*, a video game set in a world created by fantasy writer George R.R. Martin. Although Quinn didn't understand all the details, it involved characters on a journey to repair the Elden Ring and become the new Elden Lord. It involved magic spells, lots of weaponry, horseback riding, and other adventurous events in the collecting of many all-important talismans. He did not survive the quest long, being brutally killed by something called a Dark Moon Greatsword, wielded by his über-competitive teenage niece.

But this was no game. It was real life in the real world.

"You can do this," Quinn assured himself. For the first time in his life, instead of being pissed off by all the years of ragging he'd gotten from his brothers about being the "perfect" overachieving big brother, he now viewed that family reputation as a talisman.

"You *will* do this."

AMANDA MISSED QUINN. Terribly. She'd kept her phone on vibrate the entire time that she was in DC, not wanting to disrupt any of the workshops she'd attended, but couldn't stop herself from checking for texts.

One of the advantages of her career choice was that it didn't depend on tourists. As she'd told Piper the night before the Mannions' barbecue, she did keep a few loose flowers on hand for arrangements that people might buy when the farmer's market— where Jim Olson, from Blue House Farm, kept a booth—was closed.

Every season, there were tourist couples in need of last-minute bouquets. People who'd been living together quite happily, some for years, who'd come to the Pacific Northwest on vacation and suddenly get caught up in the wedding season, impulsively deciding to make their relationship official. But generally, she was either working in her office, creating plans that were similar to construction blueprints for a client, or out supervising her landscaping crew, often working alongside them, because she loved the hands-on part of her work as much as she did the designing.

Being her own boss, Amanda kept Wheel and Barrow open on weekends and was closed to the public on Mondays.

Since that night at the meteor shower, they'd had lunch at the Quinault Lodge in the park and explored the Hoh rainforest. She'd been there before, when she and Eric had first arrived in town, but she hadn't been back since his arrest and with Quinn taking her to see various ancient trees that were off the beaten path, she'd found it even more magical than before.

As an earnest young professor from Oregon State's College of Earth, Ocean, and Atmospheric Sciences showed charts and videos about strategies for mitigating the problematic urban heat island effect spreading cities and suburbs was having on orchards, produce, and berry farms, her mind flashed back to that Monday when Quinn had taken her out on his boat—a beautiful cruiser with a wide sleeping berth Gabe had built—for a picnic in a hidden cove that had ended up with him spending a long, leisurely time showing her a new use for the whipped cream Brianna had packed to go with the bowl of fresh summer peaches and local berries.

That first night, alone in her hotel room, not wanting to call him since she knew it was the pub's busy time, she realized how accustomed she'd become to their nightly lovemaking as she kept tossing and turning, missing listening to the soothing sound of his breathing, the warmth of his body as they spooned, the way, when needing her again, he'd wake her and make love so tenderly that in the morning, her sleep-hazed mind, which had been dreaming of him when awakened, often couldn't be sure if their lovemaking had actually happened or been part of her dream. The same type of dreams she had the second night at the hotel.

On the third day of the conference, as she stood at the far side of the stage waiting for the lengthy introduction to finally end, a latecomer entered the conference room, giving her a view to the dining room across the hall where servers were setting the tables for the noon awards luncheon. As one worker deftly snapped a white linen cloth onto a large circular wooden table, Amanda's mind flashed to a Monday date night at Luca's. She'd worn a silky red dress, another new purchase from the Dancing Deer, that hit at midthigh. As they'd sipped their predinner wine, sharing the events of their day, she'd felt his fingers slip beneath her skirt under the tablecloth and trace little designs on her knee. Then slowly, those wickedly seductive fingers began trailing up her thigh. She'd wondered how far he'd intended to go. Wondered too, how far she'd let him. Or if she'd even want him to stop.

With her father having been gone so much of the time, providing little to no parental control, Amanda could have grown up a wild child. But that incident with the thugs that had sent him to the hospital, which, in turn, had landed her at the police station, followed by her few days of homelessness, had taught her that following the rules, and keeping quiet and out of trouble, was an easier way to live.

She'd done her best to remain nearly invisible during college, dating occasionally, usually double dates set up by friends, but never seriously. And later, during her marriage to a man who could, in his mania, find fault in the most minor, often imagined offenses, Amanda had continued to strive to be a "good girl." But with Quinn, she felt safe enough, like that night in the restaurant, to embrace her newly discovered inner "naughty girl."

She'd never known exactly how naughty she might have allowed that night to get because, just as his fingers were inches from the lacey leg band of her panties, the waiter had arrived with their anti-pasto and the moment had passed. They spent the rest of the meal talking about ordinary date things: work, Piper who seemed to be accepting the change in her life with surprising teenage aplomb—and the upcoming wedding of his uncle and Jolene's mother. But beneath that casual conversation, there'd been a hum of sexual energy between them that had him taking her against the door as soon as they'd entered the house, not even making it to the lumpy rented sofa.

She realized that she'd made a mistake bringing along that dress, which she was wearing that day with a very professional black blazer, when it took her a moment to realize the woman introducing her had finally finished talking and the hushed room was waiting for her to speak.

As the week wore on, at night in her lonely hotel bed, her hands kept being tempted to wander places that would take the edge off her sexual need, but she didn't merely want release. She wanted one of those long, rolling orgasms, or the explosive ones that sent her flying, that only Quinn could create. Or those sharp, multiple climaxes that had her feeling as if she was shattering into pieces.

And so, she forced herself to wait, even though the hotel TV guide had an "adult" channel. After all, wouldn't that be all she'd need? Though, as the desire for Quinn built, the temptation to take care of her problem herself did, as well. But having experienced the real thing, she resisted, instead watching a team of lovely British people compete in a competition involving something called choux pastry that looked a lot like the cream-filled, chocolate-topped eclairs she'd get from the brawny guys at Cops and Coffee.

She'd watched a rom-com on the flight back to the West Coast, and while it had been reasonably tame, it had her yearning for Quinn in a different way than those restless nights in her lonely hotel room had. It wasn't only the mind-blowing sex she'd missed. But being with the man she loved. He wasn't the type of man who'd go into grand, romantic gestures to win a woman over, but even as he'd accused her of making him sound boring, to Amanda, his dependability, his unbending sense of right and wrong, his willingness to shoulder so many others' problems on those broad shoulders, and knowing that he'd be in her corner, whatever might happen in her life, was a love far deeper and more valuable than flashy diamonds, a room filled with hothouse flowers, or a surprise trip to a tropical island on a private jet, like in the movie she'd watched.

Which was why, when she saw him standing there, waiting for her at Seattle's SeaTac baggage carousel, she tossed all propriety to the winds and ran across to him, jumped into his arms, wrapped her legs around him, and kissed him. Right there in public, not caring who saw them, or what people might think, because all that mattered was being back with this man whose broad hands were holding her butt as he returned the kiss with an equal fervor. She was vaguely aware of more than one phone camera pointed their way, knew they could very well end up on TikTok or Instagram, but didn't care. Because she was back home. Not yet in Honeymoon Harbor, but in Quinn Mannion's arms. Where she belonged.

"I suspect we created a scene," he said, as they waited for her bag to come sliding down the chute.

"I know we did. I'm sorry."

He linked their fingers together and lifted her hand to his lips, pressing a kiss in the center of her palm, which, like so many other places on her body he'd discovered, she'd never realized could be an erogenous zone. "There's nothing to be sorry about. I do have to warn you about something, though."

"Oh?"

"Remember that night at Luca's?"

"Of course I do." She'd tell him later about how

the memory had caused the glitch in her carefully rehearsed presentation.

"By the time I get you back to your place, we'll be lucky to make it to the door like we did that night." His eyes were a deep blue flame as they looked down into hers.

Rather than take the ferry, they drove back to the peninsula, the sexual tension building as she told him about her conference, which, as important as the topics had been to her, undoubtedly sounded boring. In this case, that was a good thing, because the closer they got to Honeymoon Harbor, the more desperate Naughty Amanda was tempted to have him pull over to the side of the road and let her attack those damn five buttons again. Keeping them out of trouble, Good Amanda resisted.

When they finally reached her house, if parking hadn't been on the street, rather than some remote driveway like the one at Quinn's house, Amanda might have experienced her first car sex.

And wouldn't that make a banner headline on the Facebook page and Mildred's "Seen Around Town" column?

Instead, they'd managed—just barely—to make it inside the house. Their coupling had been fast and hard, and exactly what she'd needed. Later, after catching their breaths while collapsed on the floor, they finally stumbled into her bedroom sanctuary, where, having gotten the edge off, they spent a long, leisurely night making up for those lost days they'd been apart.

THE NEXT DAY, despite jet lag, and too little sleep, anticipation for their trip to Victoria had her waking early, and, for a welcome change, Quinn was still in her bed, lying on his side, propped up on one elbow, looking down at her.

"Good morning, Sleeping Beauty."

"Good morning, sweet talker." She loved Quinn for many things, but wouldn't have guessed, when she first started falling for him, that he'd turn out to be a romantic at heart. "How long have you been awake?"

"Long enough to come up with ideas as to what I wanted to do when you woke up." His hand brushed over her bare shoulder. His touch was light as a feather, which was all it ever took for her body to respond. Other body parts, which should have been exhausted from their reunion night sex marathon, were also stirring.

"We have a ferry to catch," she reminded him. "And reservations at the gardens."

"As much as I want to spend a long, leisurely time in the shower, you're right about the reservations. So, I was thinking that perhaps a morning quickie would be in order, given that I should be entitled to some celebration to mark this milestone of waking up in your bed. Of watching you dream." His long fingers skimmed along her collarbone, his thumb pausing where her heartbeat quickened at his slight touch. "Watch your skin flush." As if reading her mind, he drew down the sheet and caressed her breasts. "Were you dreaming of us? Together this way?"

She'd never been untruthful to Quinn. Not that she'd ever been tempted to be, but also because she knew that what people said was true. Somehow Quinn knew everything. But even were she to attempt to lie and say that she'd been dreaming of what plants to use in landscaping the summer home a new Seahawks tight end was building for his family, her body would give her away.

"That's all I dreamed of my entire time in DC," she said. "I was so missing you, I almost paid for an adult channel."

His lips had been creating havoc at the hollow of her throat until he lifted his head to look down at her. An ebony brow arched. "Did you?" A blue flame of desire flared in his eyes, even as he smiled at that idea.

"I said *almost*. Partly because the conference committee was paying for my room, and I didn't want that channel showing up on my bill. But also because I knew that it would've been a waste of money. Because after being with you, after us being together the way we are, how we fit—"

"As if we were created for one another," he finished her thought, drawing her against him.

"Exactly." She skimmed her nails lightly down his back. "How quick?"

"You're not the only one who was dreaming," he said, rolling over on top of her and fitting himself between her thighs. He was granite hard and every bit as ready as she was. "I suspect," he said, as he slid into her, back where he belonged, "we just might set a world land speed record."

CHAPTER TWENTY-ONE

QUINN WAS AT the stove, frying bacon, dressed in only Levis when Amanda entered the kitchen. How bad did she have it that she even found his bare feet sexy? Drinking in the sight of his tight butt and biceps, she decided, not for the first time in the past weeks, that she was the luckiest woman in Honeymoon Harbor. The state. Country. Planet. Because Quinn Mannion was hers.

Over the four glorious weeks since they'd first become lovers, he'd literally changed her life. Amanda found herself smiling during the days at work, even laughing during the nights they spent together. She'd never, ever, laughed while making love until these days, when her heart felt as light and buoyant as the iridescent soap bubbles Kyle and Mai's darling daughter, Emma, had been blowing from a plastic bottle at the Mannions' barbecue.

He turned the flame off from beneath the burner, came over, took her into his arms, touched his lips to hers, then put her a little away from him.

"I like that dress. It makes you look like you should be in a shampoo commercial, running through a meadow of flowers."

"Thank you. It's new." Although it wasn't her usual style, she'd snatched up the bright yellow floral print sundress the moment she'd seen it in the window of the Dancing Deer. Its ruched bust, fitted waist, and flared short, ruffled skirt made her feel cute. And sexy.

"You look so darling!" Dottie had exclaimed, clapping her hands when Amanda had come out of the dressing room. "Like summer."

"That shade works beautifully with your hair," Doris had said. "It brings out your natural highlights from working outdoors. If we'd realized you'd be interested in it, we'd have held it back and called you." Pointing out, not unkindly, Amanda had thought, how very different it was from the jeans or capri pants she usually wore. Thanking her for the compliment, she kept to herself that she'd been feeling recklessly romantic since Quinn's lovemaking had not only lived up to her fantasies, but overachiever that he was, had surpassed them.

Velvet's opinion had, unsurprisingly, been more to the point. "Quinn's toast. Maybe you should pick out your wedding dress now, so we don't accidentally sell it to some less deserving bride-to-be."

"Oh, we're not talking about any wedding," Amanda had replied. "Just, well, living in the moment."

"Good for you," Dottie had said. "I'm a firm believer in making the most of every moment."

"It's wise to take your time," Doris offered.

"FYI," Velvet had jumped back in, "unlike Thorn, who surprise proposed to me from the stage in the middle of a concert in Walla Walla, where his band, Savage Sasquatch, was performing, Quinn Mannion doesn't exactly seem like a live-in-the-moment type of guy. I'm betting that he'll propose before Labor Day."

"Oh! September is such a lovely time of year here," Dottie, the more romantic of the twin sisters, had enthused. "It's perfect for an outdoor afternoon wedding."

"I don't know anything about fashion." Quinn's voice dragged Amanda's mind back from that conversation in the Dancing Deer as he skimmed an index finger over one of her shoulders bared by the sundress's spaghetti straps. "But this somehow makes you look sweet and hot at the same time. And reveals just enough to make me want to explore more."

That wickedly clever finger trailed down to brush a featherlight touch along the crest of her breasts. The first time she'd undressed in front of him, that night at the coast house, she'd worried that he'd find her A cup breasts lacking, but his murmured comment as he'd palmed them, showing her how perfectly they fit in his hands, had alleviated that concern.

Having checked her weather app after a breakfast of bacon and scrambled eggs, she retrieved a sweater from the closet by the front door and they were on their way.

"I've wanted to go to the gardens since before we arrived here," she said on the way to the ferry terminal in Port Angeles. "But Eric didn't want to waste time looking at flowers, and afterward, well, I just never got around to it."

The entire truth was she'd have had no one to talk to about all the wonders she'd be seeing. And to be honest, while some clients liked to inject their opinions into her plans, especially when she was building an outdoor kitchen, other than juniper bushes and a handful of pine and fir trees, most men weren't all that interested in flowers and probably couldn't tell a rhododendron from a hydrangea.

"My parents took us a few times over the years when we were kids," he said. "Mom loves flowers, and Dad, as you discovered at the barbecue, lives and breathes horticulture, so it was always fun and there was always something new to see over the seasons."

"I read that the developer and her husband had moved from Ontario to build a cement plant. Then, after a few years, all the limestone was depleted, leaving a huge quarry."

"That's true. Mrs. Butchart envisioned reclaiming it as a garden and had topsoil brought in by horses and wagons to fill it, and thus was born the sunken garden. It's still there over a hundred years later."

"I can't wait to see it. She was truly a visionary."

"You probably would've been besties," he said. "I can easily see you creating gardens all over the peninsula if you had the chance."

"Aha. Just when I thought you had everything figured out about me, you're wrong. I'd never try to compete with the diversity of Mother Nature. This peninsula has over fifteen hundred species. Over a hundred are listed as rare and nine are only found here.

"We have salt marshes, bogs, stunning mountain meadows, tundra-like alpine, all within old-growth forests which represent several species of record-sized trees. Like your father, I love this place with a passion and even during the bad times, there were still mornings when I'd wake up and feel as if I'd landed in Nirvana.

"So… I'm just going to enjoy all the wonder this part of the planet has been gifted with, joining with those who are working and fighting to save it, and keep my focus on making home yards and public spaces more beautiful and sustainable. That and making people happy."

"You make me happy. Whenever I think about you." He glanced over at her, his gaze warming her from the inside out. "When I look at you."

"Including that night when I got home late from work covered in dried mud just as you showed up to take me to a movie and dinner?"

"Especially that night." It turned out that with Jarle in the kitchen, Piper running the front of the house, and a recent graduate from the college's Food, Beverage Arts, & Hospitality Department filling in behind the bar, service without him had continued without a hitch. "Especially washing you clean in the shower."

She laughed, remembering how messy and slippery the mud had gotten when wet, and how they'd painted each other with it, each spreading it over the other's body beneath the hot, streaming water. Then, once the last of it had disappeared down the drain, slick with the foamy liquid soap she'd bought from Jolene's skin care line—the scent that Burke had told her made her smell like a piña colada—he'd taken her hard and fast against the tile wall.

Afterward, they'd had cold cereal with fresh blueberries from her garden for dinner. And once she'd put the bowls and spoons in the dishwasher, declaring himself still hungry, he'd untied her short silk robe, spun her around, and bent her over the granite counter. It was one of the few times she'd experienced a dreaded flashback, but when she'd stiffened, Quinn, having learned her body well—the same as he'd discovered erogenous zones she'd hadn't known existed—paused and ran a slow, soothing hand down her back.

"We can stop," he'd murmured, his lips nuzzling that place behind her ear she'd never realized was directly connected to that part of her that had, only seconds earlier, been aching for him. Again. "Just say the word."

"Don't stop," she'd said. She'd taken a breath, blown it out, and felt the fear dissolve like spindrift bubbles on the sand. "I want you." It was time, she'd told herself, to replace a painful memory with a glorious one. Which they had. Stupendously.

"After finally getting to bed, we made it a trifecta," he said, his deep voice warm with memories. "That was one great night. But I think last night beat it."

"As did this morning." For someone whose life had

been a sexual desert for so long, Amanda was definitely making up for lost time. There were occasions she wondered if she was turning into a nymphomaniac because it seemed she couldn't get enough sex. No, she amended. She couldn't get enough Quinn.

They had a long wait for the ferry, which gave them time for her to tell him about the conference, and for him to catch her up on happenings at home, including the preparations for the wedding at the farm.

"My folks didn't plan any performances for the day, and for those who might just see it driving by, they've added signs that it's closed for a private event. It's supposed to be sunny, so they're planning the ceremony and reception dinner outdoors. But the guest list is small enough that it won't take that much work to move everything into the barn if it does start to rain."

"It's wonderful that Gloria is getting a new start at her age," Amanda said as the huge grey, red, and black ferry—so different from Washington's snowy white and green ones—arrived at the dock and walk-on passengers deboarded and cars drove off. "Not that midforties is old."

"Gloria Wells will still be young at ninety," Quinn said. "But yeah, after all she went through, it's nice that her life's turned out so well."

"Jolene told me that her mother put off accepting Mike's proposal for such a long time because they were so different."

"That's not necessarily a bad thing. Look at my parents."

"True. But it was their lifestyles she was worried about. Apparently he'd been quite the jet-setter, hob-nobbing with the rich and famous."

"Also true. But don't forget, he grew up here. And when the gloss of wealth and fame wore off and became boring, he came back home."

"Which seems to be a Mannion thing. Maybe you should get one of those fake family shields of honor they sell online. With Latin words reading 'Mannions always return home.'"

"Mannions *semper revertetur in terram suam*."

She'd been watching a seagull perched on a piling cracking open an oyster shell with his beak when she turned back toward him. "You speak Latin?"

Quinn shrugged. "I was a lawyer, which is an *advocatus* in Latin, which isn't necessary to know, but since the Romans had, at one time, conquered most of what's currently Europe, and our legal system comes from the first European colonists, Latin terms that had been used in the law of Rome were adapted to our legal system. Same with government and medicine. Anyway, rather than having to constantly look terms up, I decided to take Latin in high school."

"What's the Latin term for planning ahead?"

He thought a moment. "*Consilio praemisit*."

"Which is what you do. Brianna told me that you even took a course in brewing at the college when you came back."

"It only made sense and I learned a lot."

"That's not one of my strong suits," she said. "I'm incredibly detailed when it comes to planning landscaping, because I learned that in college. But, in my real life, I struggle with planning too far ahead." Like moving in with Quinn, she thought. It would, admittedly, give her a longer drive into work, but, in truth, much of her design work was done at home where it was quiet and his home was large enough that she wouldn't be constantly interrupted.

"Proving my point about people not needing to be exactly alike to be a perfect match," he said, starting the engine as the cars in front of them were being waved forward to start loading. "Once we get parked and up on deck, maybe I'll share a few of my plans for tonight with you." He put a hand on her knee, bared by her skirt. "Others, I think I'll keep as a surprise. I wouldn't want our sex to become predictable."

"Like that could ever happen," she murmured, feeling that now familiar tingling triggered by anticipation at whatever he might have in mind when they arrived at his house, where she'd agreed to spend the night for the first time since the star shower.

"It says here that the gardens cover fifty-five acres with over a million bedding plants in some nine hundred varieties," Amanda said as she read the brochure they'd been given when they arrived. "Can you imagine?"

One of the skill sets of being a lawyer was knowing when to speak and when to shut up. Which is why Quinn decided not to say anything, as they entered

the gardens, about her expression being nearly as ec-
static as the one that would flush her face when she'd
orgasmed. They started with what the brochure referred to as the crown jewel of the gardens, the five-
acre Sunken Garden created from that limestone pit,
which had a mound in the middle, accessible by a
stone staircase.

"It has one hundred and fifty-one beds," she said
in awe, looking around as they walked the stone path.
"It's the highest density of flowers and borders than
any place in the gardens. And they plant sixty-five
thousand bulbs every spring. Just imagine."

"That's a lot of bulbs," he said. As lovely as all the
flowers were, they couldn't compete with the beauty
of her face as her brown eyes were trying to take it
all in. As they strolled, hand in hand, she pointed out
lilies, marigolds, begonias, and various other flowers, some of which he recognized from his mother's
gardens, but except for roses, tulips, and daffodils,
he was pretty clueless about names and knew he'd
never remember all these.

She'd taken a notebook out of her bag and was
busily making notes about plants that she must have.
"You do realize that your tiny yard at your rental
place won't support all you're writing down," he said,
after dropping a quick kiss on her lips beneath a wil-
low tree at the small lake.

"That doesn't mean I can't plant them in other
people's yards."

"You could start with mine," he suggested casually. "Did I mention I have five acres?" She'd only

seen the lake side of his house the night of the star showers. That and his bedroom and kitchen.

"You have that much land?" Her eyes widened even as he watched the thoughts racing through her head.

"That much," he confirmed, knowing that she'd be mentally planning a garden at his place before they left. Which had only been part one of his plan to win her. "It's not all lakefront. Much of it is behind the house, with some lawn and most left natural."

"Natural is good," she said. "You could put in a fountain," she suggested, as they stood at the graceful one even he had to admit was super cool. "Nothing this extravagant," she added as the water shooting up in cycles had the fountain appear to be dancing. "But something in a place that would let you hear it from the bedroom. It'd be soothing to go to sleep to."

"Sounds good to me." Though he figured it wouldn't beat the sleep that came after multiple rounds of sex. He could practically see the wheels turning in her head, showing that she was already on board with the idea and they'd only made it to the first of the gardens.

Although the gardens were unsurprisingly crowded due to summer tourists, to preserve the tranquility, the brochure had advised people to keep their conversations low. Which most had, their voices reverential, as if in a church. Observing others whose expressions were as rapt as Amanda's, Quinn supposed that to many, the gardens felt like a church. He'd certainly always found more peace out amidst nature in the forests and mountains, surrounded by the towering trees or beside one of the many lakes of the Pacific Northwest than—despite being head altar boy for a time— he'd ever felt at Saint Peter the Fisherman's church.

"I'm glad we didn't tour this with a group," she murmured as they watched one such group pass by, the leader pointing out the various flowers. "It's undoubtedly more efficient, but I prefer it being just the two of us."

"Me too."

Quinn could smell the rose garden before they reached it. "Okay," he admitted, as they walked through a tunnel of arched red roses. "This is pretty spectacular."

"It won the World Rose Garden of the Year award in 2018 from the World Federation of Rose Societies," Amanda read from the brochure. "And features twenty-five hundred plants and two hundred and eighty varieties. Even I didn't know there were that many varieties of roses.

"I'll have to do some research on which ones could grow on the peninsula," she mused, and although he'd cut his tongue out before admitting it, he was relieved that she wasn't going to take that notebook back out and make them search for all two-hundred and eighty rose plants.

"Everyone always asks for roses, and I've found several varieties that thrive, but they still need a lot of tender loving care due to the variations of soil conditions and controlling the pests and diseases that come with our maritime climate." She pointed toward tall bright blue flowers. "Those are delphiniums. Since they can grow to six feet tall, I've used them before for summer backdrops behind shorter plants."

Leaving the roses, they passed another fountain. This one featuring a dragon. "'The Dragon Fountain was a gift from China celebrating the thirty-fifth anniversary of Victoria and its sister city, Suzhou,'" she read. "'It represents the friendship and good-will of the Chinese people and signifies wishes of peace and prosperity as well as good weather for the crops.'" She glanced up at him. "A dragon fountain would probably be overdoing it at your place."

"Definitely. Though I do like the heron one you had made for Bri's garden."

"It turned out well," she agreed. "Brianna wanted a peaceful respite, and fountains definitely offer that, along with a place for birds to bathe and drink. Last month, she had a frog who croaked all night for a week, calling out for a mate," she said as they moved on beneath the tall torii gate into the moss-covered grounds of the Japanese Garden.

The winding pathways between the tall bamboo trees, the soft rustle of the maple and beech leaves, along with trickling streams, provided a quiet haven after the dazzling variety of colors and flowers of the previous garden that had been crowded with tourists all stopping to take photos.

"I'm so impressed," she said. "I could never pull all this off."

"With fifty-five acres, they had a lot more space to work with," he pointed out.

"True." She glanced up at him. "Though I have to admit those five acres of yours are tempting. Maybe when we get back to your place, I'll take a look. Though I'd want to go all native to stay with your meadows. Milkweed would bring you migrating monarchs, which are endangered."

"I'm all for saving butterflies."

"Hmm." He could hear her thinking again as they wove their way through the tranquility of the quiet garden. Because they somehow, suddenly found themselves alone, he pulled her closer for a quick kiss beneath a maple tree shading them from the bright summer sun.

"How many more gardens do we have to go through? Because I'm about to start croaking."

"Frogs are very faithless lovers," she said. "You're supposed to be monogamous."

"Why would I want any other woman? When you're perfect for me?" From the heat in his eyes, he was about to kiss her again, then gave her a playful pat on the butt instead, right before a little girl, who looked to be about that age of Kylee and Mai's Emma, came running into the garden.

"I'm really starting to feel for that frog," he said as they moved on. "Because I want you. Now."

"I can relate," she admitted. Amanda fantasized a lot about him during every day. But after having him spend the night so often, and agreeing to stay over at his house again, the dynamics of their relationship had changed. The intimacy had been there since the day he'd served her that "birthday" glass of wine. But it was growing deeper, more serious. "It's not just sex," she murmured.

"It never has been," he agreed. "Though that's really great."

"The best the hotshot lawyer who can speak Latin and knows all the best words can come up with is great?" she teased.

"Okay. I'll accept your challenge. How about exceptional?"

She shrugged. "True. But rather ordinary, don't you think, for a man with your prolific vocabulary?"

"Incomparable?"

"True. And you're getting closer."

"If I get it, what do I win for a prize?"

She thought a minute. "A bubble bath," she decided.

"Seriously? That's it?"

"With me. In that hedonistic Jacuzzi tub you have in your bathroom." Her small rental only had a narrow shower. "For as long as you want. However you want."

That flame that could warm her all over flared in his blue eyes again as he put his thumb to his chin, looked down at her, and considered that idea for a long, silent moment. "Well, that prospect certainly has me rising to the challenge."

Amanda couldn't help herself. She glanced down and saw he wasn't using a metaphor.

"Transcendent," he said triumphantly.

"You win," she said on a laugh, even as she knew they'd both won.

Leaving the tranquility of the Japanese Garden, they climbed a flight of stairs up to the Star Pond, which Amanda read had originally been designed for Mr. Butchart's collection of ornamental ducks. The designers had planted brightly colorful annuals between the points of the star, and Amanda and Quinn drew curious gazes from other visitors as they burst into laughter at the frog fountain rising from the star's center.

"Don't say a thing," she said as they left for the last stop on their self-guided tour.

"I was merely going to mention that I don't remember this place being so kinky when my parents brought us here. I also have to wonder if playing with his ornamental ducks was the only thing Mr. and Mrs. Butchart did at the Star Garden."

"I never realized, in all the time we've been friends, that you have such a dirty mind."

"Tell me you weren't thinking the same thing."

"I wasn't thinking the same thing."

"You're a liar." He put his arm around her waist. "A beautiful one, but a liar just the same. Your face is an open book... I've decided what I want," he said.

"For your prize in the tub?"

"No. The ornamental thing in my fountain. Like Bri's heron."

"Don't tell me you want a frog?"

"I absolutely do. But not a single one because he'd be lonely. We need two."

"That'd have me thinking about sex every time we sat out there."

His eyes were wickedly laughing as he grinned down at her. "And your problem with that is?"

Honestly, as they walked beneath the two white arches taking them into the final and most formalized Italian Garden, Amanda couldn't come up with an answer.

"Fun fact," she said instead. "This garden was completed in 1926. Prior to that, Mr. and Mrs. Butchart's tennis court took up the space,"

"They were probably too busy playing other games up at the Star Pond to have the energy to play tennis," he said, making her laugh again, which drew more curious looks.

He'd reserved a table for high tea in the dining room, a classic, turn-of-the-century building that had once been the Butchart family home.

"They named it *Benvenuto*," Amanda read. "The Italian word for *welcome*... Oh," she breathed, as they were led to the table window he'd requested overlooking the Italian Garden, "this is like one more gift garden indoors."

There were flowers on the white draped tables, potted plants and bright flowers lined up on the shelf atop the wainscoting, painted the same color of the walls. More plants hung from ceiling hooks. And potted trees added to the sense of being outdoors. "I think I could live here. Imagine this having once been a private home."

They'd no sooner sat down than a waiter arrived, wondering if sir or madam would enjoy a cocktail or wine pairing. "I think I'll stick with tea," Amanda said. Since he'd be driving the long way home, Quinn seconded that order. They were faced with a wide variety, including the 100th Anniversary blend that the server described as a light mix of Darjeeling, black Hunan, and gunpowder tea.

"The chefs worked with a team for six months to come up with a perfect blend to celebrate the gardens being in bloom for a hundred years," he told them. "It's our best-selling flavor."

"As a brewer who appreciates the work that goes into blending ingredients, I'm going to have to go with that," Quinn said.

"If you don't mind me asking, would I have tasted your beer?"

It was not the first time Quinn had been asked that. "My brewery's across the border in Washington. Honeymoon Harbor, to be exact."

The server, who'd been behaving in a friendly, but semiformal way, responded with enthusiasm. "You'd be the same Quinn Mannion who created the excellent Captain Jack Sparrow? That was the first legal beer I drank. My cousin Mike brought it back from a trip to Bellingham. And your summer brews have got me listening to the Beach Boys. Are you going to keep brewing to that theme every summer?"

"That's the plan," Quinn said, slipping Amanda a quick, apologetic look that wasn't missed by their server, who'd been behaving as if she were invisible.

"I'm sorry, ma'am. We get a lot a famous people here, but never one that I've felt a personal connection to. I'd always planned to play pro hockey, but my final year playing for University of Alberta, I blocked a slap shot with my foot and ended up breaking my ankle really bad. It never did heal quite right. At least not well enough to play at the pro level."

"I'm sorry," Amanda said.

"Yeah, I was too. But life moves on, eh? So, I had to come up with a plan B and decided the thing I liked best after playing hockey was craft beer, so I'm thinking of becoming a craft brewer myself."

Having heard that too many times to count at the beerfest, Quinn pulled out one of his business cards and handed it to the kid. "If you ever decide to look into it seriously, I have some connections in Vancouver who would be willing to talk with you. I learned a lot from brewers in Seattle before I took classes."

"Thank you, Mr. Mannion!" From his wide smile, he could have just won the Stanley Cup.

"No problem," Quinn said. "What would you like, Amanda?"

"I apologize again," the waiter said. "Yes, ma'am. What would you care for?"

She ordered the Teaberry, which was described as a black Ceylon tea flavored with strawberries, blackberries, currents, and stevia.

"You certainly made his day," she said, as they watched him nearly run between the tables back to the kitchen.

"While he made me feel ancient. I always wanted to be a lawyer, but I'd never been that excited about it. It was just the path I was on. And got stuck. I hope he makes it."

"I do too. And if he does, you'll have had something to do with it."

"I doubt that."

"Sometimes all it takes is a word of encouragement from someone who's been there," she said. "And as for feeling ancient, he called me ma'am. Twice. Also, Piper asked me yesterday if you and I got married, how I'd feel about being her stepmum. I got the sense she was worried I might think she'd be in the way. Or interfere in our relationship."

"What did you say?" Quinn kept his voice casual.

"That we hadn't discussed marriage, but anyone would be proud to have her for a daughter."

"That's pretty much the same thing I told her."

"We should bring her here," Amanda said, looking out at the glorious view of the garden. "Jamal is apparently jammed with work finishing up that boat Gabe's restoring and another fishing boat just came down from Dutch Harbor, so he doesn't have as much time to spend with her. The boat's owner, who made millions in oil up there, wants it restored for an Alaskan museum he's creating."

"Gabe mentioned something about that."

"While we're talking about new starts, his life has definitely done a one-eighty. I don't know what he was like when he was on Wall Street, but he's certainly a poster boy for what a husband and father should be."

"Honestly, he surprised us all."

"Life happens. Things change," she said, smiling up at the waiter who returned with two pots of tea and two servings of Chantilly cream, followed by a light sponge cake and berry compote, topped with yet another dollop of cream. "It signifies of heritage," he told them. "Jennie Butchart served it to the thousands of guests who visited the gardens, and our chefs have wanted to keep the tradition alive."

"It's a lovely tradition," Quinn said.

Amanda took a taste. "And, oh, my goodness, it's heaven in a glass," she said. "I can't imagine what the chefs will come up with next."

"I'm sure you'll be quite pleased," he said. "The first thing I was taught when I came to work here was that we all have a standard to live up to." And then he was off to refill a glass of champagne at a neighboring table, where a couple appeared to be celebrating a special occasion.

"Thank you," Amanda said.

"For what?"

"For too many things to count. But for now, this day. I knew I was right not to go alone. But I'd never imagined how much better it is being here with you." She reached across the table and took his hand. "And as wonderful a day as this was, and still is, I'm looking forward to spending the night with you."

Another server, this one a young girl, who looked about Piper's age, arrived with a tall three-layered tray. "These house-made sausages are very popular," she said. "As is the smoked salmon, which is locally wild and sustainably caught in BC. Everything, including the ham, is both sustainable and local, all sourced from within thirty miles of here. We're proud of that."

"As you should be," Amanda said as she chose

a small slice of tarragon quiche from the bottom of the tray platter.

"The best way is to eat up from the bottom plate," the girl said approvingly. "Although a lot of people can't resist our signature candied ginger scones with house-made preserves and Devon-style cream on top. The chefs found the original family recipe while researching the archives."

"I think she talked me into it," Amanda said, as the server left. The scent drifting up from the just-out-of-the-oven scones was irresistible. "Oh, wow. You have to have one. If there is a heaven, it would include these scones."

She held it out to him, and he took a bite from her hand. "That's damn good."

Amanda studied the middle plate. The one with the pastries. "I'm glad we walked all those acres. Because I can feel myself gaining weight just looking at this level."

"Don't worry. I'll help you work the calories off when we get home."

Home. He'd said it so casually, as if he was thinking that now that he'd talked her into one night, she might leave her rental house and move in full-time. And truthfully, she'd begun to wonder, why not? There was also the case that she paid month to month. Her landlord was one of those greedy real estate speculators from Portland and Seattle, who'd been buying up properties like crazy. She could wake up tomorrow homeless. Again. This time, she knew that he'd help her by giving her a place to stay. But then, would he always wonder if she was only there because she had no choice? Instead of because she wanted to be?

Which she did. Quinn was right. They weren't truly sharing their lives, which would be fine if they were casually dating. But they'd gone way past that.

She'd tell him, she decided, as she bit into a tangy lemon tart. Tonight.

CHAPTER TWENTY-TWO

THEY'D HAD THE server box up the leftovers, which saved them from having to cook when they got back to Honeymoon Harbor. Convenient, as Amanda had teasingly reminded him as they'd walked back to the parking lot, because—his seduction dinner had already worked.

"Thank you for bringing me here," she said again. "It'll go down as one of the most special days of my life."

"It was quite the experience," Quinn said, although he wasn't as blown away by gardens as she was. Which, he'd decided, made sense. He'd certainly gotten a lot of pleasure going through various breweries when he'd been planning the next stage of his career. "And I just realized that the gardens remind me of a trip my family took to Disneyland, back when I was in middle school."

"I've never been to Disneyland, or Disney World, but I've heard the gardens are remarkable."

"I guess. The thing is, my mother, who's quite the gardener herself, kept remarking how perfect they all are."

She looked up at him. "You make that sound like a negative."

"It works for them. Because it is, after all, billed as the Magic Kingdom, where everyone can escape from their ordinary lives, and little kids can get a hug from Snow White."

"Snow White kissed you?"

"No, she kissed Burke. On the cheek. He talked about it for months." There was still a framed photo of the memorable event in the framed gallery going up the stairs in his parents' house. "These gardens remind me of that." They'd reached his SUV.

"Did the brochure say how many gardeners the place has?" he asked as they drove out of the lot.

"Fifty year-round. Seventy in the summer, when they employ part-timers."

"All those people," he said. "To create perfection." He glanced over at her as they turned onto the road leading to the ferry dock.

"To be truthful, having seen them, I would've expected even more workers," she said. "There wasn't a weed showing or a leaf out of place."

"That's my point. Although they are impressive, I still prefer your work."

She turned toward him. At least as far as the seat belt would allow. "You're just saying that to make me feel good."

"I have plans to make you feel *very* good later," he said easily. "But no, I meant it. Yours are actually more magical."

"How?"

"Because they seem to have sprung from the ground naturally. As if planned by Mother Nature rather than an army of horticulturists."

"You really mean that."

"I don't say things I don't mean." He glanced over at her. "Especially to you."

"Wow. That's the nicest thing anyone has ever said about my work. If I wasn't wearing this seat belt and the armrest wasn't in the way, I'd kiss you."

"Later," Quinn suggested.

"Most definitely," she agreed.

AMANDA COULD FEEL an odd tension radiating from Quinn on the trip home. Not the same sexual tension that she was feeling, but something else that she couldn't put her finger on. Although their conversation covered things from the gardens, including facts from a book she'd bought from the souvenir shop, along with several packets of seeds, which she'd have to declare entering back into Washington, but had been assured by the clerk that she'd have no problem with customs.

"Of course, I can buy the same types here, in the US," she said. "But I think it would be special to plant seeds from those gardens in my work. And on some of your five acres."

"Sounds good to me," he said. "So long as I get my frogs."

It wasn't that unusual a request. She still occasionally consulted on gardens from San Francisco to Seattle and had installed two frogs in a fountain for a novelist living on South Puget Sound. One frog was drinking a glass of wine. The other—unsurprisingly, given the owner's occupation—was lying on a stone boulder, reading a book. But neither had caused her to think of sex.

"Jennie appeared to have been a woman ahead of her time," she said, returning to the book. "She enjoyed ballooning and flying. And later in life, became a qualified chemist."

"As unusual as that would've been for a woman in the 1900s, I imagine being married to a millionaire would have allowed more opportunities for entertaining hobbies. Several of my former clients had runways or helipads on their estates. One, who lived on the Sound, had a float plane."

"It's true that the wealthy have more privileges," she agreed. "And although they helped support us during times that Eric was out of work, except for clients like Brianna, and Kylee and Mai, I do prefer creating public places that can be shared by everyone."

"That's why Teddy Roosevelt saved so much of the peninsula as a federal preserve. To protect the native elk—which were known as Olympic elks back then—and the trees. If it weren't for him, what's now the park could've been clear-cut, taking away the habitat of at least nine large terrestrial mammals, fifty small ones, and fourteen marine mammals."

"I'm seriously impressed that you knew that off the top of your head."

He shrugged. "I worked as a lifeguard at Sol Duc Hot Springs during summer vacations from UW and would occasionally fill in on my days off as a tour guide. Memorization is part of being a lawyer, and I'm fortunate to have a good memory. So, that just stuck with me."

"Probably because you had an interest in them. The same way I remember plant species."

"Probably." She also suspected that, on the days he was on that lifeguard stand, a lot more women would decide to spend the day swimming or just lounging beside the pool. And she had not a single doubt that his tours would gain a record amount of female visitors who were more interested in their guide than elk, marmots, bears, or otters.

"Anyway, Jennie was obviously one of the generous wealthy because, when word of the gardens got out, people would flock to see them, and she'd have her staff serve tea to everyone who came. In 1915 alone, they reportedly served tea to eighteen thousand people."

"That's a lot of tea."

"Not up to the millions the gardens get today, but she must have had a special staff just for the visitors. It says here that she'd occasionally served the tea anonymously herself, dressed as a waitress. And reportedly was even tipped."

"True or not, that makes a good story and adds to the lore," he said.

She sensed that she was losing his interest.

"Is everything okay?" she asked after a near-silent twenty minutes passed. Every once in a while, she'd ooh and aah over a pod of black-and-white orcas or dolphins frolicking alongside the ferry as if racing it, and while he'd respond that they were cool, that was about all she was getting from him.

"I'm fine."

She started to think back over everything she'd said, worried about whether she'd offended him, then she remembered how self-destructive that old behavior could be and returned instead to reading the book and looking at all the wonderful photos. Some in black-and-white during the family's earlier days, and more recently, the more colorful ones.

"I'm sorry," he said after taking a call that lasted all of ten seconds. "I was just concerned about some work Seth was doing at the house. Although his crews are very good at cleaning up at the end of every day, I didn't want you having to deal with a bunch of workmen when we arrived."

"So, I take it this mysterious job is done?"

"It is. We both had to get to work the morning after the meteor shower, so I didn't get to give you a full tour of the house. It's admittedly too big for me, but it works as a gathering place when the kids come spend time at the lake and want to sleep over."

Amanda wanted to ask him if he'd also bought the house with his own kids in mind, but she didn't want to get ahead of herself. Today, she'd tell him she was moving in. That was a major step and they had plenty of time to get accustomed to the change. It wasn't as if either one of them was going anywhere.

With his remodeling, whatever it was, completed,

his seemingly brooding mood had lifted and their conversation during the rest of the ferry ride and on the way home had been as normal as any couple might have after an extraordinary day. They'd both spoken with Piper about how she'd fit into their relationship, and although the M-word wasn't mentioned, they'd decided that her idea of taking Piper to the gardens was a good one.

"I still want to do that," he said as they drove along Lakeshore Drive, headed to his house. "And I know she'd love it, but I was thinking, perhaps next Monday, the three of us go out on the boat. Have a picnic, maybe see some whales. November to February is usually the best time. But it's also the worst weather. So, let's just take it easy and play it by ear. All she needs to know right now is what we know. That we're in a relationship, and we both want her to feel comfortable and included."

"Now you're talking like a lawyer."

"I *was* a lawyer," he reminded her. "Although I don't remember any door-slamming with Brianna, Gabe tells me that teenage girls are often a riddle wrapped in a mystery inside an enigma."

"Winston Churchill regarding the Nazi-Soviet nonaggression pact," she placed the quote. "And before you ask how I knew that, or that it fell apart when Hitler invaded Russia two years later, I did study more than flowers in college."

"I wasn't going to ask that at all. Especially since you're probably one of the few people visiting Butchart

Gardens in a year who knows that along with planting flowers, Jennie Butchart was a chemist."

"I like to read. And I hung out in the library a lot whenever I'd end up in a new school, because I never fit into any of the already established cliques. There's also another way of looking at that quote with regard to Piper."

"And that is?"

"When you handled my marriage breakup, you said that you typically didn't take on divorces because they're messy."

"I never handled any divorces except for yours, because they do tend to get messy. Especially when custody of children is involved."

"You know I appreciate you making an exception in my case, especially handling it pro bono, after Eric's manic spending left me in such debt."

"Friends help each other," he said as he pushed the button that opened the gate to his driveway. "I was happy to be able to help you extricate yourself from a rough situation. Well, not happy, because I'm sorry you were in that trouble, but—"

"I get it. And since Piper's of age, there are no legal custody issues. But despite you and her mother having made a pact to get along with each other and share her, issues will still arise. Who does she spend Christmas with? What about summers? Who'll walk her down the aisle if she gets married?"

"That's obvious. It'll be David. Because he's been her father for sixteen years of her life. I've been her employer, and now birth father, for a few weeks.

And she's already asked what to call me, so we discussed it, and I'm going to stay Quinn to her, but I'd
be proud for people to know that I'm her birth father. As for holidays and vacations, we'll just have
to leave that up to her, and depending on where her
parents might be posted."

"You were very angry when you showed up at my
house that night."

"I can't deny that. And I still regret missing those
important years of her life. But Burke told me that
when you blow a pass, you can't dwell on it because
it'll affect your mindset for the rest of the game. I've
decided that's not a bad way to handle a bad mistake.
Not that I consider the situation with Piper anything
like a blown pass."

"I know. I felt your pain. But Burke's very wise."

"For a guy who had Gabe and me write his reports
for his summer library reading program because he
insisted he couldn't waste time better spent honing
his football skills, I'd agree."

"Well, I can't fault him on that one," she said. "So,
you and Fiona are okay with all this?"

"So far, I'm optimistic. What about you?" he asked.
"Are you okay with another woman being in my life?
One I had a child with?"

"That's part of the point, isn't it?" she asked. "You
didn't have a child with her. Because she never told
you, then lied to her daughter about it. And to be perfectly truthful, I'm angry on your behalf because I
love you and believe she owed it to you to be involved
in your daughter's life. But I've spent most of my

life trying to grasp onto the concept of bygones. My Mother. Dad. Eric. My therapist has helped me realize that I didn't need to carry all that baggage around with me. Since you said that you don't feel anything for Fiona, or have an emotional connection—"

"I don't."

"I believe you. So, I think a boat trip to hopefully see whales next Monday sounds lovely."

QUINN'S HOME WAS as beautiful as she'd remembered it. Created of logs milled on the site, it boasted what he told her were five bedrooms and six and a half baths. The open concept great room featured a towering beamed ceiling, a monumental stone fireplace, and a dramatic staircase that led to the upper floor. Tall folding glass doors led out to a raised deck. They, like the walls of windows that let in both light and the spectacular panoramic vista of the lake and the mountains beyond, were triple paned to keep cold out. "The previous owner had heating installed beneath all the floors, which are great in the winter."

"You have an elevator!"

He shrugged. "I had it added when I moved here. For when Gramps and Gram visit for family things. I worry about them on those stairs."

Once again, she thought, above all else, the most important thing to Quinn was family. If they hadn't so embraced her, she would have been envious.

He led her down a long, wood-hewn hallway, then pressed a button that had a huge plank door opening. When she saw what was on the other side, she gasped.

"This is what Seth has been working on for you?" she asked, as she stared around the solarium that two of her rental houses could have fit in. The walls and ceiling were all glass. It was empty except for a lone hibiscus tree and several pieces of forest green wicker furniture covered in leafy prints and white iron tables and chairs. There were also varying levels of stone pillars, obviously designed to be bases for plants.

"Seth and my mother, who chose the furniture, did it," he said. "Seth borrowed another crew from a friend who does remodel and renovation work in Oregon. The floors, like the rest of the house, are heated, but the thermostats are separate because none of us knew what temperature they should be and if I'd have asked you, it wouldn't have been a secret."

She turned around. Still stunned by the space. "You did all this for me?"

"Well, not exactly just for you. I kept thinking while we were at the gardens today, what it would be like to make love in whatever you turn the space into." He bent down and folded out a mattress from a love seat, turning it into the size of a double bed. Which wasn't nearly as large as the king he had up in his bedroom, but she doubted they'd do much sleeping in here.

"I don't know what to say."

"There are going to be a lot of unhappy guys who worked hard to get it done if you hate it."

"How could you even ask that?"

He brushed the pad of his thumb beneath her eyes, then trailed his hand down her face.

"You're crying."

"I am?" She lifted her own hand to her cheeks and felt the tears. "They're happy tears. No, that's not a strong enough word. Transcendent," she decided, borrowing his. "I thought you didn't do grand gestures."

"I never did before you. So, I take it you like it?"

"I love it," she said. "More than I have words for."

"Maybe you could show instead of tell," he suggested.

"I have every intention of doing just that. But first, I have to tell you something."

"Something's wrong? Seth and I consulted with a lot of contractors who do this type of work, trying to get it right."

"No. It's perfect. Better than perfect. I've honestly dreamed of this, but I always thought I'd have to get a job at some conservatory. I never imagined I'd have one of my own."

"It's going to take a while to fill it," he said.

"It will. And that's what I want to tell you." She went up on her toes and kissed him. A long, hot kiss, filled with all the joy that had her heart rising up to the top of the paneled glass ceiling. "I'd already made the decision, earlier today, to move in with you. So although this is the most gloriously perfect gift I've ever received, it's not why I'm moving in."

She wrapped her arms around his neck. "I'm moving in because I love you. More than I ever thought possible. And, right now, I'd like to do my best to repay you with that bathtub sex."

"Again we're on the same page. But first, there's one more thing." He moved a folding Japanese screen painted with cherry blossoms his mother had found in Seattle aside, revealing a door. "Go ahead and open it."

She did as instructed and gasped again as she viewed a fully equipped workshop. "Jim Olson helped me plan this," he said. "He took me shopping for all the basics. He said you probably had a few of your favorite things you'd like, so we didn't entirely buy out the shop."

"Jim went into a busy shop for you?"

"Not me. For you," he said.

That started the waterworks again. "For a guy on the spectrum, who doesn't always grasp social cues, he sure nailed this."

"I'm taking that as a yes, you like it," Quinn said. "And you can thank Jim in person later. But right now, I'm going to claim my prize."

Scooping her off her feet, he carried her out of the solarium, down the hallway, up the curving stairway to the master suite, where he dropped her unceremoniously on the bed, causing her to bounce.

"I'm going to start filling the tub," he said, "while you get out of those clothes."

He didn't ask. Nor was it a suggestion. What it came very close to, Amanda considered, as she heard the water begin to flow into the deep tub, was an order. A demand.

Oh, yes, she thought, as she practically tore off the dress she'd been imagining him slowly, seductively taking off her, they'd both definitely won that challenge.

CHAPTER TWENTY-THREE

VELVET HAD BEEN right about September being a perfect month for a wedding, Amanda thought, as she watched Gloria Wells and Michael Mannion exchange vows in the garden she'd created to enhance the entrance to the barn after the family had turned it into a summer theater. Butterflies danced on the colorful annuals, bumblebees buzzed harmlessly on the lavender as they gathered the pollen that would become the lavender honey served in Brianna's B and B, and every so often a hummingbird would zoom by after drinking from one of the feeders that Sarah Mannion had hung around the farm.

Caroline Harper had returned home to perform the wedding, as she'd done for Kylee and Mai. Amanda watched as Michael took Gloria's hand in his then slipped the platinum band that matched the dazzling engagement ring he'd given her a few months earlier onto her finger. As Amanda listened to him pledge to love, honor, and cherish her for all time, she felt Quinn, who was seated beside her, glance over. Not daring to risk looking back at him, she kept her eyes on Gloria—her still youthful face lightly enhanced by her Emmy-nominated makeup artist daughter, resplendent in a dress that looked as if it had been inspired by the gardens she and Quinn had visited—as she returned the promise.

Amanda knew that Quinn wasn't hearing those solemn vows as mere ceremonial words. To him, they were much, much, more. He was the most responsible, dependable, honorable man she'd ever known. And, wonder of wonders, he was hers.

The gathering of friends and family—Amanda had noticed earlier that Piper, seated on the other side of Quinn, was holding hands with Jamal—all stood and applauded as the couple danced down the aisle to The Black Eyed Peas' "I Gotta Feeling."

The dinner was served in a casual buffet style, as Bastien and Desiree sang a medley of songs Gloria, with Jolene's input, had chosen. Before owning their co-joined Cajun restaurant and bakery, they'd belonged to a popular blues rock band. Along with singing at Kylee and Mai's ceremony, they'd also performed for Seth and Brianna's and Jolene and Aiden's double wedding.

"Those two are becoming the Mannions' on-call wedding singers," Quinn said as he and Amanda danced to Rihanna's "We Found Love." They were moving much slower than the song inspired, but given that his hands were wrapped low on her waist, and hers were around his neck, their lips nearly touching, to her, it was perfect.

"They seem to be." She brushed her lips against his. "I was thinking, while they exchanged vows, about that question you've been holding back asking me."

"And what would that be?" he asked as his lips moved to nuzzle behind her ear—yet another erogenous zone he'd discovered.

"Am I wrong thinking that you've been planning to ask me to marry you?"

He drew back his head and looked down at her. "No, you aren't. But—"

"You were waiting for me to be ready."

"Yes. I thought, when you agreed to move in, that was a good start, and—"

"Stop." She cut off his words with a finger against his lips. "I have a suggestion… I'm going to take my finger away in a minute, and when I do, why don't you just ask? Are you on board with that?"

Hope flashed in those Mannion blue eyes, followed quickly by a love so deep, and so powerful, it almost knocked Amanda to her knees. They were so intent on one another, neither noticed Desiree grab her husband's arm and point toward them.

Quinn stopped dancing and, unaware they'd garnered an audience, took both her hands in his. "Amanda Barrow, will you please marry me?" The proposal was neither flowery nor romantic. It was pure Quinn. The man she loved. Just as he was.

"It's about damn time," she said. "Yes, Quinn Mannion, I will definitely marry you. As soon as legally possible." And didn't that set off another round of applause?

"I'm sorry," she mouthed to Gloria, who was clapping along with the others. She hadn't meant to have a public audience that took away attention from the bride. But Gloria merely laughed, put one hand on her heart and blew them both a kiss with the other.

As Amanda flung her arms around Quinn's neck and kissed him, Bastien and Desiree broke into "At Last." How perfect, Amanda thought. They'd already wasted too much time, each waiting for the other. Waiting, as Michael and Gloria had vowed, to love, honor, and cherish each other for all time.

But for now, at this moment, on this day designed to celebrate eternal love, they were beginning their own happily-ever-after.

EPILOGUE

Five years later

MOTHER NATURE HAD graced Honeymoon Harbor with a perfect day for the Mannion family's annual Fourth of July barbecue. The sunny sky overhead was a bright cerulean blue with only a few puffy clouds drifting by to add visual interest. A soft breeze carried scents of pine and fir, salt air from the harbor, and grilled meat and seafood that mingled with the sound of laughter.

As always, Quinn and Jarle were manning the double grills. This year Jarle was wearing a black apron his wife had gotten him for an anniversary present. Although he was probably the last man in Honeymoon Harbor anyone would have imagined wearing an apron, Ashley had chosen well. The message—*Your opinion is not in the recipe*—was a perfect accessory to the butcher's chart of a cow tattooed on his beefy arm.

As a noisy flag football game took place on the far side of the lawn, Brianna and Desiree lay on folding lounge chairs, watching their children splash around in a large blue, yellow, and red blow-up pool.

"You have to bow down to me," Abella Broussard—named for the Cajun grandmother who'd raised Bastien, Desiree's husband—said. Wearing a pink and white polka-dot two-piece bathing suit with a ruffled skirt, she was seated astride an inflatable unicorn. "Because I'm princess of all the mermaids. So you must obey my every command."

She lifted a closed fist, as if holding up the sparkling wand that had come with the princess costume Bastien had bought her for her birthday. Her long ebony curls had been pulled back into a ponytail and her eyes, a deep, dark chocolate inherited from her father, were royally stern.

"Your son is definitely smitten with that girl," Harriet, who was busily crocheting a soft bed shawl for the local volunteer hospice care group, told Brianna.

"He is that," Brianna agreed. "Ever since he was old enough to talk, we've heard, 'Abella did this. Abella did that. Abella says...'" She smiled. "Wouldn't it be lovely if they grew up and got married someday?"

"Abella Broussard-Mannion," Desiree mused. "It has a nice ring to it."

"I've never been much for hyphenated last names," Harriet said.

Brianna restrained a smile. Her grandmother had opinions on seemingly everything, and had never been hesitant about sharing them. Until that one memorable, life-changing day, when they'd learned that Quinn had a daughter he'd never been told about. One who'd fit into the family as if she'd grown up a Mannion all along. But at the time, Harriet had not been happy, at which time her husband had surprised them all by sternly instructing her to keep any negative thoughts to herself.

"I think it would be lovely to add Cajun and Creole roots to our Irish/Scandinavian family tree," Brianna responded mildly.

"Humph." Narrow shoulders shrugged. "It won't matter what marriage you two might try to plan. Children grow up and make their own decisions." She shot Brianna a look. "Like your parents."

"I fell in love with Seth when I wasn't much older than Abella and Jerome are," Brianna said. Just as Bastien and Desiree's daughter had been named for his late grandmother, she and Seth had named their son for *her* grandfather, who'd passed peacefully in his sleep after Christmas Day two years ago.

"I was nineteen when I fell in love with Bastien," Desiree said. Blue eyes, a contrast to her tawny, Creole/Caribbean island complexion, softened at the memory. "When he talked me into joining his band. Later, it took us some years apart to realize that we were meant to be. That he was my *coeur de mon coeur.*"

"Heart of your heart," Brianna translated. "The title of only one of the many songs he wrote about the two of you."

"That's it." The same song they'd sung together on their first album as a married couple this spring. She'd always suffered performance anxiety on stage, but after Bastien had Seth build a studio where they could record in private, before releasing the song on the internet to resounding success, they were already collaborating on another.

"My Jerome was never one for grand gestures like writing a song for me," Harriet said. "But I always knew he loved me. After he passed, I found a stack of faded journals he'd locked away in his workshop. All those early years he'd been away from home fishing, he'd written to me every night in those little books. Mostly just about his day. But every entry ended with him writing that he missed me. And loved me." Her voice cracked a bit on the telling.

"Damn it, Gram," Brianna said, touching a finger to her eye where a tear had formed. "You're making me cry. You never told us about that."

"I wasn't ready to share," Harriet said. "I needed to hold those words close to my heart for a while." The hand holding the crochet hook covered that heart she'd been protecting.

There was a slight silence, disturbed only by the splashing caused by young Jerome pushing Abella around the pool on her unicorn. Brianna glanced over at Desiree and knew they were thinking the same thing. That they should be so lucky as to live long enough to celebrate as many anniversaries as Jerome and Harriet Harper had been blessed with.

Then a cheer broke out, shattering the shared moment as former Super Bowl–winning quarterback Burke threw a long floating pass to Jamal, who took off like a gazelle, dodging defenders to score what appeared to be the winning touchdown. On the sidelines, Piper was jumping up and down, waving the pair of University of Washington purple and gold pom-poms she brought out every year.

"My hero!" she shouted.

After spiking the ball, Jamal ran over, lifted her off her feet and spun her around as she awarded him with a celebratory kiss.

"You'd never know," Brianna said, "that laughing cheerleader is off to the International Criminal Court next week."

After having graduated from Clearwater Community College, then summa cum laude from UW, Piper had finished her first year of law school, and had won a summer internship in The Hague. Wanting to stay together, as they had been ever since the Mannion barbecue when they'd first met, as talented in his own way as his fiancée, Jamal had landed a summer job at a shipyard only thirty minutes from The Hague.

Then the plan, which they'd worked out together, was for her to finish her law degree while he returned to working for Gabe, after which they'd get married here on the farm, before moving to the Netherlands together.

"I'm going to miss her," Harriet said.

"We all will," Amanda agreed as she joined the trio after placing little clay pots of yellow-faced daisies, mixed in with the pure blue roses Jim Olson had succeeded in creating two years ago to great horticultural acclaim, on the long tables. "But it's not as if there aren't planes flying back and forth, and this also gives Piper the ability to spend time with her other family. At least this summer, with her mom and dad now being posted to the British embassy in Belgium, right next door.

Having established a new Mannion tradition, Fiona and David Lowell had continued to join the family for Thanksgiving every November. David, proving that even British trade diplomats had a fun side, had added an extra week to their yearly trip, which he spent wearing a Santa suit while driving Christmas Festival attendees around the tree farm in the sleigh, singing along to the carols merrily belting from a set of speakers.

Quinn rang the iron dinner bell, announcing the meal was ready to be served. Continuing their own tradition, rather than sit at one of the tables Amanda had decorated, Piper and Jamal took their plates to the bench beneath the tree not far from the others.

After Harriett said grace, as she had every year for as long as Quinn could remember, he took in the sight of his large, still growing family, and decided that life was about as perfect as anyone could wish for.

Then, as all those gathered together raised their glasses for a toast his dad called for, Quinn gazed down into the uplifted face of his adored wife, who he'd fallen in love with at first sight, but never would have met if fate, and yes, possibly the universe, hadn't had him returning here, home forever to Honeymoon Harbor.

* * * * *

Get 3 FREE REWARDS!

We'll send you 2 FREE Books <u>plus</u> a FREE Mystery Gift.

FREE
Value Over
$20

Both the **Romance** and **Suspense** collections feature compelling novels
written by many of today's bestselling authors.

HARLEQUIN
PLUS

Try the best multimedia subscription service for romance readers like you!

Read, Watch and Play.

Experience the easiest way to get the romance content you crave.

Start your **FREE TRIAL** at
<u>www.harlequinplus.com/freetrial</u>.